A LOT OF PEOPLE WANTED PAUL JENSSEN DEAD

The C.I.A. had orders from the highest authority to terminate with extreme prejudice its former operative.

The K.G.B. had placed him on top of its international hit list. Nowhere was safe for him . . . not London, where he unearthed the first clue . . . nor South Africa, where he plunged into a maze of lethal subterfuge and unexpected love . . . nor Switzerland where in a vault beneath the streets of Zurich, the ill-gotten wealth of a nation threatened to topple the American government. Paul Jenssen found himself fighting alone against an omnipotent force that could assume any form, deceive and steal without challenge, and slay with impunity. . . .

THE
MIDAS ACCORD

THE
MIDAS ACCORD

DOUGLAS EASTON

A SIGNET BOOK

SIGNET
Published by the Penguin Group
Penguin Books USA Inc., 375 Hudson Street,
New York, New York 10014, U.S.A.
Penguin Books Ltd, 27 Wrights Lane,
London W8 5TZ, England
Penguin Books Australia Ltd, Ringwood,
Victoria, Australia
Penguin Books Canada Ltd, 10 Alcorn Avenue,
Toronto, Ontario, Canada M4V 3B2
Penguin Books (N.Z.) Ltd, 182–190 Wairau Road,
Auckland 10, New Zealand

Penguin Books Ltd, Registered Offices:
Harmondsworth, Middlesex, England

First published by Signet, an imprint of New American Library,
a division of Penguin Books USA Inc.

First Printing, December, 1991
10 9 8 7 6 5 4 3 2 1

PUBLISHER'S NOTE
This is a work of fiction. Names, characters, places, and incidents
either are the product of the author's imagination or are used fictitiously,
and any resemblance to actual persons, living or dead, events, or
locales is entirely coincidental.

*For all of my parents
and for Doctor Doom and
the Little Samurai.*

THE
MIDAS ACCORD

1

April 1939

Like a small dog curled at its master's feet, the city nestles at the base of the Atlas Mountains. It is a crossroads, a way station for the Berbers and the nomadic Bedouin and the mysterious Blue Men from the encroaching Sahara. It is a meeting place, has always been so, a place with an affinity for secrecy and discretion. It is a city of great antiquity, yet constantly shifting. Only the mountains are still.

In the alleys of the tapestry-covered souk the eerie wail of the muezzin calling the faithful to evening prayer replaced the hawking cries of the shopkeepers. The violet sunset sent strange shadows dancing across the ancient cobblestones of the Kasbah, the old quarter, bathing the city in the weird dusk peculiar to Marrakech.

In the sitting room of a small windowless house, an indistinguished link in the souk's chain of abutting buildings, two men sat oblivious to the activities just outside. The house, little more than four whitewashed clay walls, was an unlikely site for a meeting of importance. It had been chosen carefully.

An ancient servant placed coffee and honeyed pastries on the low brass table, while the two men waited for him to leave. The two could have continued speaking in his presence, for he was deaf, and nearly blind, but they did not do so. He silently padded out of the smoky, poorly lit room.

The men had exercised extraordinary precautions to arrive at the meeting unobserved. Each had taken several extra flights, following highly circuitous routes. New identities had been created, documented in credibly weathered passports. Dirtied djellabas, the hooded robe of the North Africans so reminiscent of a monk's cassock, further concealed their wearers.

The man from Washington spoke. "I am afraid that I am not empowered to grant a delay to your decision. When I return home tomorrow morning, I must, and shall, take with me news of either your agreement or your refusal. You have had more than ample time to consider the advantages of our proposal."

The man from Johannesburg inhaled joylessly from his cigarette and glared through thick-lensed glasses. He was unaccustomed to being on the receiving end of ultimatums, and the haughty desk jockey from the State Department, with his soft-looking hands and pompous manner, aroused his full contempt. The American's offer, however, overrode any personal feelings of dislike. Quite simply, it was a miracle. He found it difficult to remain calm.

"What guarantee have I that you will keep your word, assuming the victory of which you seem so confident?" His English, although grammatically correct, was heavily laced with the guttural accent of his native Afrikaans.

"You have my assurance as a representative of the United States government. The president has personally approved the proposed agreement."

"I see." The South African took another drag off the cigarette and inspected a portion of the ceiling. His almost totally hairless pate and pendulous jowls gave him the appearance of a humorless bulldog.

The American continued. "You may rest assured that my government would hardly propose such an accord unless we were prepared to follow through on our share of the agreement."

"I can imagine many things. In wartime, much is said and promised. Much is forgotten in peacetime. I regret that I can not accept verbal assurance. Even from an American." The man from Johannesburg permitted himself an imperceptible and mirthless smile.

The man from Washington leaned forward. "It seems to me that you are rather in need of our assistance."

The Afrikaner calmly took another puff and slowly exhaled the bluish smoke. "Not half as much as you are of mine."

It was the American's turn to stare. After several minutes of complete silence, punctuated only by a hungry donkey's bray from somewhere in the now quiet souk, he sighed. "Very well." From under his voluminous djellaba he withdrew a slender oilskin pouch. "I need hardly inform you that the existence of both our accord and these papers can under no circumstances become public knowledge. There can and will be no leakage."

"That sounds rather like a threat."

The American shrugged eloquently. "My government, like most governments, does not take kindly to being embarrassed. If London catches word of this, it won't be pretty. I'm sorry if that sounds threatening to you. But I won't rephrase my warning."

"You Americans would sell your mothers to save your good name." The South African scowled. "But you've no cause for worry from me. I'm not stupid enough to let the world in on our little covenant. So if you've brought along one of those fancy American ink pens, I'll make my mark."

The men signed both copies of the document the American had produced from the case, the South African reading each thoroughly to ensure their identical wording. Each man took one and stood. The American proffered a hand. The Afrikaner shook it. "Sonny, why don't you leave first? I'll tell Mohammed to show you out of the souk." He left the room.

The old servant reappeared and gestured to the American to follow. They stepped through the wooden doorway into the snaky alley and began to walk toward the Place Djemaa el-F'na, the Assembly of the Dead, where the American's driver waited. The souk still dozed in the heat of the sultry Marrakech afternoon. They passed the now closed doors where, during the cooler hours, hard-nosed shoppers could be found haggling over the price of brass and copper bowls, spices, fruits, and perfumes.

The souk seemed endless as the old man rounded yet another labyrinthine corner. Without warning they entered the eerie open square of the Place Djemaa el-F'na. The American spotted his car a short distance away and handed the old man a few centimes. The servant silently nodded his thanks and watched as the emissary of the president of the United States walked to the carefully battered Citroën. The chauffeur was nowhere to be seen. After staring around the Place for a few seconds looking for him, the man shrugged, opened the door to the driver's seat, and placed himself behind the wheel. The keys, hanging from the ignition, were hot to the touch, the driver having neglected, incredibly, to open a window. The car was a sauna. He turned the key.

The man saw the movement next to his feet before he felt anything.

The Egyptian cobra is not the largest member of the cobra family, nor is it the most venomous. Those distinctions are enjoyed by the eighteen-foot king cobra and the extraordinarily toxic Cape cobra, respectively. Nevertheless, the bite

of the six-foot Egyptian cobra, *Naja Haje*, is, bar-
ring immediate treatment, usually fatal. The
fangs are large and therefore likely to inject
more venom than a smaller-toothed snake.

Snake venoms vary widely, some causing massive bleeding, others causing internal clotting.
Cobra venom, with its lethal neurotoxins, shuts
down a victim's central nervous system. Death
comes in minutes.

The bite itself is not particularly painful, but
soon afterward, the victim's brain begins to lose
its ability to control respiration and heartbeat.
Shortness of breath, severe heart palpitations,
and convulsions ensue. Death follows shortly
thereafter. Prompt treatment with an antivenin
is therefore essential.

The American stared at the two new holes in
his djellaba, just below his knee, and at the
swaying serpent hissing vigorously on the floor.
It was angry at its incarceration in the over-
heated car. Very slowly, he opened the car door
and cautiously lifted his legs.

The serpent lunged again. Two parallel nee-
dles again embedded themselves an inch into the
flesh of the American's right thigh.

The man began to scream. He was screaming
even as he stumbled out of the car into the
deserted square, fell gasping on his side while
clutching his erratically pumping heart, and
died.

*　　*　　*

The old servant placed upon the low table the brown oilskin pouch he had taken from the corpse lying in the Place, and trudged out of the room. On the shabby couch, the bald man stretched forward to pick up the pouch, and leaned back comfortably. He smoked deeply. A huge grin split his heavy features almost in two: He had many reasons to be elated. His name was Daniel Malan, and in exactly nine years he would become the fifth president of South Africa.

2

May 24, 199—

The man stood motionless, gazing silently at the painting of a band of maidens in Greek costume lounging on the banks of an English river. Its lush greens and blues evoked an extraordinary feeling of tranquility. He wished that he were lying by the edge of the river.

A few moments later he gave a last glance at the Turner landscapes and walked out of the museum. He found himself on Millbank, the curvy road bordering the Thames on which the sedate Tate Gallery is located. The street was clogged with lunch-hour traffic and with commuters creeping out to the suburbs for the three-day holiday weekend in honor of Prince Edward's marriage. The London drizzle tamped his reddish blond hair to his head, accentuating his pleasant face and almost tiger-like green eyes. He had neglected to bring an umbrella. In spite of the rain, he found a cab, and gave an address in Kensington Church Street.

The passenger's name was Paul Jenssen. He was glad to have had some time to stroll through the Tate prior to his two-thirty appointment. The museum had been nearly devoid of visitors due to the holiday, and he'd virtually had the place to himself. As an amateur painter, he found it both educating and stimulating to examine the works of the masters.

The roomy London cab crept forward in the traffic, edging onto Constitution Hill past the Mall and Buckingham Palace. The royal standard was not flying over the squat building; the queen had already left with her family to Windsor for the weekend, to be with the horses she preferred to people.

Police protection around the palace seemed denser than usual, probably in anticipation of some weekend IRA mischief. The sovereign and her family lived under constant threat of assassination. After her cousin Lord Mountbatten was blown to bits in 1979 aboard his boat, the queen had begun to take a more personal interest in her family's security.

The cab meandered left past Piccadilly onto Knightsbridge, the green expanses of Hyde Park and Kensington Gardens on the right. Through the new spring foliage Paul could glimpse Kensington Palace, London home of both the Prince of Wales and the queen's sister.

Paul leaned forward as the roomy London taxi veered right onto Kensington Church Street. The street was lined with antique stores and curio shops of every sort. "It's number thirty-two."

The driver nodded and pulled up shortly before a row of quaint boutiques. Paul paid the driver and let himself out of the car. His lanky frame moved with the smoothness of a natural athlete as he strolled to the doorway of a small shop whose front window was crammed to the limit with dusty books and yellowed papers. He pressed the bell.

The shop appeared to be empty. The door was locked. Paul waited a minute and rang again, pressing the buzzer for several seconds.

A tiny, raisinlike gnome teetered unsteadily out of somewhere in the back of the shop and fumbled with the lock. He was clothed in ancient khakis and a fascinating bow tie which had been created by someone who obviously enjoyed using all of the secondary colors together. The lenses of the little man's glasses were at least three eighths of an inch thick. Paul bit his lip and was reminded once again of a cross between a munchkin and Menachem Begin.

The gnome finally managed to get the door open. He peered up into the visitor's face. "Paul! How are you, m'boy? Wonderful to see you. Looking splendid. Come in and have some tea, we've just put the kettle on." Paul felt a tiny vice clamp onto his forearm, and he was dragged into the shop. "Now, you just sit right there and I shall be back in a jiffy." The creature gave a throaty chortle and hobbled out through the doorway at the back of the cluttered shop. The sound of a breaking dish, followed by a "Damn!" issued from the back.

Paul gazed around. The three or four chairs in the congested room either had all the cane missing from their seats or were stacked with several feet of large volumes badly in need of dusting.

The little man presently returned, precariously balancing an old tin tray. It held a bowl of sugar, a pitcher of milk, a wonderfully ornate Georgian teapot, a large plate of chocolate cookies, and two fragile saucers and teacups. The milk sloshed onto the tray as the old man threaded his unsteady way through the morass of antiques to his visitor.

Paul transferred several dozen pounds of books to the floor from a rather abused Queen Ann night table, and his host deposited the tray. After five more minutes they had cleared two of the more intact chairs and sat down.

As he served the tea, the gnome spoke. "I was so glad to find you in town. I believe you'll find the letters most interesting. Milk with your tea?"

"No, thanks, Arthur." Paul shifted his tall body in the confining chair and accepted a cup of the steaming drink. "Well, you got lucky. I flew up from Johannesburg last week to do some research at the British Library." He hesitated. "Are you sure they're genuine?"

His host, who had begun to gnaw on one of the enormous chocolate cookies like a myopic squirrel with a particularly oversized walnut, gaped in astonishment. "Am I sure? But, of course, m'boy, how can you even ask such a thing? I may not speak Afrikaans, but I've been around long enough to spot a counterfeit. Of course they're the real goods. Trust me. Here, never mind the tea, I'll show you right now."

Arthur Jones made what seemed a valiant effort to spring to his feet and tottered over to a toaster-sized cherrywood box which lay toward the back of the shop. He retrieved it and triumphantly placed it on the table next to the tea service.

"Just look, m'boy. If those aren't genuine, I shall retire."

Paul slowly opened the hinged lid of the box. Inside lay two letters, still in their original envelopes. On each of their flap sides was a black wax seal, in which was impressed the peculiar image of a two-headed phoenix writhing in flames. They had been opened with a letter opener and were in good condition, although obviously old. Both were addressed to Mr. Anton du Preez, Post Office Box 81, Carletonville. Paul recognized the town as a gold-producing site in the Witwatersrand area adjoining Johannesburg. He carefully opened the top letter. It was written in Afrikaans.

The old man was silent as he watched Paul read. The only sound was the ticking of an immense grandfather clock which stood in a corner of the shop, unvaryingly giving one-thirty as the time of day.

"Well, what does it say?"

Paul did not answer for a few minutes as he

continued reading. Then he looked up, an incredulous half smile on his lips. "Remarkable. My Afrikaans is far from perfect, but this appears to be a handwritten letter by Hendrik Verwoerd, president of South Africa in the late fifties and early sixties. Arthur, I apologize for doubting you. Where'd you find them?"

Paul's host glowed. "Yesterday, a young woman came into the shop. South African, Afrikaner, but married to an Englishman, lives in London now. Pleasant girl. Quite attractive, actually. Dark hair, pale complexion." He gave a prunish grin and then paused, his face gone blank. "Anyway, she'd discovered this chest of letters in the attic of her father's house near Johannesburg. She mentioned that she became estranged from her father when she married outside the Afrikaner community. I gathered he'd been a widower who lived alone. Apparently he died several months ago, and she went down to sort through his papers and to ready the house for sale.

"The woman realized that the letters were old, and suspected that they might be valuable. So she brought them back to England where she hunted in the telephone directory for a dealer in letters, and that's how she found me. She asked me to sell them on consignment. The rest is history: When I remembered that Verwoerd had been some high muckety-muck Boer, I thought that you might be interested, what with your book in progress about South Africa. And here you are."

Paul shook his head in amazement. "Arthur, I'd like to translate one of these carefully, with a dictionary, before I decide whether or not to buy them. Would that be all right?"

The little man nodded. "Of course, of course. Take them both if you wish. Your face is known to us, as they say." He chuckled throatily.

"What is the asking price?"

The gnome smiled coyly. "I was hoping you'd be able to tell me what they're worth. I'll trust you to give a fair assessment."

Paul grinned. "You put a lot on faith, old fellow. But I'll try and be objective about it." He rose to leave, pocketing the letters. The tiny shopkeeper patted him on the back as they approached the door. "I'll call you tonight, if that's okay."

"Certainly, certainly. Ta." He waved good-bye and disappeared into the gloom of the shop.

Paul hailed another taxi and gave the address of his short-term rental studio on a quiet Chelsea side street. The city had calmed, the rush-hour traffic having abated and many of the city's inhabitants now away in the country.

The cab let him off after a short ride and he hurried up the three flights of stairs to the flat, where he began several hours worth of laborious and painstaking translation, frequently consulting an Afrikaans-English dictionary.

By nine he had finished one of the letters and paused to grab a beer from the kitchen. Returning, between swallows, he reread it and placed it slowly on the desk. He meditated for several minutes and then, noticing the time, picked up the telephone.

The silvery voice of Arthur the shopkeeper intoned, "Hullo?"

"Hi, Arthur, it's Paul. Listen, these letters are interesting. Does two hundred pounds sound fair?"

"I think that sounds all right. The owner should be happy with the price."

"Great. Will the shop be open this weekend so I can drop off the money?"

"Of course, m'boy. We antiquarians, pun intended, do not observe modern holidays."

Paul laughed. "Fine, I'll drop by tomorrow morning." He replaced the receiver and took another swig of beer.

He thought quietly to himself for a few minutes, absently tapping with a pencil. He then pocketed the translated letter and strode to the door. Downstairs, he headed for the scarlet-painted phone booth several feet from the apartment building's entrance. Inside, he picked up the telephone receiver and dialed a Mayfair exchange. After several rings, a woman's voice, afflicted by a heavy Texas accent, answered, "Haylow."

"Hi, I'm calling for Dean McWhirter, please."

"Shoah, y'all hole awn jus' a minute." The sound of a phone clanging was followed by a soprano shriek. "Dean! Tel'phone, hawny!"

A man's voice came on the line. "Hello?"

"Hi, Dean, it's Paul Jenssen."

There was a momentary silence. "Paul! How've you been? Where are you?"

"I'm fine. I'm in London, researching a book I'm writing. I'm only here for a little while. How're you and Priscilla doing?"

The man's voice was pleasant but tentative. "Fine, just fine. Cilla just got back from a visit with her mother in Forth Worth. Not much going on. What's up?"

"Dean, I was wondering if I could drop by tonight. I know it's an imposition, but I'd like a word with you."

There was another pause. "Is everything okay?"

"Dean, I wouldn't ask on such short notice if it weren't important. I've come across something fascinating. I want to talk to you about it. Hush-hush."

The pitch of the man's voice altered almost imperceptibly. "Company business? If it is, Paul, I don't think it's such a great idea. Given what's happened and all."

"C'm'on, Dean. This is something else. It's wild. We've known each other too long to let those jerks you still work for stand in the way."

McWhirter chuckled dryly. "How soon can you get here? It's number eight Mount Street."

"I'll be there in fifteen minutes."

The slender, chic, and very southern Priscilla McWhirter welcomed Paul Jenssen into her elegant corner town house with the unquestioning and nonchalant demeanor of a veteran CIA wife. She ushered him into a walnut-paneled study off the thickly carpeted main hall and closed the door.

Inside, a tall, silver-haired man with tortoise-shell reading glasses perched upon his patrician nose stepped forward to warmly shake Paul's hand. "Hi, guy. Looking good. Whiskey?"

"Yes, thanks. Nice place you have here."

"The taxpayers wouldn't have it any other way." He grinned. "Ice?"

"Just a little water. Sorry to intrude on your weekend like this."

"Nonsense, it's great to see you. I apologize for being so cautious about meeting. You know how tight-assed they can be at Langley."

"Diamond-from-coal tight."

"Exactly. But screw it."

McWhirter handed his guest the drink and gestured to a pair of leather armchairs. They both sat.

"Dean, today I came across a couple of letters. I translated one of them." Paul tapped his breast pocket. "Give me your word as my friend that you'll keep this to yourself and I'll show it to you. I want you to tell me what it means."

McWhirter smiled down at his drink. "Paul, you know I can't make you promises I may not be in a—"

Paul interrupted. "I know. I haven't forgotten what it was like. If you can't tell me about it, so be it. But promise me you won't go to Langley on this."

McWhirter sighed. "Fine. It's just my job. Shoot."

Paul pulled from his pocket the letter he had transcribed. He handed the document to McWhirter, who read it aloud.

18 February 1959

Dear Anton,

I am writing to you in response to rumblings of discontent which have come to my attention regarding payments by our Brothers into Elizabeth. I have been led to understand that in certain quarters there is talk questioning the wisdom of placing such vast sums in one fund, under the ultimate control of one individual, our honourable Treasurer.

According to the bylaws of the constitution of our most sacred fraternity, such divisive and treasonable talk, outside of major meetings appropriate to the discussion of important issues, is punishable by expulsion from the Order.

To those ill-advised or misinformed Brothers who doubt my resolve to bring them before the Executive Council for such serious transgressions, I say, BE WARNED. They will shortly find themselves stripped of membership with complete loss of privileges and standing in our community.

As Chairman of the Brotherhood's Secret Committee on Conduct, Anton, it falls to you to answer such disrespect to our constitution with a stern and swift response. If we are to attain a position of invulnerability, we cannot allow a handful of cretins to ruin our noble and holy bounty. You may consider yourself under instruction to identify those misguided Brothers described above and to have your enforcers warn them of the tenuous position in which they have placed themselves. You are authorized to show this letter when you deem it necessary. You will of course dispose of it properly when you have no further need of it.

These out-of-meeting snipings must cease immediately.

With best regards for you and your family,
H. F. Verwoerd

McWhirter slowly looked up from the letter. "Paul, where the hell did you find this?"

Paul smiled. "From an old friend here in London. What do you think?"

"Well, it looks genuine. If it is, we both know what it means. What a coup. You said there's another letter?"

"Yes, also by Verwoerd. I haven't translated it yet. But you think this is the real thing?"

McWhirter gazed down at the letter. "Oh, I think so. I definitely think so. There are a lot of people who'd love to get their hands on this."

"I know I can trust you to keep this quiet, Dean."

"I gave you my word, Paul." He waved the letter. "So what are you going to do with it?"

"I'm going to investigate and see if this fund is still around."

"Some friendly advice, Paul?"

"Sure."

"Be careful. The most likely reason the fund stayed undetected all these years is because these people are so ruthless."

"Thanks. I'll be careful. You can't help me out at all, though?"

"I don't think so. It's as much news to me as it is to you. There have been rumors of a South African mega-slush fund for years, but never anything concrete like this. If it does still exist, it's been kept quiet in a way that few secrets this size can be. Obviously there are some fairly committed people in charge. Other than that I know nothing."

Paul drained the scotch and rose. "I won't keep you any longer. Again, thanks for letting me impose."

"Please, stop it. You're always welcome. Just don't tell anyone I said so." They both laughed.

McWhirter saw Paul to the door and closed it behind him. Priscilla McWhirter stood facing her husband. "That was the man that hullaballoo was about a couple o'yeahs ago, wasn't it? Paul Jenssen, right?"

Her husband nodded.

"They're gon' be s'prised at Langley he suddenly mater'lized out o' nowhere?"

"How are they going to know?"

"Why sugar, they're gon' know when you tell 'em he came by, and they're gon' be real interested in what he tol' you."

"I don't know what—"

28

"Oh, come on, darlin'. That door to yo' study isn't as thick as you think."

"Priscilla, I will not have you eavesdropping on my business conversations. For your own good."

She said nothing but merely pointed at the telephone in his study.

"If you'd listened more carefully, Cilla, you'd know I gave him my word I'd keep quiet about what he told me."

She drew herself up and placed her hands on her hips. Her tone was cold and firm. "Now, you listen to me, Dean McWhirter. If you think I have stood idly by watchin' as you get older, while men younger than y'self get promoted over you, jus' to see an oppo'tun'ty like this laind in yo' lap and have you pass it up, you ah sadly mistaken. This could be our ticket to an administrative position." She walked to her husband and stroked his cheek. Her tone softened. "I know he's yo' frien', hawny, but he'll never even know you called Langley. Now, do what you have to do. If not fo' y'self, then fo' yo' fam'ly."

Dean McWhirter gazed absently at an imaginary speck on the wall and then walked into his study. He picked up the phone and began to dial.

Paul hailed a cab and returned to his flat. Once inside, after heating a couple of leaden steak and kidney pies, he threw himself on the bed and began translating the second letter. Although also written by Verwoerd, the tone was that of a man obsessed, a paranoid and power-mad leader whose only purpose lay in furthering the ambitions of the mysterious organization he referred to as "the Brotherhood."

2 August 1965

Anton,

I don't dare telephone you for fear the call will be intercepted. The enemies of our cause, supported by Moscow, seek to destroy us insidiously, through stolen information and other such cowardly devices. They have already made two attempts on my life, but treacherous, unmanly attempts they were, by bombs placed in my sedan. But God does not yet intend for me to die, and certainly not by their filthy hand.

Nevertheless, Anton, I feel in my heart that the enemies of our Brotherhood grow stronger. They will soon try to break us, and foment rebellion throughout the country. We cannot permit this. They must be crushed. I have already placed E.F. under the deepest possible protection. What a wonderful catch the steward of the codes would be for those who would destroy us. They will never extract the codes from that one; E.F. would sooner die. A true believer.

But now the real reason for this letter. I feel sure that I shall not serve in office much longer. It is nothing concrete, and yet I am as sure of it as I have ever been, and you know how instinctual I am. Our Brotherhood must ensure continuity in the quality of leadership of this country, even when its leaders change. Yet how is this to be accomplished? Those four old men who sit on the Executive Council are known to all the Brotherhood, and, being known, are approachable by many who would wear the mantle of "leader." They can be pressured and influenced by the wrong sort of people. But you are not known. You are the king-maker, the brother to whom the Executive Council will pay heed, but who is almost as shadowy as our Treasurer. Your only office held in the Brotherhood was on a Secret Committee. You cannot be influenced. You must make them choose a strong leader, a leader who will continue and expand the current policies of growth. Perhaps someone like Vorster. But strong!

Anton, promise me that you will not fail me, will not fail the Brotherhood, in this most vital of duties.

As ever,

H. F. Verwoerd

Paul placed the note on the night table and, noticing it was well past midnight, turned in for the night.

At the same moment, five time zones to the west, a black Lincoln glided quietly through the warm spring evening as a bloody Washington sunset yielded to the cloak of night. The sedan turned onto Pennsylvania Avenue, heading west.

The passenger in the backseat glimpsed pickets and signs through the tinted windows, an assortment of causes demonstrated in vain as the car sped noiselessly past the White House. It crossed the Potomac into Virginia and entered the Parkway, the traffic now thinning after the evening exodus from the capital.

The highway veered north, mimicking the path of the river. Convenience stores and shopping centers, the victuallers of suburbia, flew by as the driver ignored exits for Arlington and Falls Church. Crowded miniature golf parks beckoned children and easily amused adults to floodlit fun.

A sign announced MCLEAN. LEESBURG. LANGLEY, EXIT 1 MILE. The sedan turned left onto the exit and a minute later curved right onto a narrow country road. The Lincoln's headlights picked up a modest signboard on the right-hand side of the road stating CENTRAL INTELLIGENCE AGENCY. The words floated above a hungry-looking eagle clutching some foliage and a small arsenal of arrows. The car continued slowly down the road onto a sycamore-lined drive. It stopped at what appeared to be a tollgate.

A guard stepped forward from the dusty shadows to examine with a flashlight the driver's identification. He aimed the light briefly at the passenger and waved the car through.

The driver parked in a remote corner of the vast lot and opened the rear door. "Mr. Williams, if you'd care to follow me, we'll go inside now." He spoke with a soft Texas accent, vowels reluctant to surrender to consonants. There was nothing gentle about him, however. The driver was a sixth-degree black belt in karate. He was at least proficient in half a dozen other martial arts and a crack shot as well. He also happened to be an excellent driver.

The passenger emerged from the rear of the car and glanced around suspiciously. He was of medium height and medium build, with light brown hair and eyes. His suit, although well made, was not so good as to attract attention to its quality. His face was pleasant. It showed its owner to be roughly in his mid-thirties. But it too was not particularly noticeable. In fact there was nothing about the man that attracted much notice. Except when he spoke. His name was George Williams, and at thirty-four he was the wonder child of the new president's staff. He enjoyed virtually unlimited and direct access to the Oval Office. In spite of his bland appearance, he was referred to in the corridors of power as the president's golden boy.

"This way, please, sir." The driver led his charge toward a squat eight-story building. Once again a guard at the entrance checked the escort's papers and nodded.

The two men entered an elevator devoid of buttons. Williams's escort produced a key and inserted it in one of a dozen keyholes set into the lift's left side. Williams felt his stomach twirl as they dropped an unexpected and rapid sixty feet. The doors hissed open, and they walked into what could have been the reception area for any Fortune 500 company, except that the receptionist was a well-built young man and there were no self-congratulatory publications lying about.

The man nodded at Williams's escort and the latter guided his charge to a smoked glass door off to the right of the reception area. He knocked softly, and then opened it after hearing a muffled "Come in."

Inside, behind a massive mahogany desk, a well-dressed man of medium height arose. "George, thanks for coming on such short notice."

Williams nodded. The escort closed the door and left.

James Bell, assistant director of the Central Intelligence Agency, indicated a plush armchair for his guest and came around to the front of his desk. He ran a hand through an iron gray shock of hair and chewed his lower lip.

"George, I apologize for not explaining to you over the phone why it was so important that we see you immediately. However, a problem has arisen which holds potentially catastrophic implications for the security of the United States. With the president out of town, you were the logical one to approach. Someone is going to have to brief him, and from what we understand you have the best access.

"Two hours ago, a man named Paul Jenssen approached our chief-of-station in London. Apparently, Jenssen came across two handwritten letters by Hendrik Verwoerd, the South African president from 1958 until his assassination in

1966. Jenssen showed our agent one letter which he'd translated.

"From its content it was obvious that both Verwoerd and the man he was writing to were members of a group called the *Broederbond*. Have you heard of it?"

Williams shook his head.

"Let me give you a little background on the *Broederbond* first. In 1978, a man walked into the offices of the Johannesburg *Sunday Times* and revealed the inner workings of a secret organization known as the *Broederbond,* 'the Brotherhood' in Afrikaans. What he revealed was subsequently smuggled out of South Africa and published overseas. The CIA, and at least a small percentage of the public, had long known of the existence of the *Broederbond,* which was openly founded in 1918 as an Afrikaner nationalist group opposed to British rule in South Africa. The crushing defeat of the Boers, or Afrikaner farmers, at the hands of the British certainly played a significant role in the group's inception.

"In 1921, however, they decided to go underground. Since that time, the group has grown to wield extraordinary power in the highest strata of South African society. Many of its leaders spent time in Hitler's Germany, learning firsthand how a defeated people could stage a dramatic and powerful comeback. It represents and works for the ideals of the National Party's hardline philosophy. And that very same National Party has enjoyed an uninterrupted streak in office ever since they first came to power in

1948. They've been running the country for more than forty years.

"For years we've tried unsuccessfully to infiltrate the *Broederbond*. We have an agent right now in Johannesburg who's coddled up to the *Broederbond* for almost ten years, supporting Afrikaner causes and so on. They believe he's a genuine convert. But they still won't let him in. The reason is that he was raised in an English-speaking environment and so is not 'an Afrikaner by birth, but by conversion.' The dissident member who told all to the *Sunday Times* revealed that admission to the group is denied to any person who has been 'significantly exposed to non-Afrikaner culture.' Members must be white, male, primarily Afrikaans-speaking, nondivorced, regular churchgoers, and rabid in their support for the system of apartheid. The member also disclosed the fact that since 1948 every South African president has been a *Broederbonder*. The group numbers twelve thousand of the most powerful men in South Africa.

"We've never had any proof, but we've long suspected that the *Broederbond* was amassing a huge fund, probably in Switzerland or Liechtenstein. Two years ago, one of our men in Cape Town heard a whisper about a secret *Broederbond* account holding the equivalent of forty-five billion dollars, U.S."

Williams raised his eyebrows and gave a low whistle. "What's it for?"

"Well, we know the Nationalists have recognized from the beginning that they would always be at risk of overthrow by the black majority. We believe that they probably built this superfund as insurance against such an overthrow, and that it was derived largely, but not entirely, from a secret tax imposed on the mine owners and other major Afrikaner-owned businesses as the price of peaceful operation. Most probably, the fund is in gold. An enormous golden parachute.

"We think that the gold is to be used to help this South African elite, the twelve-thousand-member *Broederbond,* in exile. The sheer size of the fund will bring them unheard-of power. With that kind of money, they could buy anything or anybody. The wealth of Midas."

Williams stared for a long moment at his host. "Jesus."

"I know. Scary. What was startling to our man in London was the fact that the letter he saw mentioned the existence of something called 'Elizabeth.' It didn't ring any bells but we ran a worldwide check on it anyway. Less than an hour ago, our Zurich people came up with something interesting.

"In 1952, a confidential account was opened at the United Bank in Zurich, the largest bank in Switzerland. All assets of the account were deposited as the sole property of a corporation named Elizabeth, Ltd. Corporate offices were registered as a Zurich post office box. Three directors were listed, each authorized to withdraw funds. In addition, a particular progression of numbers and letters in sequence, when presented by any individual, not just a director, would be sufficient authorization for the bank to release funds to that individual. The fund exists, George. It's called Elizabeth.

"Within four weeks of the account's opening, all three directors mysteriously died. One man was discovered floating in Lake Constance. It was put down as a suicide. Another had a massive heart attack while on a train to Amsterdam. The last was found with his head blown off in a shack near the Andermatt Glacier with the words 'Zionist Spy' splashed in red on the walls. Rubbish."

"So who has the code to open the account?"

"Exactly: Who? In the letter Jenssen showed our London man reference was made to a 'Treasurer.' We have no idea who it is, or even if it's more than one person. It appears from the evidence, however, that whoever it or they are, the Elizabeth sequence is in their possession, and no one else's. It must be someone whom the very top party and government leaders trust implicitly, someone completely dedicated to the tenets of apartheid. Someone they would trust with forty-five billion dollars. There's no other way to touch the money.

"Furthermore, according to our source at the United Bank, whoever the financial wizards were who masterminded this plan, they apparently had a sense of foresight regarding Switzerland's banking secrecy and disclosure laws. Until several years ago, Switzerland had never once yielded, or even bent, to pressure from a foreign country to make banking disclosures of any sort. Under Swiss law, banks may only compromise the privacy of a depositor if indisputable evidence exists that said depositor had committed a crime. Even the Nazis couldn't get the Swiss to break their code of silence during World War II.

"Recently, however, the Swiss have shown a semi-willingness to freeze the assets of deposed dictators. Marcos's money will eventually be turned over to the Philippines, and Haiti has managed to completely isolate Duvalier from the money stashed in his Swiss account. The bankers in Zurich are seemingly reluctant nowadays to arouse the ire of entire newly liberated nations.

"Marcos and Duvalier understandably believed in the inviolability of Swiss bank accounts; theirs were the first cases in which abuse of power in a foreign country figured as evidence of a crime. Because of their mistaken belief, their names appear on their accounts, with no attempt at concealment.

"The Elizabeth fund can never be frozen or touched the way Marcos's and Duvalier's have been. No prominent Nationalists or anybody else with a stake in the money—or anyone alive, for that matter—are listed as the owners; the only access to that account is with a particular code which anybody could use if he gets his hands on it. That is both the beauty and the Achilles' heel of Elizabeth: It can't be impounded at the request of a new and bitter black South African government, but it can also be tapped into by anyone who gets hold of the proper access sequence."

"Incredible!"

"That it is. In the last few years, particularly large sums have apparently been added to the fund, unquestionably reflecting the emerging patterns of revolution and violence which are occurring now in South Africa. The incidence of bombings is skyrocketing. We know the Eastern Bloc has supplied the rebels with enormous quantities of war materiel; all of their weapons are either Soviet- or Czech-made. They've amassed a great reserve of ammunition, stockpiled mostly in Zambia and Zimbabwe. The confrontation is coming soon.

"We've also detected the first signs of an Afrikaner emigration. Germany and the Netherlands both received huge numbers of applications for resident status in the last four weeks, many from National Party figures and friends of the government and its policies. The state of emergency has only worsened the unrest. There's a widespread perception that this is it, that this time the violence isn't going to die down and the bombings aren't going to go away. It looks like they're getting out."

Williams stared at Bell, his eyes wide with disbelief. "Do you seriously mean to tell me that there will shortly be a black government in South Africa?"

"I'm not saying that; no one knows for sure how long the whites can last. They're extremely well armed and their army is excellent. Their firepower is definitely better quality stuff than what the guerrillas have, and they're light-years ahead in training. From a numbers standpoint, however, they're swamped: Only seventeen percent of the population is white, and not nearly all of them are pro-apartheid. Outside of a few other pariah nations like Israel and Malawi, no other country supports the ruling regime.

"George, what I want you to make the president aware of is the fact that if the Soviets find out about the fund and manage to get the code, then if the South African government falls, the new, black regime that comes in will become a Soviet military satellite. That's a guarantee. The Russians will dangle the forty-five billion, and there's no new government that's going to be able to resist."

Williams leaned forward in his chair, his palms meeting over his mouth, as if in prayer. "What if we obtain the codes before the Soviets do, or before South Africa falls? Logically we'd be in the position of strength, then, no?"

Bell nodded. "Unfortunately, we're drawing a complete blank on the identity of this mysterious Treasurer. Paul Jenssen, the man who approached our London agent, is a former CIA man himself. He left five years ago after his wife was murdered in Lisbon. He makes no bones about holding the Agency to blame, saying we were supposed to be guarding her while he was on a sensitive assignment. But it wasn't like that. The Agency wanted the whole thing put to rest, so they made him a very hush-hush, and very generous, settlement. A couple of million dollars. Anyway, that's how he knew who to go to in London. It seems that Jenssen is writing a book on South African politics and was in London doing research, which explains how he found the letters. Our London chief apparently promised his old friend he'd keep quiet about it, but he obviously placed more importance on protecting national security. We've decided our best bet to get close to the code is to locate Jenssen and watch him carefully. We haven't put out an all-personnel alert because we're afraid he might still have some friends in the Agency who might tip him off. This has the highest security classification."

Williams cocked his head to one side and squinted. "May I ask what happens to this Treasurer when you locate him?"

"We will obtain the access code from him."

"I assume that the faint possibility that he or they may not want to be a good boy and hand it over has occurred to you."

"George, you know as well as I that because of its strategic location and its mineral wealth, among other reasons, we must ensure South Africa remains friendly toward the United States. It is critical to American security interests that the Soviets fail to get a toehold there. Please understand me: When we find the Treasurer we're just going to have to make him want to give it to us." Bell gazed steadily at Williams. "If you get my drift."

Williams returned the stare. "I get the drift,

and I don't care to know any more. Jim, you'd better not let the Soviets edge us on this one. South Africa's way too important to lose."

The man sat alone in the tiny windowless room, huddled over the wireless, headphones shutting out all extraneous sound except the gibberish coming in rapidly over the airwaves. He transcribed the meaningless phrases quickly but neatly into a large ledger, stopping his fluid writing only when the eerie computerized voice abruptly ceased. From a shelf crowded with binders and reference books the man selected a slender manual bound in crimson plastic, and flipped through the well-worn pages. He placed the manual to the left of the nonsensical dispatch in the ledger and began the tedious process of decoding.

Fifty minutes later, he had double-checked his translation, the words comprised of Cyrillic characters now forming a cogent message. The man stared again at the name at the beginning of the communication.

TO BE IMMEDIATELY DELIVERED PER-
SONALLY REPEAT PERSONALLY BY
THE DECODER TO ALEXEI BARESH-
KOV DIRECTOR KGB STOP...

He grabbed the paper onto which he had decoded the dispatch and rushed out of the radio room. He raced down the long, office-lined corridor and fidgeted impatiently in the elevator as it inched its halting way to the top floor. After what seemed to the radio man to be an eternity, the heavy doors opened and he strode into the office of Bareshkov's secretary. "I have an urgent radio communication for the director."

The hard-faced woman at the enormous desk which dominated the room looked up coolly. "I will accept the message."

"I regret that my instructions are most clear. I am to personally deliver the communication into the hands of the director. Is he here?"

The woman compressed a pair of already thin lips and depressed a button on her telephone console. "Comrade Director, a communications man is here with a message for you. May I send him in?"

A gruff "Da" issued from the intercom, and she led the messenger into the spacious inner office, a sanctum which she guarded so tenaciously that her nickname in the building was Cerberus. Inside, a slender, aesthetic-looking man with steel-rimmed glasses looked up from a chrome and glass table of decidedly Scandinavian origin. "Yes, Comrade, was is it?"

"Comrade Director, this dispatch was just received from London. I decoded it and was instructed to deliver it to you myself."

"Thank you, Comrade." Bareshkov accepted the proffered document. "You may go."

The radio operator wheeled smartly and exited the office, followed closely by the watchdog secretary. The director looked at the dispatch.

TO BE IMMEDIATELY DELIVERED PERSONALLY REPEAT PERSONALLY BY THE DECODER TO ALEXEI BARESHKOV DIRECTOR KGB STOP EXTREMELY URGENT STOP FOLLOWING REPORT RECEIVED FROM CRYSTAL SWORD 0400 HOURS TODAY LONDON TIME STOP TIN FORTRESS HAS LEARNED OF NEST EGG STOP TIN FORTRESS WILL MONITOR INDEPENDENT REPEAT INDEPENDENT PROBE TO JOHANNESBURG AFTERNOON FLIGHT TODAY STOP PROBE FILE NAME PERSEUS STOP PLEASE ADVISE STOP END OF MESSAGE

The director of the Bureau for State Security, widely known by its abbreviated form KGB, wordlessly reread the dispatch and turned to stare out of the picture window behind him. Although it was May, a sprinkling of midmorning snowflakes whirled and gusted under the leaden Moscow sky. Below, in Dzerzhinsky Square, a few pedestrians in lumpy gray woolens hurried past the imposing edifice of the Lubyanka, seat of the KGB. Their faces pointed uniformly at the cobbled pavement, as if they suspected money might be found on the ground. The Lubyanka was one Moscow landmark where people made a point of not looking up.

The director spoke to his overprotective secretary through the intercom. "Summon my car immediately. Then telephone the general secretary to let him know that I will be over to see him in thirty minutes on top priority."

"Yes, Comrade Director."

"And I want to see the file named Perseus immediately."

"Yes, Comrade Director."

A quarter of an hour later, the sleek but slightly bloated shape of a black Zil limousine emerged from the underground garage of the Lubyanka. The light Saturday traffic was immediately halted by bemedaled policemen who frantically cleaved a path through the square for the imposing car. Sandwiched between an escort of two motorcycles at each end, the limousine turned onto Karl Marx Boulevard and entered the empty lane in the center reserved for VIPs. The powerful man in the curtained backseat mused on the privileges of a supposedly classless society as his glossy automobile sped past the snarl of bumper-to-bumper cars in the non-VIP lanes.

Within several seconds the battlements of the Kremlin, whose name conjures up for so many Americans the image of evil old men seated around a polished oak table, plotting the insidious destruction of the Free World, heaved into view. The onion domes of the walled inner city loomed impassive on its hill above the surrounding streets, an anachronistic witness to the passage of time, a fifteenth-century flock of czarist palaces in the Land of Lenin.

The enormous Zil circled the Kremlin's western flank, still on Prospekt Marxa, heading south. At Borovitsky Square the car turned left onto a gentle hill, passing the southern tip of the long Alexander Garden, and climbed to the Borovitsky Tower. The massive, pyramidal stone structure soared above the fortress walls on either side. The limousine glided through the Borovitsky Gate at its base and came to a halt at the imposing Grand Kremlin Palace, where the offices of the members of the Politburo were located. Scarlet-jacketed Red Guards surrounded the limousine and accompanied Bareshkov inside. The head of the KGB was escorted to the second-floor offices of the most powerful man in the Soviet Union. In the past all of the general secretaries' offices had been situated on the top story of one of the palace buildings. Nevertheless, upon his election the present general secretary had ordered his suites moved down to the second level. The reason given was that the Soviet leader wanted to "be closer to my beloved people." However, it was whispered in certain circles that he suffered from pyrophobia and wished to be as near the ground as possible in the unlikely event of fire.

"Hello, Alexei."

"Good afternoon, Comrade General Secretary. I am sorry to be the bearer of bad news."

Seated behind a nondescript pine desk, the Soviet leader flashed his famous, notoriously untrustworthy grin and motioned his guest to an armchair. "I too am sorry, Alexei. What has happened?"

"As you will recall, comrade, last year we discovered evidence of the existence of a massive financial reserve secreted in Zurich by the leaders of South Africa. We believed the United States to be unaware of this fund. Until this morning. An hour ago we received a cable from our London man who runs a plant in MI 5. That man in turn has a source at Langley. The CIA man, incidentally, believes he is only passing information on to MI 5 and does not realize that his information ultimately winds up in Moscow."

The general secretary offered no comment. He continued to gaze impassively at his intelligence chief.

Bareshkov swallowed nervously. "Anyway, our London man has learned that the CIA now know about Zurich. They got wind of it yesterday evening through information obtained from a former agent, on whom we have a long history. His name is Paul Jenssen. Our file code name for him is Perseus. He was employed by the American government for seventeen years and was a clever and dangerous opponent. He masterminded the Prektor fiasco three years ago. His wife ... died in the aftermath as a result of his involvement in that unfortunate incident. He is now a writer, conducting research for a book on South Africa. The Americans have ordered him under close surveillance, as soon as they find him, hoping to learn the Treasurer's identity. If you recall, the fund's sole trustee is known only as the Treasurer. We have not yet learned the identity of this Treasurer either."

"Alexei, do you believe this man the Americans are watching can succeed?"

The director's steel spectacles glinted as he consulted the folder labeled PERSEUS. "According to our file on him, the man is a veteran agent, and his final assignment was to South Africa. He therefore knows the country and its people. He is strong physically, highly intelligent, and extremely resourceful. During his posting to Johannesburg he taught himself Afrikaans. He is therefore capable of researching his book, and the identity of the Treasurer, in both Afrikaner and Anglo cultures within South Africa. He could succeed where others would not."

"And if something were to occur which incapacitated this man?"

"Then, Comrade General Secretary, the chance of our own man succeeding in unveiling the Treasurer before the Americans do becomes infinitely greater. As you are aware, our lack of diplomatic relations with South Africa has made it extremely difficult for us to maneuver in that country. We have recently had some success establishing an agent there, however, and we are pinning our hopes on him."

"Alexei, thank you for informing me of this unfortunate development." The general secretary of the Central Committee of the Communist Party rose and looked penetratingly into the eyes of his chief spy. "I am sure you will do whatever you feel needs to be done. Whatever that may be. Da?"

"Da, I understand. Good day, Comrade General Secretary."

"Good day, Alexei."

The message zoomed out over the airwaves less than an hour later, the instructions urgent in their simplicity and terseness.

At the Soviet Embassy in London, in a communications room almost identical to its counterpart in the Lubyanka in Moscow, a radio clerk on weekend duty quickly decoded the brief orders. He delivered the message, which ran simply ELIMINATE PERSEUS STOP END OF MESSAGE, to his superiors and returned to the radio room for a cigarette. A communications man's lot was ninety percent acute boredom.

3

Under the immense copper dome of the British Library's main reading room, Paul Jenssen sat mesmerized as he researched the *Broederbond*. For such a small number of men to have so totally and so quickly infiltrated the power structure of a major industrialized country, for all practical purposes running it, was astonishing. It was testimony to a people's single-minded determination to overcome all obstacles.

The library possessed a surprising amount of information on the group. Paul waded through the bulk of it, much of it repetitive, until an item caught his eye. It was an article from the *Times*, several years old, which detailed information leaked by an unidentified source at the Israeli Defense Ministry.

The article's main focus was the source's allegations that the *Broederbond*, in a secret arrangement with the Israeli defense minister in the mid-1970s, had agreed to supply Israel with high-grade uranium in exchange for nuclear technology.

The reporter then proceeded to list a series of curious and unexplained events including the detection, in Autumn of 1979 in the South Atlantic, of a strange light, closely resembling that of a nuclear explosion. The light caused the intelligence services of several nations, including the United States and Britain, to suspect that Israel and South Africa had collaborated on a nuclear test.

Paul was acquainted with the rumors that South Africa now had the bomb and suspected they were true. But it was a puzzling question, because the so-called frontline black African states of Botswana, Zambia, Zimbabwe, and Mozambique, the only plausible enemies of South Africa, had no real urban centers. Cities being the primary targets of nuclear weapons, it was certainly curious. Of course, there were those strategic weapons which could halt a battlefield of tanks or strike against an enemy missile silo or military base, but these too did not apply to those black African nations. As for other important targets such as bridges, railroads, factories and airports, these could easily be eliminated with conventional weapons. Yet as inexplicable as it was, Paul doubted that South Africa would spend millions acquiring the technology simply to boost national prestige. The Afrikaners he knew were far too frugal and too disparaging of international opinion to waste money in that kind of effort.

He checked the time and realized it was getting late. He returned to his flat to collect his bags and hailed a cab to Heathrow. The rainy weather slowed traffic to a crawl.

By the time he reached the terminal the flight was already boarding. The woman at the check-in counter placed a RUSH tag on his suitcase and told him to run for the plane.

Paul arrived at the gate slightly out of breath and was hustled onto the plane. The copilot at the door clucked at him in mock rebuke.

The South African Airways 747 lifted off from Heathrow Airport and retracted its wheel carriage. Like an obese bat, the huge craft nosed blindly up through the thick fog above the patchwork English countryside, guided only by radar. The airplane tilted at a treacherous angle, circled, and straightened on a southerly heading. White knuckles unclenched, cigarettes were lit, and stewardesses with unbreakable smiles began the warmly welcomed drinks service.

In the first-class cabin in the jet's extreme anterior, Paul savored a glass of Krug Grande Cuvée champagne, closed his eyes, and grinned. After accepting the money for the two letters, Arthur had attempted to interest him in a three-volume set on South African cooking from the 1920s, in surprisingly good shape but nevertheless quite useless.

He momentarily reconsidered the wisdom of his hasty return to South Africa, but reassured himself that the new lead was too promising not to investigate. Besides, he had managed to accomplish most of the needed research in London.

What was called for now was a breakthrough in Johannesburg.

The aisle seat on Paul's right was empty, the only one unoccupied in the cabin. Behind him, an elderly British couple argued about currency exchange rates. In front, two meticulously groomed children were arguing over the window seat. Their mother, an attractive young woman in a beige linen traveling suit, had wisely seated herself across the aisle, apart from her contentious offspring. The other first-class passengers were mostly businessmen returning from meetings.

A crisp voice, oozing confidence and competence, issued over the microphone. Captain van Vleck spoke in Afrikaans, his accent sharp and staccato. After he finished his announcement, he repeated it in English. The bilingual captain announced that the airplane would be climbing to an altitude of thirty-five thousand feet and that in approximately ten minutes the English Channel would be directly beneath the aircraft. He did not add that the flight would take two hours longer than any other carrier because no black African nation would allow South African Airways to traverse its airspace.

The plane continued to ascend, suddenly piercing the haze. Brilliant sunlight and a spectacular unbroken prairie of cumulus clouds caused the siblings in front of Paul to renew their competition for the window. The girl, ponytails tossing with righteous indignation, whined to her mother.

"Mummy, Alec won't let me sit by the window. I never get to sit by the window. It's not fair!"

"Alec, switch seats with your sister, please. It's her turn now."

Alec began to cry.

Alec's mother fortified herself with a large swallow of gin and tonic and leaned across the aisle to pacify her children.

A svelte blond stewardess canvassed passengers for their supper selections. Paul opted for the tournedos Rossini, agonizing slightly over having to reject both poached salmon and roast squab. "Would you please microwave it to medium rare?" The stewardess smiled wanly, evincing previous acquaintance with this weak attempt at humor.

Paul gazed at the sea of clouds and plotted his strategy. It was an incredible story. Verwoerd's letters had confirmed what he and many in the intelligence community had long suspected: that the fanatics who ran South Africa had years ago established a contingency plan. The idea of an overthrow was discussed in terms of eventuality, not avoidability. It was simply a question of when. Paul had never managed to reconcile their accepting attitude with the emotional prospect of losing one's homeland. He had intuitively sensed a fallback, a cushion to make loss less painful. Now it all made sense.

Paul pondered on the size of the fund and whether it in fact still existed, as he suspected it did. He realized he harbored a great desire to unveil the mystery of the Treasurer's identity. Yet he felt fairly sure that to ask around Johannesburg about an enigmatic Treasurer or a large fund in Zurich would be to sign his own death warrant; the sort of fanatics who owned the account would never permit him to leave the country alive.

He realized that his best avenues of investigation must lie outside the South African inner circle of power and privilege. Those in active opposition to the Nationalists would be most able to help solve his questions about the Treasurer's identity without compromising his safety.

He thought at once of Pieter Danniken, probably the country's most outspoken white critic of apartheid not in prison. Danniken's freedom was at least partly due to his international prominence as an art historian. He had been, and still was, a living institution in his homeland. His castigation of official policy had made him the bane of the Nationalists, but his patriotism had never been in question. Danniken's love for his country was immediately visible in the rousing and somewhat risky speeches he gave throughout the land, and it was this quality that caused him to be criticized, rather than vilified, by those who disagreed with his political views.

Paul had met the scholar in 1978 at a cocktail party at the U.S. Embassy in Pretoria honoring visiting American congressmen. Professor Danniken had pointedly been invited. This sort of planned irritation of the South African officials present was typical of the Carter Administration.

At one point in the evening, both Jenssen and Danniken were listening to one of the congressmen, a well-fed Democrat from Mississippi, expound at length upon the wealth of South Africa's citizens compared to those in neighboring black African countries. The congressman felt that South Africa must be doing something right given such a disparity.

Danniken said nothing throughout the windy discourse. After the man finished, Danniken asked if the congressman owned any pets. Yes, the representative from Mississippi owned a Great Dane named Dixie. And what did the dog eat each day?

With a toothy grin, Dixie's master attested to his pet's devouring several pounds of food daily.

Danniken fixed the congressman with an icy stare and quietly said, "Your pet, Mr. Congressman, obtains more nourishment than sixty percent of South Africa's inhabitants. I use the word *inhabitant,* and not *citizen,* as you did, Mr. Congressman, because to apply the description *citizen* to South Africa's blacks is to border on the ridiculous. They are serfs. Good evening." With that Danniken had walked away from the speechless Mississippian.

Later, Paul had spoken with Danniken. Without compromising his cover, Paul made it clear to the professor that he admired him, and a bond was established. They enjoyed discussing a wide range of subjects, from art to politics to the merits of South African wine. Over the course of the next few years, their friendship evolved, although

Paul never appeared publicly in the activist's company for fear of jeopardizing his cover.

Paul decided that Danniken would be his starting point in the hunt for the Treasurer. It was possible that the professor might have some ideas as to who was holding the codes to unlock the Elizabeth fund.

The unmistakable sound of a splash signaled renewed hostilities up front. The splash was immediately followed by a shrill scream, and a Coke-drenched child sprang into the aisle. "Mummy, I hate him, I hate him, he's poured his soda on me!"

A muffled "She started it" came from the aisle seat.

Paul leaned forward and tapped the clearly exhausted mother. "If you like, one of your kids can take my seat by the window. I really don't enjoy being reminded of how high we're floating."

The woman gave Paul a look of immense gratitude. "Alec, this nice gentleman has offered to let you look out of his window, which has an even better view than Laura's. Please thank him and buckle your seat belt."

The towheaded Alec emerged into the aisle and moistly mumbled something which approximated "Thank you." Paul helped the child into the seat he had just vacated by the window and seated himself in the adjacent one, on the aisle. Alec then turned and fixed Paul with a serious stare.

"Next week I shall be five." Alec held up a

plump hand as irrefutable evidence to support this claim.

"That's most impressive."

Alec nodded in agreement and turned to gaze serenely and dispassionately out the window.

Paul suddenly recalled how much he and Christine had wanted children. She had had auburn hair, cut short, and extraordinary eyes, like the deep gray of a Scottish lake in winter. They had made countless plans to raise a family once they returned stateside for good, whenever that happened.

It never did. Three years ago he had returned to their villa in Lisbon from a rendezvous in Vienna with a would-be defector, a top Russian nuclear physicist. The physicist had turned out to be a setup, a KGB diversion. The motive for the diversion was revenge, to assuage the wounded ego of an entire intelligence service. Two months earlier, Paul had masterminded a mission which had brought out of Moscow two KGB colonels, a genuine coup of immense value to the United States. In the course of the double defection, three KGB agents, one of whom had also achieved the rank of colonel, had been accidently killed in an explosion. Moscow had furiously viewed this event as a premeditated action perpetrated by the CIA, thus violating the unspoken rule of peace which normally existed between the superpowers' spy camps. It had been too great a humiliation for the Soviets.

Paul had found the two U.S. marines in the garden, just outside the villa. The CIA had had them assigned from the U.S. Embassy in Lisbon to guard Paul and Christine's home in his absence. They had been garroted. A thin loop of piano wire had been quickly and effectively dropped around their necks and yanked from behind.

Inside, it was a shambles: drawers emptied, mattresses slashed, valuables missing. Chaos. And then he had rushed upstairs to open their bedroom door and glimpse her arm emerging from under the large brass bed, motionless, lifeless. . . .

Paul clenched his eyes shut and tried to freeze out the image of Christine's murder. The Lisbon police had been unable to solve the crime, and for all he knew the case was still open. With the theft of so many precious items, it had seemed to them nothing more than a vicious and desperate robbery. He had pretended to believe that they were correct. But he had not forgotten. The guards had been incompetent, and for their incompetence they had paid the ultimate price. But the killers were free. He would bide his time. And then he would have his own revenge.

The Agency had behaved contemptibly in the aftermath. The brass had convened a board of inquiry and had played out the bad joke they had had the gall to call an investigation, only to arrive at the very predetermined decision. "Regrettable, but nevertheless not our fault." No retaliation to be taken against the killers in Moscow, the men who out of misplaced pride had wanted him to suffer more than death, and so had killed Christine.

They had transferred him to South Africa, to "get away and forget and make a new start." They were patronizing—as though to forget, much less to forgive, were that easy. He would do neither. He would wait patiently, outwardly calm and recovered. His wife's assassins would watch him, waiting. And when they were at last convinced that he was not a threat, that he had indeed placed it all behind him, he would strike. He would be avenged.

For a year or so afterward, he had buried himself in his work and had allowed himself no time to think of her. He did not think of other women, could not look at another woman. One evening, while in Cape Town, as he had gazed out from Table Mountain over the city and the bay, the endless coastline making him feel completely insignificant, he broke, and in the blue-gray twilight on the flat-topped mountain towering over Table Bay, he mourned.

Within one week he was back in Washington, leaving behind his job and almost all of his belongings, unwanted reminders of a former, happier time. He had purchased a small house near Bethesda, had settled in, and had proceeded to write a book on the similarities and differences between the American Revolution and other nationalist struggles for freedom. Surprisingly, it had been a success, enjoyable reading for the amateur historian, yet analytical enough to satisfy the coffee table pretensions of many who fancied themselves deep thinkers. Now, two years after leaving the CIA, he had returned to South Africa to work on a second book.

"Sir, if you'll open your tray I'll be able to serve your dinner." A different stewardess, a brunette, spoke to Alec. With some help from Paul, the boy unfolded his tray and the stewardess placed a supper upon it. She consulted a notepad and then turned bewildered to Paul.

"Sir, I don't show any order taken from this seat. Did you request supper?"

"Actually, I did, but I was sitting where this young gentleman is now. I believe that he has been served my supper."

"But I ordered steak!" Alec announced plaintively.

"Oh, that's no problem, there's plenty more," the stewardess reassured the child, and scampered back to the galley.

Alec tapped Paul on the shoulder and held out a knife and fork. "Will you cut my steak, please?"

Paul smiled and began to cut the child's food. The waitress returned with an identical supper for Paul.

Through a packed mouthful, Alec commented to Paul that food tasted better in the air. Paul agreed, adding that it was a noted scientific fact that the quality of food improved the higher the altitude.

"Really?"

Paul solemnly nodded, straight-faced. "Absolutely. And that's very observant of you to notice."

The two concentrated on their steaks, Alec chewing carefully while staring out at the clouds, their puffy edges limned in gold by the now red-orange sun. The last rays bathed the cabin in that blinding tangerine glow peculiar to airplane sunsets, and then vanished as the sun fell beneath the horizon. Captain van Vleck came back on the loudspeaker and announced that the plane would be landing shortly on Ilha do Sal for a scheduled refueling stop.

Suddenly Alec dropped his cutlery and turned to stare at Paul.

"I don't feel good."

"What's wrong?"

"My tummy hurts."

Paul looked over to Alec's mother and saw that she had fallen asleep. He pressed the bell on the side of his armrest and a stewardess appeared almost immediately. "Do you have any Alka-Seltzer? This young man is not feeling well."

"Certainly, I'll be right back." The stewardess vanished and quickly returned with a glass of water and a packet of the ubiquitous medicine.

"Alec, drink this, you'll feel much better." Paul dropped the tablets into the glass and offered the fizzing potion to the boy.

The child took a tentative sip and pulled a face. "It tastes nasty."

"Do you still have a stomachache?"

Alec nodded, his face contorted by an awful grimace.

"Then you have to drink this to feel better."

Alec gathered his courage and bravely gulped several mouthfuls.

"Try to finish it."

The glass slowly drained. Paul watched the boy to see if any change occurred.

"It hurts." Tears came to Alec's eyes.

Paul awakened the boy's mother. "I'm sorry to get you up. Your son has a stomachache."

Alec's mother quickly rose and knelt by her son. "Alec, darling, tell me where it hurts."

Her son had begun to roll in his seat in anguish, moaning, hands cradling his abdomen, his face a mask of pain, features a mirror of exquisite agony. Several of the businessmen across the aisle glanced over at him. The elderly English woman behind Paul leaned over the seat, said "The poor lamb," and gently stroked Alec's silky blond hair. "Here." The boy pointed at his stomach and began to weep. "Mummy, it hurts!"

"I know, Alec, it's a tummyache. It will go away in a bit if you just sit back and stay calm." She turned to the stewardess hovering anxiously in the aisle. "Have you any seltzer water?"

The stewardess nodded and hurried again to the galley, returning with a cup of club soda.

"Alec, Mummy promises that if you drink this down the tummyache will begin to go away."

The gasping child clutched at the cup, which his mother held to his lips. He swallowed the soda and then doubled forward in his seat. He looked up at his mother, head twisted strangely, and gave a barely audible cry, a low, strained moan that prompted the stewardess to race to the public address phone.

"Excuse me, ladies and gentlemen, but we have a small medical problem. If there is a doctor aboard, please come to the very front of the aircraft. Thank you."

Beads of sweat had formed on the boy's forehead. He had now ceased to move, and his hand dangled limply over the edge of the seat. He appeared to be asleep.

A tall silver-haired man strode into the first-class cabin and wedged himself through the cluster of people surrounding the ailing child. "Excuse me, I'm a doctor." Paul quickly rose, and the physician seated himself in the empty chair. He placed his fingertips on Alec's right wrist and stared at his watch. After a few seconds he looked up at the stewardess. "How long until we stop at Ilha do Sal?"

"About forty minutes."

"This child must be hospitalized immediately. The pulse is extremely irregular. He appears to be undergoing some sort of allergic reaction or seizure." The doctor turned to the ashen woman kneeling in front of Alec. "Are you this boy's mother?"

"Yes, I am."

"Ma'am, is your son allergic to anything with which he might have come in contact this evening? Has he ever exhibited this sort of illness before?"

"No, never." The woman stared blankly at her son.

"Well, I have no way of determining what's wrong with him without tests being performed. There's nothing I can do for him here. You'll have to take him off the plane when we stop to refuel."

Alec's mother stroked her son's hair and wiped the perspiration from his brow with a moistened napkin.

The boy's sister arose from her seat and knelt by her mother. "Is Alec going to be all right?"

"Yes, Laura, darling, he's just not feeling well. Go back to your seat."

The unconscious boy's body began to jerk, like a marionette manipulated by unseen hands. Quickly the doctor grabbed the boy's arms. "Take hold of his legs; he's convulsing."

The boy shuddered violently, straining to free his pinioned limbs, his small chest heaving spastically. A fleck of spittle formed at the corner of his distorted mouth.

As suddenly as it had begun, the convulsion ceased. Alec lay limply and still in his chair. The doctor again placed his fingertips on the boy's tiny wrist, shifting them to Alec's throat after several seconds to locate the carotid artery. Silence ensued for what seemed an interminable length of time.

The doctor pressed rhythmically on the boy's tiny chest, then blew carefully into the gaping mouth. He repeated this several times, but elicited no reaction.

The doctor looked down into the frightened

face of Alec's mother. "Ma'am, I'm sorry. He's gone."

Alec's mother gazed disbelievingly at her son's white face. "What? What do you mean, 'gone'? Don't be ridiculous, he's just got an upset stomach from all the excitement. Alec is an extremely excitable child." She tugged violently on the boy's wrist. "Alec! Alec!" She slapped the motionless child hard on the face. "Alec!"

The doctor stood and whispered in the ear of the gaping stewardess, who then withdrew and promptly returned with a plastic cup of water and a pill. He took both and smoothly placed the pill in the still-kneeling woman's hand.

Firmly, he said, "Ma'am, please put the pill on your tongue." The stunned woman obediently complied. "Now wash it down with this." Unthinkingly, as if in a daze, she accepted the proffered cup and swallowed the pill.

The doctor gently helped her to her feet. She wore the completely empty expression which accompanies both extreme shock and extreme boredom. The stewardess placed an arm around the woman and slowly walked her out of the cabin to the crew's seating area.

The doctor turned to the tiny flaccid body. He again touched one of Alec's wrists and, reassuring himself that the boy was dead, placed a blanket over the corpse. He glanced at Paul and nodded his head in the direction of Alec's sister. The little girl, after having been prematurely reassured by her mother of her brother's well-being, had become deeply absorbed in a coloring book.

Paul placed himself in her mother's now vacant seat and spoke to the child. "Your mother asked me to tell you that she's talking with a friend in another cabin, and she'll be back in a little bit." The girl looked up briefly at Paul, nodded, and resumed her coloring, tiny tongue protruding past her lips.

The doctor whispered in Paul's ear. "I'll have the captain radio ahead to Ilha do Sal. Watch the girl." Paul nodded silent agreement, and the doctor disappeared in search of a stewardess.

Paul turned to look at Alec's tray. The plate of half-eaten food had disappeared. He rushed back to the galley to find three stewardesses busily emptying scraps from the first-class dinner plates into a waste bin.

He asked, "Who removed that child's dinner?"

They stared at him blankly.

He glared at each of them hard. Nothing, not even a blink.

He returned to the cabin to watch Alec's sister.

The plane began to nose forward as it descended to the rocky outcropping of Ilha do Sal. The lunar landscape of the volcanic island drifted wispily into view as the jet edged under the cloud line. In the fading light Paul glimpsed the massive salt mine for which the tiny island, one of eighteen in the Cape Verde archipelago, was famous. A final circling, and the plane was rolling purposefully across the pitted tarmac to the glorified Quonset hut which served as international airport. A decaying sign in Portuguese bade a halfhearted and unconvincing welcome to the Republic of Cape Verde. Paul wondered why anyone would come here unless they had to.

As soon as the plane lurched to a stop, the main hatchway was opened and the local South African Airways agent came aboard. The dead child's mother was escorted, zombielike, from the plane, accompanied by her daughter, who wanted to know why Alec wasn't getting off as well. Her questions went unanswered by her dazed mother. Paul watched them drift forlornly into the shabby terminal.

Several minutes later two mulattoes with pencil-thin mustaches stepped into the first-class cabin carrying a grubby canvas stretcher. Their sulky dull-eyed expressions were those of the very poor performing unpleasant tasks for the rich. Silently the two placed the lifeless figure that had been Alec on the dilapidated litter and trudged out. An almost audible sigh of relief could be sensed, if not heard, in the cabin.

Within an hour the plane was once again aloft, the child's death an unreal nightmare which had ended as quickly as it had begun. The first-class travelers passed the remainder of the journey sleeping and making desultory and halfhearted stabs at conversation, awkward attempts to pretend that nothing out of the ordinary had occurred.

Paul awoke from a light and troubled sleep to find the stewardesses busily dispensing breakfast, immutable smiles offering no evidence of the tragedy which had taken place only hours before. He accepted freshly squeezed grapefruit juice and an omelet. But before he began, the food looked less appetizing when he remembered why the seat to his left was empty. He ate nothing.

Captain van Vleck once again spoke over the public address. "Good morning, ladies and gentlemen. In just a short while we'll be making our approach to Johannesburg's Jan Smuts Airport. The temperature there is twenty degrees Celsius, sixty-eight degrees Fahrenheit, with clear skies. Local time this morning is eleven forty-five. We hope you've had a pleasant trip, and thank you once again for choosing South African Airways."

The aircraft lazily descended. Below, the verdant farms and prosperous suburbs of Johannesburg sprawled across the open veld.

Farther south, the city's modern towers formed a dramatic skyline above the flat plain of the southern Transvaal. Paul felt a rush of adrenaline.

The passengers disembarked eagerly, anticipating the chance to tell those greeting them beyond the customs barrier of the grisly occurrence of the previous night. Paul made his way through immigration and headed for the baggage claim. After a prolonged wait for his luggage, he exited the terminal and entered the taxi at the head of the cab queue.

The fifteen-kilometer ride to Johannesburg

lasted only twenty minutes; the broad highway to the city lay uncongested, if unattractive, under the flawless cerulean sky of South Africa. The driver quickly bypassed the dumpy mountains of earth tailings which remind every visitor of the mines, the inconceivably vast gold mines, which are both Johannesburg's raison d'être and its lifeblood. It is otherwise an improbable city, a riverless city, a mushroom eccentrically sprouted on a once-barren stretch of desolate and windswept veld. It is the legacy of a penniless prospector who on a fateful day in March 1886 panned the first yellow metal ever taken from the seemingly limitless gold reef of the Witwatersrand.

The taxi approached the central section of Johannesburg. The ramrodlike Strijdom Tower, the tallest building in Africa, soared above the skyscrapers of the financial district. The driver observed Paul craning his neck to glimpse the top.

The driver assumed Paul was a tourist. "She's a beauty, is she not? More than two hundred and fifty meters tall and solid as they come. One used to be able to visit the observation deck on the highest story, but since the unrest began the whole tower's been off limits to the public." His accent was the broad drawl of South African English.

The taxi entered Fox Street and passed the imposing Stock Exchange and Chamber of Mines buildings. The streets were deserted. On a weekday, they would be swarming with blacks from the blacks-only suburb of Soweto; the blacks-only bus terminal was just a few blocks away.

The driver turned right on Kruis Street, then quickly left onto Main Street to the vast Carlton Centre. The porte-cochere of the legendary Carlton Hotel, and its annex, the newer but even more elegant and luxurious Carlton Court, protected an assortment of Mercedes sedans, Jaguars, and limousines from the infrequent Johannesburg rain.

Paul leaned forward. "I'm going to the Court, the next building."

The driver nodded and edged the cab another fifty yards down Main Street to the Carlton Court. A black footman in spotless gray livery and top hat opened Paul's door for him and hefted the American's suitcases into the subdued clubbiness of the oak-paneled lobby.

A studiously groomed blonde flashed Paul a brilliant smile and asked him to fill out his registration papers. When he finished she glanced at the bellhop waiting unobtrusively by Paul's baggage. "Wendell, please show Mr. Jenssen to suite number four. Mr. Jenssen, please let us know if there is anything which you require."

With a nod of thanks, Paul allowed himself to be led by the black houseman to his suite on the fifth floor, a sumptuous apartment of muted blues and grays. The houseman drew the curtains, revealing the pool and trees below, and withdrew after receiving Paul's tip.

Paul sat on the edge of the enormous bed and picked up the receiver of the antique French telephone. The hotel operator came on the line. "May I help you, please?"

"Yes, I'd like 884–5585 please."

The ringing which began at the other end was interrupted by a gruff "Hallo."

"Pieter?"

"Ja, dis Pieter." The man's Afrikaans was curt and clipped.

"Pieter, it's Paul Jenssen."

There was a pause of several seconds. "Paul! My God, it's been ages. Where are you?"

"I'm back here in Johannesburg, at the Carlton Court. Why aren't you in church?"

"Oh, I got a good night's sleep last night." They both laughed.

"Pieter, are you free?"

"Yes, of course. Let's see, it's one o'clock now. Can you come 'round for tea? Say three-thirty? Or is that too early?"

"Make it four, if that's okay. I want to wash up and run a quick errand first. Same address?"

Danniken laughed richly. "Of course. We Afrikaners aren't like you nomadic Americans—once we find a house we stick to it like limpets."

"That's reassuring. See you at four, Pieter."

Paul hung up and quickly unpacked his luggage. After a hurried shower and shave, he descended to the lobby and approached the woman at the reception desk.

"Excuse me, is the public library open today?"

"Normally no, Mr. Jenssen, but they're experimenting with Sunday hours this month, so you're in luck. The library will be open until six this evening. It's about a ten-minute walk from here. Or shall I call you a taxi?"

"No, thanks, I know where it is, I'll walk there."

Paul left the hotel and walked west on Kruis Street. After three blocks he turned left on Market Street and headed south. He passed the Old Johannesburg Post Office, and a little farther on, the grand City Hall. In a few minutes he arrived at the steps of the imposing Central Library.

Inside, Paul found his way to the nonfiction section. There he located the heavy blue leatherbound volumes entitled *Who's Who in South Africa.* They were annual publications with the year stenciled in gold on the binder. He took the book labeled 1965 to one of the many old wooden reading desks in the high-ceiling room and flipped it open. He withdrew a small notepad and pen from his blazer and slowly began to wade through the several hundred biographies whose owners' last names began with the letter *F.*

After an hour, he had perused the entire section. He replaced the volume and approached the information desk. A white-haired woman with spectacles hanging around her neck stood guard. Paul smiled to himself at how much she resembled the stereotypical librarian.

"Excuse me, I wonder if you could help me. I'd like to obtain some reading material on South Africa. On its socio-political background."

The matron looked up and smiled. "Of course, sir. Any particular aspect?"

"I'm interested in doing some research on an organization called the *Broederbond*."

The woman's smile faded to a look of surprise, her eyebrows furrowing. "Well, sir . . ." She hesitated. "I don't believe we actually have any books on the group, but we could probably find mention of it in the encyclopedia." She led Paul over to a shelf containing several dozen oversized volumes.

In the *B* book Paul located the small paragraph describing the *Broederbond*. "A now-defunct Afrikaner cultural organization founded in 1918 by two Johannesburg men, as a reaction to perceived British cultural imperialism. At its peak in the 1930s, the association enjoyed a membership of several thousand, before its virtual demise following the Second World War." He snorted and turned to the publishing information at the beginning of the volume. The encyclopedia was, as he suspected, of South African origin. A little bit of creative history, he thought.

Paul turned to the librarian hovering nearby. "Unfortunately, this doesn't help me much. Doesn't the library have anything else on the subject?"

"I'm afraid not, sir. It's not exactly something that people, um, talk much about, if you get my meaning." She looked at Paul furtively.

"Thank you for your help." Paul arose and walked outside. The avenue sweltered in the unseasonably warm afternoon. He descended the steps toward the hotel to catch a taxi.

Out of the corner of his eye, Paul noticed a

small movement in one of the cars, a gray Peugeot parked ten yards away. Inside the motionless sedan were what appeared to be two people, both reading newspapers which completely obscured their faces. The windows were up in spite of the eighty degree weather.

Paul passed the car and soon turned right onto Kruis Street. He looked back over his shoulder, and noticed the Peugeot pulling gently away from the curb in his direction. Both of the faces of the two occupants were concealed by wraparound sunglasses with mirrored lenses.

He walked to the line of taxis waiting under the Carlton's porte cochere and seated himself in the back of the first one. He gave the driver Danniken's address and the car pulled away from the curb.

As the taxi passed Market Street Paul glanced to his left. The gray Peugeot had parked again, its creepy occupants having resumed their reading. Paul watched it through the rear window.

Just as he was passing out of sight, Paul saw one of the newspapers drop. The man was speaking into a telephone, his shaded eyes looking at Paul's disappearing taxi.

4

The midafternoon dust had mixed with the oil and gas fumes of the traffic, rendering the hot African air disagreeable to inhale. The sun reflected blindingly off innumerable towers of glass and steel, like millions of facets on an enormous jewel. The refracted rays bathed the city in their harsh light.

The taxi headed north to quiet suburbs, inhabited by whites of comfortable income. The oppressive quality of the downtown atmosphere and of the congested highways which lead out of Johannesburg gradually yielded to the tranquility of quiet avenues lined with pastel houses, creating an illusion of English countryside in the middle of the Transvaal.

The cab skirted the small towns of Killarney and Rosebank, where bank vice presidents and small-business owners maintained homes on perfectly manicured lawns. It passed the charming village of Hyde Park, where well-heeled housewives complained to each other over lunch at the country club about the difficulty of engaging good cooks from the cheap labor pool in the all-black township of Alexandria five miles to the east.

The taxi rolled quietly into the lush hamlet of Sandton, in whose palatial mansions the gold and diamond barons play at country squire. A conspicuous yellow police car idled at the curb of the road, clearly awaiting nonresidents and uninvited sightseers. The masters of the policy of "separate but equal" knew enough to conceal their booty.

The car turned right onto a quiet lane edged with jacaranda trees. The houses were neither as large nor as opulent as those in other sections of the village, but they were secluded and set well apart from each other, each home hidden behind the high brick or concrete walls which in the white suburbs obscure virtually all residences from public scrutiny.

The driver craned his neck to look at Paul. "What was the number, sir?"

"Eighteen."

The cab pulled up to the high gate of a charming three-story white Victorian, complete with lace woodwork on the porch and a turret on the top floor. A large collie barked vociferously on the broad expanse of lawn behind the iron fences as Paul paid the driver.

A young woman with long, strawberry-blond hair emerged from the house onto the porch and, seeing Paul, ran nimbly to the front gate. "Yes?" She smiled at him through the heavy bars.

"Hello. I'm Paul Jenssen. I'm a friend of Professor Danniken."

The young woman swung open the gate. "I'm happy to meet you, Mr. Jenssen. I'm Beth Danniken, Pieter's daughter. Please come in."

Paul walked through the portal as the taxi drove away, and held his hand out for the enormous dog to smell. Almost immediately the great collie began to wag his tail and, jumping, placed his powerful forepaws on Paul's chest. A large and purposeful pink tongue emerged from the dog's long mouth and proceeded to moisten Paul's left eye.

"Jamie!" Beth called the dog. "Jamie come *here*." The collie reluctantly released his victim and padded over to his mistress.

Paul grinned. "Thank you. You saved me from the horrible fate of being licked to death."

The girl laughed, her blue eyes sparkling with humor. "Jamie's probably the world's worst watchdog, Mr. Jenssen. The house could be broken into and he'd be playing fetch with the burglars." She scratched the collie's ears.

"He's a great dog. And please call me Paul."

"All right, Paul. I know my father can't wait to see you. He was ecstatic that you called. He's waiting in his study."

She led him into the old house. The interior was decorated simply and attractively with antiques and heavy wood pieces, in the manner of a nineteenth-century farmhouse. Artwork was everywhere: sculptures by black African artists, magnificent tribal shields, and framed dyed bolts of Zulu wool covered most of the available wall space.

Beth knocked on a door of weathered oak halfway down the hall. A gruff "Come in" issued from within.

Inside, at an antique teak desk, sat Pieter Danniken. Intelligent and good-natured blue eyes peered out from beneath a set of extraordinary beetling gray eyebrows. A shaggy mop of white hair perched unmanageably atop a slightly oversized head, evoking an image of Albert Einstein.

"Paul!" Danniken jumped up from the chair, his big frame almost knocking over several gilt pictures on the side of the desk. "Great to see you!" He wrapped Paul in an affectionate bear hug.

"It's sure good to see you, Pieter. It's been way too long. And if you'd told me a little more about your daughter it would have been a lot sooner."

Beth blushed and offered coffee. Both men declined, and she withdrew from the room.

"Sit." Danniken gestured to an oversized brass-studded leather chair of the sort which inhabit male sanctums around the world. "What propitious circumstances bring you to Johannesburg?"

"Pieter, right now I make my living as a writer. It's been my occupation since I left South Africa two years ago. I'm—"

"No more consulting for multinational American corporations?" Danniken interrupted, placing a slightly mocking accent on the word *consulting*.

Paul's eyes narrowed to a squint. He gazed for a while at his host. "You knew?"

"I was diplomatic enough not to have asked you. But you took such pains never to be seen publicly in my company. At the same time you worked for 'American commercial interests.' Quite a nebulous catchphrase, no? Anyway, no real commercial representative would have the personal political leanings to want to even surreptitiously associate with me. You really worked for the U.S. government, didn't you? Snuggling up to our beloved South African elite and all that sort of thing, eh?"

Paul grinned at Danniken for several moments. "Pieter, you're pretty perceptive for an art professor. Does anyone else know?"

"Not that I know of." Danniken smiled. "The people in power here are so convinced of their own righteousness that they don't second-guess those who are friendly to their cause, so to speak. Your friendliness to them was probably perfectly natural and understandable in their view."

"I can't believe all those years you knew, or suspected, and never said anything."

"Is it so surprising? I figured that you'd tell me if you could, so why worry you by letting on that I didn't believe your cover?"

"I suppose so. Listen, Pieter, I've got something to tell you. Two days ago, in London, I came across two letters written by Hendrik Verwoerd. They tell a fairly amazing story."

Danniken raised his eyebrows in curiosity. He fiddled absentmindedly with his wristwatch, repeatedly buckling and unbuckling the clasp. Paul watched him, momentarily distracted.

"One letter, written in 1965, mentions a large fund, whose apparent custodian is someone known by the code name 'the Treasurer.' There's a strong indication that this Treasurer's initials are E.F. I want to find out who he or she is. Or was."

Danniken leaned forward, his chin resting in his right hand. "How much money?"

"I don't know. It doesn't say. But from the tone of the letter I'd say it was enormous. The money sounds like it's some sort of slush fund. I'm fairly sure it's owned and operated by the *Broederbond,* but for what specific purpose I have no idea."

His host whistled. "That's a relatively lethal beehive to go poking one's nose into, I can tell you from personal experience. I don't know if you realize just how dangerous the people in the *Broederbond* are."

Paul shrugged. This further agitated Danniken. "Good God, man, you've seen firsthand what happens when the *Broederbond* is involved. People just disappear. Those men are fanatics. This is nothing to fool around with."

Paul nodded. "I know. But it would be incredible to be able to expose something like this in my book. No one's ever managed to infiltrate the *Broederbond.*"

"Incredible, absolutely. But is it worth risking your life?"

Paul folded his hands in his lap, silent for a

moment. When he spoke it was in a voice charged with emotion. "There's more to it than just a great story. You never knew Christine, but she had a real passion for social justice. Prejudice, bigotry, and hypocrisy infuriated her.

"Christine was killed as a direct result of my work. I can't do anything to bring her back, but I can do a little to make the burden of her murder less painful. She'd have hated everything the *Broederbond* stands for. I want to expose what they are as a sort of honor to her memory."

Danniken realized his warnings were to no avail and crossed his arms. "But if they really amassed a great deal of money, how could it all be kept hidden?"

"Well, the Swiss are pretty tight-lipped when it comes to depositors. So are Liechtenstein, the Bahamas, and Vanuatu. It could be in a secret account in any of those countries. In fact, the letter alludes to the Treasurer holding the codes, and that would fit perfectly with a numbered account in a money haven. Therefore, it would be something the public wouldn't be able to find out about."

"Well, maybe if you ferret out the Treasurer, you can take it one step further and find out the location and size of the fund. Maybe even how to get into it. Then we could all retire to Miami, eh?"

His guest leaned back in the comfortable armchair and chuckled.

"Paul, it's a wild story. If it's true, the Treasurer must be someone who enjoys extraordinary protection by the elite of this country." Danniken rose and paced slowly behind his desk, gently stroking his lower lip. "It would have to be someone who is trusted beyond all shadow of doubt by the Nationalists. Absolutely, with that kind of money involved."

Paul nodded. "There's also the significant possibility that the Treasurer is either dead or at least retired, and that a successor has been named. I have no idea how old the Treasurer was in 1965 when Verwoerd wrote the second letter, but with a position carrying that kind of responsibility he can't have been too young when he started, which means by now he'd be pushing eighty or ninety. But even if there was a change, perhaps I can trace the current Treasurer by uncovering his predecessor. Obviously, this all assumes that the fund hasn't been dismantled since 1965. The tone of the second letter, however, makes me think that it was too firmly entrenched, and that it most probably still exists."

Danniken continued to pace, already lost in thought. "E.F., E.F., who could that be?" His forehead became a grove of wrinkles. "Paul, let me think awhile on this after our dinner. I may be able to dig up some candidates."

"Pieter, I looked in *Who's Who in South Africa* and came up with four possibilities."

"Well, then, after I think of some people we'll compare and then you'll have somewhere to begin. How's that?"

"Great. Thanks. But Pieter, there's something else. A proverbial fly in the ointment."

"Yes?"

"Somebody knows I'm here, and they're not happy about it. A few hours ago, I was at the library in Jo'burg doing a little research on the *Broederbond* and to look at the *Who's Who*. As I walked back to the hotel, I'm fairly sure I was followed."

"The government?"

"I have no idea. Actually, I doubt it. If they wanted me out they could easily have denied me entry into the country. But it's worse than just that."

"Why? What else happened?"

"Yesterday, on the flight from London to Jo'burg, a young child sitting next to me had a freaky allergic reaction to something. He had convulsions and died. It was really terrible. I never saw anything like it. And I don't think it was natural."

"Why not?"

"Right after we placed our supper orders, I offered to let the kid take my seat by the window. Fine. Except that when the food came out, he ended up taking my tray. We both had ordered steak, so there wasn't a problem. He ate the meal I should have eaten. And he went into convulsions about fifteen minutes later. During the chaos his plate vanished. Kind of a coincidence?"

"Have you gone to the police?"

"I can't. If I did that I'd have to explain my

presence here, and I'd almost certainly be deported on the next plane out of here, which I just can't afford, not right now. My reason for being here wouldn't exactly make them do cartwheels."

"Of course, you're right." Danniken jutted his chin forward aggressively. "What we need to do is to smoke out whomever's trying to stop you."

Paul nodded. "If I continue investigating, they're bound to come after me again. Then I'd be able to get a fix on who wants me to stop. Or maybe just wants me dead."

"Well, let's talk about this later. Now tell me why you're staying at the Carlton."

"I gave up my weekly rental flat in Rosebank when I went to London to do research. I thought I'd look for someplace different now that I'm back. I'm at the Carlton Court until I find something."

"Paul, why not stay with us? We have tons of room going to waste."

"Here? Pieter, I'm not here for just a few days—I'm here writing a book."

"So what? It'd be nice to have a little more life around here. Why don't you stay with us and write your book here? We'd love to have you. I also think you'd be a good deal safer here."

Paul smiled, speechless. After a minute he nodded. "Thank you, Pieter. That's a wonderful offer, and it would be great to stay with friends. But shouldn't we ask Beth?"

Danniken chuckled. "I think she'd be out of her mind to object to a good-looking young fellow staying here, but you're right. If you'll just excuse me a second, I'll nip into the kitchen to make sure it's okay." He lumbered out of the study, only to return a moment later.

"It's agreed. Now we've got a writer under our roof. You'll stay for supper, of course, and you can pick up your things from the hotel tomorrow. I think we have an extra toothbrush, so you have no excuse. And I believe Beth is making lobster for supper."

"You convinced me." Paul laughed. "I'd hate to tell you what South African lobster tails go for in the U.S."

Danniken called his daughter into the study. "Mr. Jenssen has graciously agreed to honor our humble table tonight, if it would not be too burdensome for the cook."

Beth turned to Paul. "Wonderful, as long as Mr. Jenssen refrains from making any commentaries on the backward status of South African cuisine."

Paul laughed. "I'm sure it's not, and I won't."

"Supper should be ready in about half an hour, so if you'll excuse me ..." She disappeared down the hall.

"Beth enjoys cooking for company, Paul. I hope you're hungry."

"Does Beth work?"

"Yes, she's a veterinarian with the Johannesburg Zoo, in charge of the newborn section. It's a time-consuming job, plus she's on call for off-hours deliveries. But she loves it. And she still manages to fix her old pa dinner now and then."

With mild sarcasm Paul asked, "What more could one ask for in a daughter?"

Danniken grinned and nodded. They settled back into their chairs.

"So how've you been, Pieter?"

"Oh, not so bad. Not so bad as some in this troubled land. I assume you're aware that it's becoming rather more tense than usual. The blacks grow less and less malleable, and the hard-line racists grow ever more stubborn and determined to tough it out and break their will. Our infamous secret police first manage to pummel to death some hapless prisoner who's been caught lobbing a Molotov cocktail or some such nonsense. They then do their creative best to whitewash it as a suicide, God bless 'em. 'Used his sheet to hang himself' is pretty much the standard explanation, I believe. Difficult to explain away the black and blue marks, of course.

"Then there's a funeral, in spite of the ban on public funerals, and more blacks are imprisoned, and get pummeled to death, and so on. It's the most hopeless whirlpool of blood and murder and countermurder. That cosmetic liberalization de Klerk implemented in 1989 didn't last long. The pressure from the far right was too strong. They would really rather die than live without apartheid."

"Pieter, is it worse now than during Sharpeville and Soweto?"

"My friend, those were mere warmups to the main attraction now in progress. The Soweto riots were grim, but there did not exist the utter fearlessness which is now exhibited by the blacks. They still see death at the hands of the police, but this time they do not flinch. I think, and I'm not sure, mind you, but I think they will not back down this time. What the whites have most feared throughout the short, tawdry history of postwar South Africa may at last be upon us. You can keep an entire people down just so long." The professor looked calmly at Paul. "South Africa will cease to be as we know it. Oh, I don't know how long—a year, two years, maybe just a few months. But Paul, I feel in my heart that this is not going to be just another Soweto."

The two men were quiet, each trying to imagine the changes a black government would bring.

Suddenly the powerful barking of the collie outside shattered the silence. Danniken walked over to the window and opened it. The volleys of barks were almost deafening.

"Jamie! Quiet! Jamie! What in God's name is that dog going on about?" The barking persisted.

The men left the room and walked out onto the front porch. The African heat and sun had yielded to the heavy coolness of evening and the murkey light of dusk. Crickets trilled. By some nearby pond, a frog burped.

By the iron-barred gate, the white stripe of the collie's fur was barely visible. The dog was barking crazily.

Danniken cupped his hands to his mouth. "Jamie, come *here!*" The big dog ignored him.

Across the road, a car's engine roared to life. The hazy outline of a dark green Jaguar came fleetingly into view and then vanished in the direction of the highway back to Johannesburg.

"Pieter, are you under regular surveillance?"

"Well, I believe the police keep tabs on what I'm up to. But they don't drive cars like that." Danniken shot an uneasy look at Paul. "Let's go inside." They entered the house, Paul glancing again in the direction of the road, invisible now through the darkening twilight.

The wonderful aromas billowing from the kitchen made Paul's stomach constrict. Beth emerged from the kitchen. "Gentlemen, if I may direct you to the dining room, dinner is served." She withdrew to the kitchen.

Paul followed his host to the simple and elegant dining room, its yellowwood table laid with gleaming family silver and old Limoges porcelain. Beth entered bearing a steaming Spode tureen and began to serve the soup.

She smiled at them as she seated herself. In the flickering candlelight her fair hair shone softly. "Dig in."

The soup was excellent. Danniken said nothing, other than to nod appreciatively at his daughter. Paul savored it. "Beth, this is delicious. What is it?"

"I'm glad you like it. It's cream of leek."

"Where did you learn to cook like this?"

"I taught myself. If I'd left the cooking to my father he'd be making fish and chips every evening."

"That's not a very charitable thing to say about your aged father, child." Danniken facetiously pretended to sulk.

"I'm sorry. Pa's right. We'd be going out for fish and chips every night; it would be too much trouble to make."

Her father chuckled. "Touché. Now tell us what enticing delicacy is to follow this superb soup."

She removed their plates and in a minute returned with an enormous platter of sautéed lobster tails and fresh asparagus. "Pa said you were fond of seafood, Paul. I hope you like lobster."

Paul stared seriously at her. "I do. But what are you two going to eat?"

They laughed and began to eat, the slightly crunchy asparagus the perfect foil to the succulent crustaceans. A Stellenbosch chardonnay, a crisp vintage from one of the small vineyards in South Africa's Western Cape, beautifully complemented the light fare.

The meal passed leisurely, Danniken entertaining them with stories of the Boer pioneers in the Transvaal and of the lawless gold rush era. The soft evening breeze drifted in through the open window, causing the silk curtains to billow and the candles to flicker frantically. Several times Paul found himself watching Beth. She would catch his eye, smile warmly, and then return her attention to her father.

For dessert, there was a raspberry tart, complete with an English custard sauce. They nearly finished it off, Paul and Danniken each going back greedily for thirds.

"Beth, you have got to open a restaurant." Paul leaned back in his chair and savored the remaining chardonnay in his glass.

"I just might someday. How does 'Lizzy's Bar and Grill' sound? Or maybe 'Bessy's Chop House'?"

"Hmm. Not pretentious enough. How about 'The Crystal Chameleon' or 'The Sign of The Iguana'?"

She raised her glass. "To The Sign of the Iguana."

Danniken rose from the table. "Paul, while you plan my daughter's career, I'm going to give some thought to those names you need. Beth has already fixed up your room, so I'll see you both in the morning." He patted Paul on the shoulder and walked around the table to kiss his daughter. "Don't stay up too late, you two. I don't want to eat breakfast alone." He walked toward his study.

Paul helped Beth clear the table. His offer to wash the dishes was declined, but she agreed to let him dry them. They quickly finished cleaning up and walked outside to sit on the porch steps. They sat for a long while in silence, listening to the sounds of the evening. In the sky, Paul looked for and found the Southern Cross, the beacon constellation visible only in the Southern Hemisphere.

She noticed him staring at the heavens. "The aborigines have an old wives' tale that if a mother gives birth outside under the Southern Cross, her child will have a long and happy life. Sounds sort of like a fortune cookie."

"It a beautiful constellation." They said nothing for several minutes, and then he asked, "Have you always lived with your father?"

She nodded. "My mother died a month after I graduated from the university ten years ago. Pa's never really come to grips with losing her. He wraps himself up in his teaching and in working for change in the political situation, so that he doesn't have time to miss her.

"I used to get so angry that he couldn't pick himself up and face her death," she continued. "But he loved her too much. So I stay here and look after him. It doesn't stop me from having my career."

"Your father mentioned that you're a vet at the zoo. The baby animals, right?"

She brightened. "Yes. We had four births today, a record. One of them was a snow leopard, our first. She's a real beauty. I was tempted to swipe her and take her home."

"How long have you been at the zoo?"

"Two years, since I finished vet school. I love my work. Baby animals are a zoo's biggest attraction, so the administrators treat me well. It's a great job."

There was an awkward pause. Her eyes met his for a tense moment and then looked away. "You must be exhausted. Come on, I'll show you your room."

They went into the house. Beth led him

upstairs to a cozy guest room complete with canopied bed. "Please let me know if you need anything. Good night. Sleep as late as you like." She withdrew down the hall to her own room. He heard her door click shut.

Paul quickly got into bed and fell asleep immediately. The house was silent. No one was awakened several hours later by the slow creak of the front door opening downstairs, nor was there an audible sound from the rubber-soled shoes softly entering the house through the front hall.

The tiny cottage on the outskirts of Johannesburg had only one large room. It was starkly devoid of all decoration. Except for the five straight-backed wooden chairs placed in a circle around the plain coffee table, there was no furniture. The absence of windows prevented the first cold rays of dawn from piercing the murky interior.

On the small oak table, an old Dutch Bible lay open, its faded passages gloomily lit by a single candle. Adjacent to the Bible reposed a dagger of wrought silver, its haft deeply blackened with many decades of tarnish.

The five figures moved their chairs closer to the improvised altar. Their aged and craggy faces were dwarflike in the candlelight, mouths hard and unforgiving, eyes cold, glittering flint.

In soft Afrikaans, one of the five began to intone the words of the Twenty-third Psalm. The other four joined in. Slowly, purposefully, they spoke the prayer, their frail breath hardly disturbing the solitary flame. ". . . in the presence of my enemies. You anoint my head with oil; my cup runs over. Surely goodness and mercy shall follow me all the days of my life, and I will dwell in the house of the Lord, forever."

The leader who had begun the prayer looked stonily into the eyes of each of the others. "Let us begin."

"We shall follow." The four chanted automatically.

"We meet in these early hours for a council of war. At hand is a time which we have always dreaded and for which we have long prepared. Our nation grows restive.

"There is a spy in our midst. We are watching him. He sleeps, even at this moment, at the home of Danniken, the traitor to his own people." The speaker pressed thin, desiccated lips together in a faint smile. "When the time is right, Danniken must be removed." The four listeners glanced at each other furtively, not bothering to conceal their smug pleasure.

The leader continued. "We have decided not to hinder the spy, but to watch him closely. He knows of the existence of our sacred Treasury and seeks to learn its guardian's identity. If we were to remove him, our enemies might send a replacement, whom we might fail to recognize as such. Better the devil we know . . ." There were nods.

"If the unrest throughout our land becomes much worse, I fear that you, the Executive Council of our beloved *Broederbond*, will be forced to issue the formal notice of evacuation to our full membership. Some have left already.

"Today is the twenty-fourth of May. Let us fix June the fifth as the tentative day of notice. All members will then have ten days to leave South Africa. June the fifteenth will thus be the Day of Surprise. To reiterate, the fifth is only tentative. I am fully cognizant of the finality intrinsic to the notice. Let us pray this does not come to pass. Are there any questions? Then let us close in prayer."

The speaker began to recite the Thirty-fourth Psalm. The other four listened now in silence. The voice was eerie in the unsteady candlelight. ". . . Many are the afflictions of the righteous. But the Lord delivers him out of them all. He guards all his bones; not one of them is broken. Evil shall slay the wicked, and those who hate the righteous shall be condemned. The Lord redeems the soul of His servants, and none of those who trust in Him shall be condemned. Amen."

"Amen," the seated figures whispered.

"This meeting is concluded. Good morning, my Brothers."

"Good morning, honored Treasurer."

5

Paul awoke to the smell of bacon frying. Hundreds of birds chattered in the jacaranda tree just outside his window. The sun streamed into the room between the semi-drawn curtains. He smiled.

After quickly showering and dressing, he joined his two hosts downstairs in the white-tiled kitchen. On the set table beneath an enormous bouquet of pink and white daisies rested a large basket of freshly baked scones, wrapped in yellow linen. Next to it lay silver platters of kippers, grilled tomatoes, and fried potatoes. On a sideboard, a mixed grill of farmer's sausages and smoked ham sat in regal splendor.

Pieter Danniken, wearing khakis and an old tweed jacket, was seated at the table's head, a newspaper in one hand and a glass of orange juice in the other. Beth Danniken was behind the large old-fashioned stove, an old blue apron draped over her jeans and sweatshirt. She was frying a large skillet of mushrooms. They both looked up as Paul entered.

"Good morning, Paul. Pa and I were about to dig in and leave you an appetizing selection of cold cereals." Beth smiled at him sweetly.

Paul gazed at the feast. "I'm sure that would have been a good thing for my waistline. This looks wonderful. We don't exactly get breakfasts like this in America."

Danniken motioned Paul to a chair to his right. "That's why there are so many psychiatrists there. Nothing like a solid breakfast to boost one's spirits."

Beth spooned the crisp and juicy mushrooms into a large delft bowl and placed them on the table. "To say nothing of one's cholesterol count." She winked at Paul and sat down across from him on her father's left.

Danniken glared at his daughter over his spectacles, his enormous eyebrows furrowed. "Cholesterol, hah! If people would stop worrying about extending their stays on earth by a few weeks and try and enjoy a little more of what life has to offer, they'd be a lot happier. Here, Paul, try these. They're Beth's specialty." He pointed at the bowl Beth had just placed in the middle.

"I absolutely never, ever worry about cholesterol," Paul said, deadpan, and helped himself to a portion of the enormous mushrooms.

The three dug into the large breakfast, making a creditable inroad into the mountain of hearty fare. Danniken nodded with approval when Paul helped himself to a second helping of the kippers. "Nice to see a fellow eat a proper meal, not pick at all this oat bran and whatnot like they all do nowadays."

Paul patted his stomach. "If this is proper, I'd hate to see what you South Africans call a pig-out. That was great, Beth."

She beamed at him.

Danniken said to his daughter, "Beth, I have to catch the three o'clock flight to Cape Town. If you need anything, you can reach me at your Aunt Mavis's; I'm going to stay with her. I'll be back tomorrow evening after I give the other speech in Durban."

"I'll be here, working in the garden. I have off today and I'm on call tomorrow, but we're not expecting any births."

After finishing off the pot of strong coffee, the three of them cleaned up. Paul washed the dishes while Danniken dried. Beth put away the breakfast things and cleared the table. Afterward, her father took Paul into his study and shut the door behind them.

Danniken seated himself behind the old desk and pulled on a pair of antiquated reading glasses. He pointed to a pad of notepaper lying on the desktop. "Paul, I came up with three possibilities regarding the identity of that Treasurer we spoke of last night. Each of them was a powerful figure in Afrikaner society in the nineteen sixties. All three are still alive. They all have the initials E. F., and they all live here in Johannesburg. Here." He tore the paper from the pad and proffered it.

Paul, seated in the leather chair in front of the

desk, took the paper and examined it. "Pieter, all three of these are on my list." He pulled a folded sheet of paper from his pants pocket and consulted it. "But I also thought Eisso Friedrikson might be a fourth possibility worth thinking about. Did you consider him?"

"Friedrikson? Really? Actually, he never even occurred to me. From what I know of him, he hardly seems likely. What made you pick him out?"

"According to *Who's Who* he's the head of the Dutch Reformed Church of Johannesburg. His grandfather was a founder of South African Railways. He's perfect. What would disqualify him?"

"Did *Who's Who* say anything about his marital status?"

Paul examined his notes. "No, it didn't mention anything in particular."

"Well, he's unmarried." Danniken smiled at him.

Paul smiled back. "Which automatically disqualifies him for membership in the *Broederbond*. Bang, he's out of the running."

"Exactly. He couldn't possibly be the Treasurer if he weren't even admitted to the *Broederbond*."

"So we're left with these three." Paul looked again at his notes. The three biographies other than the discarded bishop's read like stereotypical pillars of society.

Falkenhaus, Ernst; government official. Born 18 October 1907, Johannesburg. Son of Rolf and Berthe (van Hennig). Married Anna von Dienen 1935. Educated University of the Witwatersrand and Heidelberg University. Served in the Army 1928–1930. Joined Diplomatic Service 1930. Consul-General, Edinburgh, Scotland 1941–1943. Deputy Chief of Mission, Bern, Switzerland, 1943–1946. Ambassador to Spain, 1946–1952. Deputy Foreign Minister 1952–1958. Press Secretary to the President 1958–1962. Professor, University of the Witwatersrand, 1962–1965. Minister without Portfolio 1965–1975. Address: 33 Eyck Street, Sandton City (home).

Feldberg, Erich; businessman. Born 2 January 1903, Durban. Son of Erich and Wilhelmina (Haymerle). Married Marlene de Weese 1924 (deceased 1988). One son, two daughters. Educated University of the Witwatersrand. Served in Navy 1926–1930. Joined De Beers Corporation 1930. Vice President for Operations 1943–1948. Vice President for Production Control 1948–1951. Administrative Vice President 1951–1956. Senior Vice President 1956–1959. Board of Directors 1958–1972. Counsel to the Corporation 1962–1972. Club: Kruger Club, Johannesburg. Address: 14 Van Nostrand Avenue, Rosebank (home).

Fortner, Erich; ecclesiastic. Born 10 March 1910. Son of Jan and Sigrid (van Wyck). Married Anthonia Merwe 1939. One son.

Educated University of Stellenbosch. Served in Army. Ordained in Dutch Reformed Church 1925. Named bishop 1940. Served as chaplain with Army forces in North Africa 1942–1943. Assistant Archbishop of Johannesburg 1955. Founded *Afrikaners for God*, 1958, conservative religious-political organization. Address: c/o Afrikaners for God, 18 De Witt Street, Johannesburg (office).

"Pieter, do you know any of these men personally? I'm going to need an in."

"Unfortunately, I know them only by reputation. We move in different, or, to be more precise, opposing political circles. I don't know that I can be of much help to you. Getting close to these people won't be easy."

Paul was silent. Abruptly he arose. "Pieter, where's your telephone book?"

Danniken pulled a well-used volume from his bottom desk drawer. He handed it to Paul and slid the telephone across the blotter toward his guest.

Paul flipped through the pages, located a number with his finger, and dialed it on the telephone.

Almost immediately, a crisp female voice answered. "United States Consulate. May I help you?"

"Yes, would you please tell me whether Patricia Ryan still works there?"

"Yes, she does. Shall I connect you, sir?"

Paul gave a thumbs-up sign to Danniken and said, "Yes, put me through, please." Cupping his hand over the mouthpiece, he said to Pieter, "I got to know this woman when I was attached to the embassy."

Another woman's voice, deeper in pitch, came on the line. "Political section, Pat Ryan."

"Pat, it's Paul Jenssen."

"Well, Paul Jenssen. How the hell are you?" The woman laughed huskily.

"Great. I'm here in Jo'burg working on a story. And how are you, ma'am?"

"Not so bad, and don't you ma'am me. I'm definitely not a ma'am." She interrupted herself with a violent smoker's cough. "So does this mean I get to see your ugly mug, or are you too busy to have lunch with an old lady?"

"Well, Pat, dear, I am extremely busy, but it's not every day that I get invited to lunch by an old lady of such unusually advanced age. Thus, I will make time."

She snorted. "Thanks a lot, sport. I love you, too. Are you free today?"

"Sure, say around twelve-thirty?"

"Perfect. Drop by my office, and we'll decide where to eat then."

"Fine. Will you be wearing something bright and colorful so that I can recognize you? Say a big red hibiscus tucked behind your left ear?"

"Smart-ass. Twelve-thirty, don't be late." She hung up.

On a cramped vinyl couch in the waiting room immediately adjoining the office of the director of the Committee for State Security, two men sat, waiting. They were, outwardly, a study in contrast. On the left-hand side of the sofa sat Colonel Georgi Vasylich, tall and slight of build, impassively smoking a dark brown cigarette crammed with Crimean tobacco. His dark hair, graying at the temples, was neatly combed and carefully parted. He gazed coolly at the shut door leading into the sanctum, wherein his boss, the chief of the KGB, sat in regal solitude while he made his fearful underlings sweat.

To Vasylich's right sat Colonel Vladimir Lubichoff. Colonel Lubichoff was short and fairly round, with a curiously compressed nose which looked as if it had been inserted inadvertently into a duck press. He fidgeted. He inspected his fingernails, his jacket buttons, his nose. Colonel Lubichoff made no effort to conceal the feelings of nervousness which swarmed like bumper cars in his tightly knotted stomach.

Colonel Vasylich wanted to slap his colleague Colonel Lubichoff's plump, wandering hand. But he knew that this would not help matters. So he took another languorous drag on the cigarette and exhaled as slowly as he could.

They had received messages at their respective homes the previous evening. They were tersely ordered to appear before the Comrade Director at the Lubyanka at eight the following morning. This allowed them no rest, as merry images of Siberian wasteland, or worse, prevented them from becoming drowsy, much less sleeping. Even though they knew from experience that this was a favorite ploy of the chief's, it did nothing to ease their minds.

It was now nine-fifteen. Colonel Lubichoff's left forefinger was busy probing the less visible recesses of his left ear. Colonel Vasylich lit his tenth cigarette of the day.

The door opened. In its frame stood Alexei Bareshkov. He wore no expression on his face. As those who worked for him knew only too well, that meant nothing, of course.

The men rose instantly and saluted, Vasylich dropping his lit cigarette into the butt-filled ashtray on the coffee table in front of him.

"Inside." Bareshkov curtly ordered the two colonels into his office.

The colonels stood motionless before the glass table that was the director's desk. The director did not ask them to be seated. He ensconced himself behind the desk and began to read from an oversized manila folder. There was no sound in the room save for the ticking of the clock on the desk and the shuffling of Bareshkov's papers as he read.

After a grueling ten minutes, during which the statuelike colonels prayed in earnest that punishment would be nothing worse than exile to Vladivostok, the director looked up from his file. Quietly, almost in a whisper, he asked, "So, will one of you two please explain to me this report you've filed? Will somebody please tell me how this could have happened?" It was a rhetorical request.

Colonel Vasylich and Colonel Lubichoff continued to stare unwaveringly at a point on the wall some six inches above the director's head, although Colonel Lubichoff found himself unable to restrain an audible gulp.

The head of the KGB continued. His audience virtually had to strain to hear him. "I am afraid that I do not see that your assignment, as critical as it was, posed any significant difficulty, at least for two veterans of the world's most powerful intelligence service. Incomprehensible."

Bareshkov glanced again at the folder. "I see here, my dear comrades, that the simple task of incapacitating Perseus, while he was essentially cornered on an airplane, failed miserably. Not only that, but your imbecilic agent accidentally killed a child. A child! What conclusions am I to draw from this—will you please answer me that also?" The director's voice rose dramatically in pitch.

Colonel Vasylich bravely ventured a reply. "With respect, Comrade Director, the agent on the plane—"

The director slammed his right fist against the glass desk, which, by some fluke, failed to shatter. A large magenta blood vessel bulged an inch above his right eyebrow. He began to scream. "Don't talk to me about the agent on the plane. I don't want to hear about the stupid agent on the plane. Do you know why? I'll tell you. Because the agent on the plane is an incompetent idiot."

Bareshkov caught himself. He inhaled deeply. Colonel Vasylich thought he was counting to ten.

He rose from his seat and walked around the desk so that he stood facing his subordinates' backs. He tapped each one gently on the shoulder with a forefinger. They did not flinch.

He resumed speaking again, only softly now. "I would think, after this man masterminded Butov's and Dentev's lovely double defection three years ago, that it would be a matter of personal pride to execute him efficiently and cleanly, now that you have a green light. If your staff is unable to accomplish this, do it yourselves. But do it, immediately.

"I do not think I have stressed enough to you the importance of this assignment. You have no need to know the specifics, but suffice to say, if you two cannot put Perseus out of operation, I will put you out of operation. You have one more chance. Now get out of my sight."

The consulate of the United States in Johannesburg is located in the city's downtown business district. It is merely a suite of offices, not even remotely attaining the grandeur of the U.S. Embassy, an imposing mansion located in the capital city of Pretoria, some fifty miles to the north.

Yet, despite the obvious differences in appearance, the consulate in Johannesburg represents an extremely valuable asset to the interests which rely heavily on it to supply commercial assistance and information. Its primary purpose is to facilitate for American business the sensitive but immensely profitable prospect of operating within South Africa.

Paul Jenssen rode the elevator to the third floor, where he was greeted by a birdlike South African woman.

"Would you please let Pat Ryan know that Paul Jenssen is here? I have an appointment with her."

With a nod of her sparrow-shaped head, the receptionist dialed an extension on her telephone, spoke a few words into the intercom, and within seconds a plump cherubic woman in her early sixties appeared behind the desk.

"Paul, let's have a hug, right now! Don't hold back, honey." They burst out laughing and gave each other a big bear hug.

"Christ, Pat, you'd better lay off the weight lifting; if you get any stronger you're going to injure your next huggee."

"Just call me Rocco." She flexed a biceps beneath her navy silk business suit. "Let's go to lunch. Bodybuilders need a lot of food, as you may have heard." They rode the elevator to the lobby and walked into the brilliant noonday sun.

"Is Indian okay with you, Paul? There's a pretty good place around the block."

"Fine, but won't it be too spicy for you? I seem to recall how frail and delicate your stomach is."

"Very cute. Let's go." They turned the corner to find a small, family-run establishment decorated aggressively with red velveteen wallpaper in a jacquard pattern, red velvet curtains, and somewhat worn red carpeting.

He turned to whisper to her. "Can you get me the decorator's name and number? I'm having my house done."

"Shhh. Don't worry, the food's good. Just keep your eyes closed and you won't have to look around."

They were seated by an obsequiously smiling Bengali who proceeded to recite for five minutes a lengthy list of specials. After the man had finished, Paul said, "I'm sorry, I didn't catch that. What were they again?"

Pat tapped the waiter's arm. "Don't mind this guy. He's not from planet earth."

They ordered an assortment of dishes. Pat self-consciously explained that lunch was her big meal of the day. Paul merely smiled politely.

She leaned across the table and placed a hand gently on his wrist. "You're looking a lot more at peace than you were two years ago. I'm happy to see you feeling better."

The waiter reappeared, bearing a platter of *samosa,* crisp dumplings filled with mashed spiced vegetables, accompanied by half a dozen small dishes of condiments and relishes in which to dip them. With this he brought a pitcher of mango-flavored *lassi,* a pale, creamy iced drink somewhat resembling yogurt or kefir, as a counter to the spicy food.

Pat took a triangular *samosa* and, clutching it delicately by a corner as if she were administering a bath to Achilles, plunged it into a bowl of apricot chutney. She popped the dipped half in her mouth and mumbled, "So what's up, guy?"

Paul dunked one of the dumplings in the sauce and meditatively chewed it. "Pat, when's the next big bash at the embassy?"

"Well, there's one tonight, a biggie. I can't believe they're doing it on a Monday. It's in honor of our new ambassador. Do you know him?" Paul shook his head. "His name is Dr. Philip Hawthorne, and he insists on everyone using 'Dr.' even though he got the degree in economics, not medicine. My mother always used to say that was terribly pretentious, but I suppose times have changed." She sniffed. "Anyway, he arrived last week, and the embassy's putting on the customary welcome bash. All the glitterati should be there. I'm going up to Pretoria this evening. Hey, sport, would you like to go?"

"That would be great. But I need to ask you a favor first. Are there any embassy cars at your disposal here?"

"I can get the Ford Escorts, no problem. The limos I should be able to get with some fancy footwork. But, of course, all the boys always told me I was a terrific dancer." She touched her hair coyly.

"Pat, what I need is this: There are three South Africans living in the suburbs of Johannesburg whom I'd like to meet at this reception. They're VIPs, and if they get an invitation this late they're going to wonder what's going on. But if somebody from the embassy were to call them specially, as if it were a follow-up, they'd probably buy it. We could say the invitations must have been lost. The calls must be profusely apologetic and flattering, with an embassy car placed at the disposal of each guest for the round trip to Pretoria. That should be enough for most egos."

She said nothing, gazing down at the prawn curry the waiter was now ladling onto their plates. When he left she looked up. "Paul, what's this all about? This is not your ordinary can-you-get-me-a-couple-of-extra-tickets kind of request."

"These are three people whom I want to bump into, as if by accident. I'm investigating an interesting tip I picked up for the book I'm writing, but they can't know that. That's all there is to it. Very simple."

She slowly swirled the tines of her fork in the curry. "Is there any reason you know, assuming I do this favor for you, that this might blow up in my face and jeopardize my all-important and impending pension, which, my dear, is exactly four short years away?"

"I can't image anything like that occurring. If these people objected to the questions I put to them—that is to say, if what I say means something to one of them—the absolutely last thing that person would do would be to raise a fuss. It would only call attention to himself. But let me set your mind at ease. The questions I'm going to ask are based on information the U.S. feds would love to acquire. If something were to happen that put you in a tight spot—which, as I told you is extremely unlikely—I'd swap the info to get you back on track for the pension.

But, again, there's no logical reason why anything like that would or could take place."

"Why does that sound like a virtual guarantee of something going wrong?" She nibbled at her curry. "So tell me what's so special about these guys. Why all this hocus-pocus?"

"Pat, don't take this the wrong way, but I think you'd be better off not knowing the specifics. Will you trust me that my telling you is just not a bright idea?"

"Fine, mystery man, I trust you. But don't forget you owe me a biggie, and we of true Irish extraction aren't shy about calling in our vouchers."

"It's a deal." He extracted the list from his shirt pocket and slid it across the greasy surface of the table. "These are the three men. If they want to bring spouses, that's fine, anything to get the men there. Whatever you need to do."

She perused the names, her face registering no recognition, and placed the paper in her handbag. "Okay, sport, you're on. Walk me back to the consulate, and I'll give you your ticket for tonight."

Paul signaled the waiter, and in a few minutes they were in her office. She handed him a ticket shaded in red, white, and blue. "Paul, is there a number where I can reach you in case there's a problem?"

He nodded and wrote down Danniken's phone number on a slip of scrap paper. "I'm staying with friends in Sandton. If I go out, I'll let them know where I'm headed."

"Do you need a lift for tonight?"

"No, thanks, I'm just on my way to rent a car. Patricia, you have my undying thanks for this."

"Baloney. I'll see you up there."

He kissed her cheek and took the elevator to the ground floor, where he hailed a cab to the nearby Carlton Hotel. There he picked up his gear and checked out, after renting a green mid-sized BMW at the travel desk. It boasted a car phone with a retractable antenna. He reasoned that even if he were being watched, no one would think to ask whether his car was equipped with a phone, and it would thus provide a "safe" line.

He placed the luggage in the trunk of the car and headed to a nearby detective agency he had known during his Johannesburg posting. He explained to the owner what he wanted and was soon driving to Danniken's home in the suburbs, encountering minimal traffic in the early afternoon lull.

Beth met him on the porch as he carried a suitcase up the steps. "Nice car you've got there." She held out a key. "Pa already left for the airport, but he said to tell you that this is so that you feel like family and not like a guest."

"Thanks." He accepted the key. "I can't think of a nicer family to belong to."

Paul walked inside. He deposited his bags in his bedroom and pulled out his dinner clothes from the suit sheath he had just hung in the closet. The fine black wool of the jacket and pants was miraculously unwrinkled. He went in

113

search of Beth, whom he found viciously pulling weeds from a vegetable garden at the side of the house. The collie, seemingly comatose, lay nearby on the lush lawn. It was snoring.

"Hi. Showing the weeds no mercy, I see."

"It's incredible how quickly they appear. I just did this bed two weeks ago." She wiped a smudge of dirt from her cheek. "Do you like to garden?"

"I like to pick berries and eat them. Does that count?"

"It's a start. Where were you all day?"

"I went into town to meet an old friend. She wangled me an invitation to a reception tonight at the American Embassy in Pretoria. I wanted to go because there'll be some people there I want to meet. I was wondering if you'd like to go."

"An embassy party?"

He nodded.

"How glamorous. I'd love to."

"I don't know about glamour. Boring is probably more like it. I certainly don't promise anything exciting, but I'd be happy to have you with me."

She clapped her hands. "Do I need a ball gown?"

"No, just an evening dress."

"I'd better run inside and see what I've got to wear." She dropped the trowel and disappeared into the house.

The afternoon sun warmed the fragrant air and caused the crickets to chirp energetically in the pond toward the rear of the house. A bullfrog leapt from the water and landed on a lily pad, gulping loudly and guiltily as he basked in the heat. Several feet from Paul, the collie still slept, his ginger eyebrows twitching, while his paws alternately flexed and relaxed. He was dreaming of cats.

Straightening for a moment, Paul's gaze fell on the five-foot brick wall which separated the lane from Danniken's property. Just beyond it, half hidden by the overhanging branches of the trees, the dark green Jaguar sat parked. Two men were talking quietly in the front seat; they did not notice him. Paul dropped to a crouch and crept to the inner edge of the wall.

At the far edge of the estate, the wall formed a ninety-degree angle with a huge hedge which divided Danniken's land from his neighbor's. Several feet back from the point at which the hedge bisected the wall, a large gash, wide enough to permit passage, had been hacked into the dense bushes, forming a shortcut between the two properties. Paul inched toward the hole, keeping his head well beneath the top of the wall.

He passed through the hedge and emerged onto an enormous expanse of lawn. Almost a quarter mile back from the road sat a grand Tudor mansion, half hidden in trees. There was no one in sight.

Paul raced two hundred feet along the wall, which appeared to guard several additional estates along the quiet lane. He arrived at an imposing wrought-iron gate and opened it a crack, enough to see out between its solid double doors. To the left, across the road, the Jaguar still sat. He glimpsed its two occupants in the front seat, talking to each other.

On the opposite side of the lane, a vast wood filled the land in both directions as far as visibility allowed. Carefully, Paul opened the gate and, after ensuring that the two men were unaware of him, sprinted across into the forest. He burrowed his way through the huge brambles and assorted undergrowth until he had proceeded some thirty feet straight back from the road. He then turned to his left, and as quickly as possible without making any noise, he headed in the direction of the Jaguar, now walking parallel to the lane.

When he had advanced what he judged to be about two hundred feet, Paul turned left again, so that he now faced the road. Silently and painstakingly he padded through the tangled brush. He could see nothing.

An explosion of wings two feet in front of him shattered the stillness as a pheasant burst from its sylvan shelter. Paul froze. He remained motionless for several minutes, in case the men had heard the noise. But there was no further sound.

He continued walking. A glint of dark green metal flashed in the sunlight several feet ahead and a little to the right. He adjusted his direction so that he was now heading toward the car. As he inched forward he could just make out the outline of the form of the man in the right front seat. He was speaking.

Five feet from the Jaguar, Paul heard the buzz of voices. The reason was immediately apparent: The rear windows were half rolled down to allow a cross breeze in the warm afternoon. He crept closer, until he crouched barely a foot from the edge of the wood. The car was less than three feet away. The conversation, in Afrikaans, drifted out clearly through the right rear window.

". . . makes the best fried chicken around. Nothing can beat it."

"Well, I'll be lookin' forward to supper with you. I'll bring a bottle of wine and we'll have a party. Just tell me when." The two men laughed quietly.

The driver continued. "Yes, she's a fine cook. After the honeymoon's over that becomes mighty important. Not like these girls nowadays who can't boil a decent egg. No respect for family life anymore."

His companion nodded sagely in agreement. "Too true, too true. Times are changing fast."

The driver gave his partner a slow, sidelong glance. "Very fast, if there's any truth to the rumors going around. I heard the Executive Council's even met over whether or not to give the order."

"Come on. They wouldn't do it. It's final if they do. We're not even close to needing that. It's just some more unrest, same as always. The problem is, those stupid blacks don't know they're gonna be *really* poor if they ever force us to leave."

"And they won't listen to reason. They just have to have everything or nothing. Shortsighted, that's what it is. They're too damn shortsighted to realize how good they have it."

"Well, at least if we did leave, we wouldn't have to worry, you and me. I'd hate to think about all the poor fellas who aren't members. They'll be in for a rough time."

The driver shook his head slowly. "Anyway, I don't think this is just another false alarm. I know for a fact that the Executive Council had a special meeting last night, because Chris de Wet, the number two guy at South African Broadcasting, told me so."

"How do you know Chris de Wet?"

"Because, my friend, I'm married to his lovely sister."

"Yeah? So what else did your brother-in-law tell you?"

"He said that the bigwigs set a standby date of June fifth. If the order is given, he said, whatever happens, we wouldn't want to be in South Africa ten days later. Apparently they've got some beautiful presents ready for the blackies." They both chuckled. "Yep, it should be some kind of party."

They were quiet a few moments. The driver paused to light a cigarette while his companion strummed idly on the dashboard with his fingertips.

"So who is this American guy, anyway?" The passenger broke the silence.

"I don't know. Muller just gave me a snapshot and said to watch him like a hawk."

"He's probably a commie-lover if he's a friend of Danniken's. The guy honestly makes me sick to my stomach. Moscow probably gives him an allowance. Christ, why not just hand the country over to 'em on a silver platter?"

The driver nodded his head like a yo-yo and took a puff on his cigarette. "Yep, yep."

They lapsed again into silence. Paul waited for a while, and then, realizing the conversation was probably at an end, withdrew into the wood. Hurriedly he retraced his steps and, after crossing through the snarl of trees and brambles, darted back across the road. The iron gate was still ajar, thanks to the small stone he had carefully placed at its base.

Emerging from the tunnel onto Danniken's land, he saw the front door of the house open, and Beth walked onto the porch. He raced to the side of house and stretched himself on the lawn next to the collie. Beth strolled up to the flower bed several seconds later.

"I'm all set. I'm going to wear one of my mother's dresses."

Together they decimated the few remaining weeds and returned to the house. Paul did not glance backward at the two pairs of watching eyes. He gave no indication of his awareness of their existence.

* * *

The waiter lifted from the table the empty plate, upon which, some five minutes earlier, he had served to Herr Neuhaus a generous, some might say obscene, portion of warm sautéed foie gras studded with raisins macerated in Armagnac. The waiter, whose name was Franz, poured into Herr Neuhaus's gold-rimmed crystal flute a little more of the Louis Roederer Cristal Rosé champagne, and disappeared. Franz personally felt champagne, even a champagne as fine as the Cristal, to be a less than perfect match for the foie gras; he himself would have selected a fragrant sauternes, with its much higher sugar content, as a more appropriate complement to the goose liver. But Herr Neuhaus drank only champagne with his meals.

Gerhard Neuhaus took his lunch every weekday at precisely twelve-thirty and always sat at the same corner table at the Restaurant Kronenhalle, the undisputed doyenne of Zurich's restaurants. On the wall next to his table hung a portrait of James Joyce, whose favorite restaurant had been Kronenhalle.

Herr Neuhaus always dined alone; he found it embarrassing to endure the comparison between the size of his meal and that of a lunch companion. For he was what is kindly referred to in French culinary parlance as a gourmand. He liked to eat, and he looked it.

The restaurant was conveniently located on Ramistrasse, only a fifteen-minute walk from the international headquarters of the United Bank of Switzerland, although Gerhard Neuhaus never walked. His Grey Ghost Rolls Royce and driver waited in his accustomed spot directly in front of the restaurant.

Today, he had begun his gustatory adventure with a clear soup, a most excellent lobster bouillon perfumed with saffron. This had preceded the outstanding foie gras, the last morsel of which he had just washed down with a swallow of the Cristal. Franz now exchanged the empty plate for one laden with an extra-thick veal chop, medium rare, with a dollop of béarnaise sauce. Next to the huge cut of meal sat an enormous grilled tomato stuffed with minced mushrooms, bread crumbs, smoked ham, and local Emmentaler. The little room on the plate left unoccupied by these items was jammed with what Franz had described as "those superb new seed potatoes from the island of Jersey in the English Channel, available only in spring." Afterward, there would be a refreshing salad of lambs' lettuce and Belgian endive. He would finish with a vanilla soufflé, its puffed, almost crisp exterior concealing the steaming aromatic mass within. The dessert would be quickly but delicately spooned, so as to minimize the soufflé's collapse, onto a puddle of raspberry sauce.

Lunch at Kronenhalle was invariably the highlight of Herr Neuhaus's day. It was a welcome respite from his position as chairman of the United Bank. This was a position he had neither desired nor sought, but for which he had been groomed and, at the age of forty-five, forced to undertake. This occurred because his father, the bank's largest individual shareholder and previous chairman, retired, but only after carefully maneuvering his son into place to succeed him. Short of inviting disinheritance, Gerhard had not discovered any alternatives to this course of action. Although he would have much preferred a career as a restaurant reviewer, he had had the foresight not to confide this curious and aberrant ambition to his father.

In reality, the situation was not so awful. The directors of the bank were acutely aware that their new chairman was less than interested in his job, and so they had surrounded him with a formidable staff. These hyper-capable aides kept him informed of important bank business, but essentially they ran the show. His management style, or lack thereof, had led to his nickname, in Zurich banking circles, of "Chairman Reagan."

There was, however, one facet of the bank which did intrigue Gerhard Neuhaus, and that was a certain private account. It was by far the bank's largest, into which hundreds of deposits had been made over roughly a thirty-year period, all in gold. There had never been a withdrawal. The account was in the category known as Red-One, a classification which the United Bank applied to those accounts which both topped one billion U.S. dollars and which were accessible only by presentation of a prearranged bank code. At the time of the account's opening in 1952 by a corporation named Elizabeth, it had been classified Blue-Three, which signified an account of at least fifty million U.S. dollars and accessibility by at least two specific individuals, as well as by the prearranged bank code. Shortly thereafter, however, the classification had been altered to Blue-One upon the United Bank's receiving, anonymously, newspaper clippings announcing the deaths of all three of Elizabeth's directors. Although this had greatly alarmed the then-current chairman, there had been no one left to question, as all of Elizabeth's known directors were, quite obviously, dead. As the deposits continued to arrive regularly, if untraceably, over the years, the United Bank had not tried terribly hard to investigate. The color part of the account's bank code changed from Blue to Red several months after its opening, when its assets passed the billion-dollar mark. Actually, the bank was not particularly interested in knowing too much, as long as the Elizabeth account, with assets now exceeding forty-five billion U.S. dollars in gold, stayed put with them.

Gerhard Neuhaus wanted to know all about the account. Every aspect of it was mysterious. His father, upon retiring, had handed him an envelope, sealed in black wax. The imprint in the wax showed a graceful and fantastic bird, a two-headed phoenix, being consumed by flames. From the bird's ashes, according to legend, the bird would be reborn to live another five hundred years. He often found himself staring at the strange image in the wax, pondering its meaning.

His father told him that the envelope contained one of the bank's three copies of Elizabeth's secret access sequence, the other two being in the possession of the chief of security and the clerk of the board of directors. Given the astonomical sum of money involved, it would fall to the chairman for ultimate approval to release any or all of the account's assets, should anyone ever try to make a withdrawal. Aside from the envelope, there was absolutely nothing. The gold deposits arrived frequently, if unexpectedly, in a rented, unmarked truck. The bank sometimes tried to follow and/or trace it; this was now a perfunctory exercise. The story never varied. The renter had paid cash. No rental agency was ever used more than once. The driver was always the same, an ordinary-looking man in his mid-thirties who seldom spoke. Unfailingly, after collecting his receipt for the gold, he would return the truck to the place of rental, where he would be met by a taxi. He would be driven to a crowded airport or train station, and disappear. The bullion itself was always in standard 12.5-kilogram bars, unmarked, and so provided no information. In short, there were simply no clues as to the owner or owners of Elizabeth, Ltd.

At his table in the corner of the restaurant, Gerhard Neuhaus meditatively chewed a cube of veal and wondered for the millionth time about the identity of his bank's largest depositor. There was no hope of knowing until someone showed up to institute the account's first withdrawal. He would wait. He was not going anywhere in the foreseeable future.

6

Dr. Ernst Falkenhaus carefully replaced the telephone receiver and looked at his wife, who was busy constructing a needlepoint wall hanging. When completed it would read GOD BLESS THIS HOUSE. She was completely immersed in her sewing.

"Anna, we've been invited to a party tonight."

She slowly raised her head from her work. "Tonight? Whose party?"

"It's at the American Embassy, in Pretoria. They're welcoming their new ambassador, and they want us to attend. Rather badly, from the sound of it."

Mrs. Falkenhaus looked puzzled, her bunched wrinkles becoming even more pronounced. "But why?"

Her husband shrugged his frail shoulders. "I have no idea. Having retired more than ten years ago, I can't imagine why I should be of interest to them. Anyway, they said if we'd go they'd even send a car. An embassy car. Funny, eh?" He chuckled. "Well, would you like to?"

"Is it black tie?"

"Yes. I can polish my medals."

She smiled gently. "I think it would be fun. We haven't been to a proper function in ages. I think I'll go see what I have to wear." She placed her needlework on the sofa beside her and disappeared with an audible giggle.

Dr. Falkenhaus contemplated the telephone and, after peeking into the hallway, quietly picked up the receiver again and softly began to dial.

Keller the butler began meticulously laying out the master's dinner clothes in preparation for the embassy party that evening. He hesitated over the cummerbund. Although his master was nothing if not conservative in his sartorial selections, perhaps a small dash of color might not be out of the question. Americans, after all, were known to appreciate a modest amount of deviation in dress. Kelly golf pants and whales on neckties and whatnot.

The choice was between black and a deep maroon-burgundy. The latter was unusual, but somber enough not to attract either stares or wisecracks. Yes, Keller felt, that would make a nice statement. He replaced the black cummerbund in the bureau.

The master, Erich Feldberg, was at that moment in the garden playing with two of his grandchildren, who were visiting for the week. Keller looked forward to their departure with immense anticipation. They were outrageously spoiled, and worse, showed him no respect. The little girl in particular was unquestionably a fiend. Keller fantasized throughout their stay about administering a sound and prolonged spanking, punctuated by loud, copious, and highly gratifying weeping. He ground his teeth with relish.

His thoughts returning to the party, Keller mused how strange it was that the American Embassy hadn't called earlier to invite the master. Bureaucratic inefficiency was the sorry reason. It was everywhere. These days, people didn't know the meaning of service—not real service, anyway. Of course, he reasoned, there weren't many people nowadays who could afford such service as he, Keller, provided. But then Erich Feldberg, retired millionaire businessman and member of the Oppenheimer clan, founders of the De Beers diamond company, hardly had to worry about something as mundane as money.

Anyway, he thought as he finished preparing Feldberg's clothing, it would be lovely once the embassy car arrived to collect the master for the ride up to Pretoria. Then, for at least one evening, there would be a bit of discipline around the house. Otherwise, a certain pair of snotty brats would be rather disappointed with their suppers. If they got any at all. He would see to it personally.

Anthonia and Erich Fortner sat at the kitchen table in their Rosebank home just outside Johannesburg while the black maid cleared away the remains of lunch. They were both quiet, trying to deduce why the embassy of the United States would call shortly before an important reception and go to fairly great lengths to entice the bishop and his wife to attend. An embassy car was, after all, a sign of unusual favor, period.

Bishop Fortner couldn't help but wonder whether somebody had confused his name with somebody else's. He objectively admitted that his archconservative viewpoints would not make him a first-choice guest for the Americans. They must be aware of how he railed out repeatedly in his sermons against their unsolicited and unwelcome interference in South Africa's domestic affairs. Apartheid specifically. And yet they were practically begging him to show up. Maybe they now wanted to make a show of talking to all parts of his country's political spectrum. It was most peculiar.

And what did he have to lose, anyway? He might forge some important contacts, likeminded people who could be helpful to the cause. He and Anthonia would go and make the most of it. Ulterior motives be damned.

The two men regarded each other across the large desk, upon which lay scattered several flat files and assorted notes and scribblings. They were dressed in civilian clothes, although both worked for their respective governments. Dean McWhirter, the CIA station chief in London, was meeting on urgent business with Alistair Crowley, the MI5 liaison man to the CIA.

Crowley listened politely to his guest's requests and inwardly reflected that he would have no choice but to comply. MI5 was simply too dependent on American intelligence to say no too often. There was no question of cooperation in circumstances as seemingly pressing as these. Whatever it was that the Americans were after must be important. But they weren't sharing. They had made that much perfectly clear.

"In addition, we'd like to see the list of telephone numbers he called from the apartment. You shouldn't have any difficulty with that, right?" McWhirter looked up from the wish list on his lap from which he was reading.

Crowley delicately smoothed an eyebrow with his forefinger and shook his head. "No, no, I don't see why we should."

"Finally, we'd like to see the full report from your boys on the apartment, although I doubt we'll find anything of interest. Still, you never know. Do you think you can get all that for us?"

Crowley smiled thinly, the master of artifice. "We aim to please. Should have it over to you in a few hours."

The men rose and shook hands, and Crowley saw his visitor to the door. He then returned to his chair. In the distance Big Ben chimed ten o'clock. The morning was already awful.

He pressed his intercom and began issuing orders to his secretary. ". . . and I need them on my desk very quickly, say twelve-thirty. If you need help pulling it all together, get Wendy to help you. Okay?" He turned to deal with the frighteningly high pile of paperwork on his desk.

At a quarter past twelve, Crowley's secretary entered his office grasping a manila folder. She placed it on his desk and sulkily withdrew, irritated at the pressure he'd placed on her. Opening the file, he perused its contents quickly and then pressed the intercom. "Mary, why don't you grab lunch now? Take an extra half hour for the good job you did." She vanished immediately.

Crowley cautiously opened his office door and, finding the reception area empty, strode to the copying machine. He hurriedly made a photostat of the page he had culled from the file, and then returned to his office. He replaced the page and inserted the copy in his inside jacket pocket. Crowley folded his raincoat over his right arm and walked to the corridor. Several secretaries from other offices were waiting, discussing lipstick shades. The elevator arrived and they herded into it in the bovine way people affect in elevators.

Crowley waded through the lunchtime crowd in the lobby and left the building. It housed mostly small advertising companies and public relations firms, and thus was favored by MI5 for its ordinariness. The intelligence unit occupied the top three floors. The name on the brass plate read DENTON STANFORD AND PARTNERS, LTD. It was a satisfactory cover; very few people wandered in without an invitation.

The Knightsbridge street was clogged with

pedestrians. Crowley elbowed his way to a phone booth and stamped his foot waiting for the Pakistani using it to conclude an emotional conversation with his lady love. After a prolonged argument, the man slammed the phone and stormed off. Crowley dropped in his twenty-pence coin and dialed.

A man's voice, notable in its complete lack of tone or accent, answered, "Yes?"

"Hello, my friend. I thought you might care to look at something pertinent I've come across. It has to do with that fellow you and the opposition are so keen on. Would you care to meet?"

"Yes, of course. Very good. The usual spot, in one hour." The man hung up.

Crowley strolled to nearby Hyde Park, stopping along the way to buy a copy of the *Times* and a tongue and mustard sandwich. He found his way to a secluded park bench overlooking the Serpentine, the large pond in the park's center. He sat there quietly, munching his sandwich. After he finished he began to read the front page of his paper.

Crowley did not look up when a tall, mousy-haired man sat on the bench to his right. They did not speak. The man opened a crinkled brown paper bag and produced with the air of a conjurer a cold meat pie wrapped in foil. He proceeded to attack it as if he hadn't eaten for days. He emitted loud grunting noises.

Crowley looked at the man, visibly appalled. The ogre continued to gorge, seemingly oblivious of his audience. Crowley slammed down his newspaper and stomped off disgusted in the direction of his office.

The man on the bench noisily finished his lunch and burped. He then turned to pick up the copy of the *Times* which Crowley had left, and strolled to nearby Brompton Road. There, in front of Harrod's, he hailed a cab. He leaned back and carefully opened the newspaper. Snuggled between the pages of the editorials was a single sheet of photostat paper. On it was a list of phone numbers, and the corresponding owners and addresses.

The man leaned forward. "Eighteen Kensington Palace Garden, please. The Soviet Embassy." He patted the paper with his left hand and thanked God for Mr. Alistair Crowley, faithful husband, loving father of two, and part-time mole.

The late afternoon drizzle fell softly on the cobbled streets of London, forming a confetti of puddles. The antiques district of Kensington was virtually deserted, most shoppers having fled the cold spring damp for a roaring fire or a pint at a cheery pub. London at its most depressing.

A car, an ordinary gray Morris, stopped in front of the old-books-and-letters shop on Kensington Church Street. Two large men emerged, both clad in raincoats. They held their umbrellas low over their heads, thus placing their faces out of sight to the few remaining stragglers on the street.

One of them rang the bell, his gloved hand protected from the wet. After a prolonged pause, a tiny old man shuffled from the back of the shop to open the door.

"Yes, good afternoon, may I help you?"

The man who had rung said, "Yes, we're interested in acquiring some old letters. We hoped you might be able to help us in our search." His English was good, but could not conceal his Eastern European origins.

The shopkeeper nodded his head vigorously. "Well, you've come to the right place. Do come in, please. How frightful it is outside, what?"

The old man led his two guests into the dusty shop. One of them, the one who entered last, turned quietly and closed the door. He latched the bolt, locking it securely. He then began to untie the ribbons which bound the rather shabby curtains of the solitary window looking onto the street.

The shopkeeper, Mr. Arthur Jones, failed to notice, although the shop became progressively darker as the dull gray light was blocked off from outside. He was engrossed in conversation with the other man. "And in what sort of old letters are you interested? Anything specific?"

The man slowly removed his raincoat, leaving his gloves on. "Actually, we're interested in anything you may have which is written in Afrikaans, say from around 1940 on. Got anything like that?"

Arthur Jones peevishly snapped his fingers. "What a pity! You know, only three days ago I had two letters in Afrikaans. Chap I sold them to was quite pleased to get them. Don't think I have anything else, but if you'd care to wait I could go through my things to make sure. Afrikaans again! My, my, when it rains it pours."

The store's front window was now completely closed off by the curtains. The shop was dark. The second man rejoined his companion and the old shopkeeper. "What sort of letters were they that you sold?" The man's Russian accent was heavier than his gloved companion's. His last three words sounded like "dat yew solt."

"Well, they were both written by a man named Hendrik Verwoerd, who was the South African president or prime minister or some such office. Late fifties, as I recall. They were really quite a find."

"And what exactly did they say?"

"You know, I really don't think I could say."

The men unconsciously stepped forward toward the old man, who took a corresponding step backward. The man who had shut the curtains asked, "Why not?"

"Well, you see, I don't speak Afrikaans. Not one word."

"How could you judge the value of the letters without knowing their content?"

The man's companion began to flex his fingers inside his black deerskin gloves.

Arthur glanced at the man's hands and became suddenly nervous. He stepped back again. "If you must know, the simple fact is that I trusted the buyer enough to fairly assess their value for me. I am afraid that I am unable to provide you with any other information."

The man wearing gloves placed his right hand on the shopkeeper's shoulder. "I am afraid that you do not understand. The letters that you sold are very important to my friend and me. We need you to tell us what you know about them. We shall be happy to pay you. But we must know."

"But my dear fellow, as I've just told you, I don't know anything more. I have nothing else to tell you." Arthur tripped backward over a footstool and landed in a heap on the dusty floor.

The man in gloves leaned forward and effortlessly yanked the frail Arthur to his feet. "You are not adopting the proper attitude today. However, I assure you that this will change momentarily." Clapping a hand over Arthur's mouth, the Russian half dragged, half carried him to the small kitchen at the rear of the shop. His companion cast a last glance at the locked door and closed curtain and joined them out back. He switched on the aged radio perched above the stove and moved the dial to a hard rock channel. He adjusted the volume to its highest setting. Anyone listening at the door would have heard only a loud and staticky recording of "Satisfaction" by the Rolling Stones. The high-pitched shrieks of Arthur Jones as he rapidly approached his unnatural and premature death would have been completely inaudible.

The KGB killers left him on his back on the kitchen floor, lying in a pool of blood surprisingly large for such a small man. The telltale circles of cigarette burns speckled the palms of his pale wrinkled hands. The right side of his face was splotched with dark purple bruises. That was the state in which the two gentlemen from the Central Intelligence Agency found him when they visited the shop the following morning, fifteen hours too late to listen to whatever it was that Arthur Jones might have been able to tell them.

7

The embassy glittered. Candlelight flickered flatteringly on the rouged cheekbones and powdered necks of diamond-encrusted dowagers. Old men with brilliantine-saturated hair puffed out their chests, enjoying the sensation of their military decorations swinging gently at their breast pockets. A quartet of violins played inoffensive pieces of Mozart and Vivaldi. Waiters in tails drifted through the crowd, offering silver trays of unmemorable hors d'oeuvres which looked better than they tasted. Several younger women, flushed with the elegance of the evening, were laughing too loudly. The party was in full swing.

Paul held Beth's arm and guided her past the brass-buttoned marine guards to the hubbub inside. The sheer immensity of the reception room, coupled with its high white ceilings and enormous chandelier, lent a grandeur and stateliness to the festivities which could not help but impress those invited. Beth clapped a hand to her mouth in girlish delight and turned to him.

"Paul, this is wonderful! I feel like Ginger Rogers." Her gown of apricot satin was both understated and elegant, and accentuated her lustrous golden hair. The heads of more than a few men turned admiringly as she passed.

They waded through the bemedaled, beribboned crowd toward the packed bar. Paul ordered two glasses of champagne and handed one to Beth. He sipped it and shrugged philosophically. "It may be cheap and it may be sweet, but at least it bubbles." They turned to face the floor. The guests were mingling in small groups, the conversations trite and meaningless. Those not talking half listened, while surreptitiously watching other guests out of the corners of their eyes.

At the far end of the room, back near the entrance, Paul caught a glimpse of Pat Ryan. He turned to Beth. "I'm afraid I have to deal with the business portion of this evening, as promised. Remember, if I'm not here by the time you want to go home, take the car." He passed her his keys. "Will you be all right?"

"Fine. Have fun." She lifted her glass to his and smiled up at him.

Paul strode through the throng and sidled up to Pat. She was trapped near the door, held captive in conversation by a plump British diplomat with a walrus mustache. He was busy delivering a monologue on the benefits which English Common Law had brought to Britain's former colonies. Seeing Paul, she adroitly introduced him to the garrulous Englishman, and then steered Paul away by the shoulder. "Thank God you arrived. That man could launch a whole fleet of hot air balloons. When did you get here? I didn't see you arrive."

"Just a few minutes ago."

"Did you get my message? All three of your invitees agreed to show."

"Yes, your secretary called just as I was getting ready. Listen, I may not have time to thank you later, so I'd like to let you know now how much I appreciate all of your help. It means a lot to me."

"Sport, you're very welcome. Did you see your three targets yet?"

"No, I don't know what they look like. You did talk to the invitation checker at the front, didn't you?"

"Such faith, I'm so flattered you trust me. Of course I did. Let's go find him." They set off for the front entrance, traversing the long parquet foyer connecting it to the reception hall.

At the heavy oak door stood a young black marine in dress uniform. He was inspecting invitations. After verifying that they were legitimate, he crossed off the person from the master list on the clipboard he held in his left hand.

"Hi, cutie."

The marine gave Pat a wide grin. "Hey, cutie, y'self. Why ain't you out hoofin' on the dance flo'? Nice lady like you not dancin' don' seem right."

"I appreciate the vote of confidence. Paul, this is Sergeant Mason. This good-hearted marine is the fellow who's keeping an eye out for your friends." The two men shook hands.

"Yo' friends ah all heah. All three of 'em."

"Great. Can you take a minute now and point them out to me?"

"O' coss. Hey, Jones, c'm'ere."

A fresh-faced corporal, standing on guard duty several feet away, approached them.

"Jones, take over fo' a minute while I'm gone. You know how it works." The corporal nodded and accepted the clipboard.

The marine sergeant led Pat and Paul back to the party. The reception room's entrance was placed two steps above the level of the floor, so it allowed them a commanding view of the throng. Mason scanned the crowd carefully, and then discreetly spoke to Paul without looking at him. "Now, you see over there, on yo' left in back, that lady in the dark green dress? Tha's Missuz Fortner, and that man on her right is her husband, the bishop. Got it? Okay. Now, look straight back. See that guy with the cigarette? He jus' took a puff. He's holdin' a drink in his other han'."

"The one with the mustache?"

"That's the cat. That's Mr. Feldberg." He consulted a small slip of paper and looked up again. "Okay, now, Mr. Falkenhaus, where are you?" Mason slowly inspected the crowd, his eyes like searchlights. They came to rest on an elderly couple standing at the far right of the room, against the wall. The sergeant jerked his head in their direction. "See 'em? The Falkenhauses.

Mr. and Missuz. They jus' watchin', not talkin' to nobody. The missuz is wearin' a gray dress, an' pearls."

"I see them."

"Okay, then, there are yo' people. Now I got to get back."

Paul held up a hand. "How'd you like to make an easy hundred dollars?" When the sergeant frowned, Paul added, "Nothing illegal. I just want to try a little experiment, and I don't want the guinea pigs to see me. What do you say?"

The man smiled, his teeth large and white. "I'm always interested in easy money, as long as it's legal. What do I have to do?"

"I'm going to give you three notes. What I want you to do is hand one of them to each of the three men you just pointed out to me. Space them out by no less than sixty seconds. I'm going to watch their reactions when they read them. If they want to know who asked you to deliver them, just say some man who left the party immediately afterward. Nothing shady at all. Sound okay?"

"Yo' on."

"I'm going to pay you up front because I may have to leave in a hurry." Paul produced a hundred-dollar bill and discreetly offered it to the man. He then pulled from his dinner jacket three unmarked sealed envelopes and slipped them into the marine's hand.

"Now?"

Paul nodded. "Remember, not a word about

141

Ms. Ryan or me—you don't know anything. Just doing a stranger a favor."

"Got it. Hey, thanks for the job." The sergeant descended the steps to the level of the party. Paul watched him as he threaded his way toward the rear of the hall on the left. The marine made his way to where Bishop Fortner stood talking quietly with his wife and another couple. The black man tapped the clergyman on the arm. They spoke a few words to each other, after which Mason extended one of the notes to him.

Wheeling around on the ball of his foot, the marine headed to the center of the room's far side, where he walked up to Erich Feldberg. The man was talking animatedly and volubly to a young, flirtatious blonde. Feldberg stopped speaking in midsentence and looked irritably at the black man who had interrupted him.

"Yes, what is it?"

"Message for you, sir. Gentleman asked me to give this to you." Mason extended an envelope to the surprised Feldberg and marched off to the right, in the direction of Ernst Falkenhaus.

The former diplomat was leaning against the wall with one hand on the shoulder of his wife, who was seated next to him in a plush arm chair.

"Mr. Falkenhaus?"

The elderly man nodded.

Mason relinquished the last of Paul's notes and swiftly left the party. He gave no indication of knowing Paul as he passed him on his way out.

From the main door, Paul carefully watched

the three men open their messages successively. Each of the identical notes, written in Afrikaans, read, *This is to warn you. The Treasurer and that which he guards are in jeopardy. Do what you must immediately to guarantee the security of his noble charge.* (signed) *A Friend.*

Feldberg unfolded the piece of paper and read the message. Paul saw the man's expression change from blankness to puzzlement. The woman to whom he had been speaking touched his arm, apparently asking if everything was all right. He nodded distractedly and shrugged his shoulders. Pocketing the note, he looked quickly around, as if to see if he was being watched, and then resumed his conversation.

Meanwhile, Bishop Fortner was showing the note to his wife. He wore a dry smile on his narrow face, and she too appeared to find humor in the message. He pointed at part of the writing and she nodded. Clearly they felt it to be a practical joke by someone they knew. After nodding their heads a few times, they turned back to the other couple with whom they had been chatting and resumed the conversation where they had left off when the black marine had approached them.

Paul shifted his attention to the far right wall of the reception hall, where he observed Mr. Falkenhaus extracting the buff note from its unmarked envelope. The diplomat unfolded the letter and began to read. His wife neither asked him about it nor tried to read it with him. Paul thought that somewhat unusual.

The reaction visible on Falkenhaus's face was electrifying. The man's eyes bulged and his mouth gaped. He sucked air into his lungs like a fish. His wife turned to look at him and instantly she was holding his shoulders, asking what was the matter. He shook his head, did not wish to discuss it. Paul watched as Falkenhaus quickly gained control of himself and patted his wife's arm soothingly, reassuring her that everything was fine. He eased her back into the armchair and after whispering into her ear stalked toward the exit, where Paul stood. Paul averted his face to the left and the elderly man passed him without a glance.

In the hallway, Falkenhaus accosted a waiter bearing an enormous salmon mousse, molded into the shape of a fish. It was swimming in a golden sea of aspic. "Is there a public telephone anywhere in this building?"

The waiter pointed to a door at the end of the hall. When opened, a light automatically clicked on, revealing a small cubicle. It contained a pay telephone and an Empire armchair upholstered in olive green velvet which had seen better days.

Falkenhaus marched to the booth and closed the door behind him, shutting out all sound. Paul watched from the reception room entrance farther up the hall.

After several minutes, Falkenhaus emerged from the cubicle and headed back to the party, once again passing Paul on his way to rejoin his wife. A short interchange ensued between the couple. They then hurried toward the exit and

144

unhesitatingly proceeded to the building's front door. Following at a safe distance, Paul observed them as they climbed into the embassy car and were driven away to Johannesburg. He ran back to the phone booth.

Inside, below the telephone, a curved marble ledge supported several heavy telephone books. Paul leaned forward and groped with his hand underneath the shelf, until he felt two cold hard boxes, each about the size of a dollar and half an inch thick. They were connected by a thin wire. He yanked at them as delicately as possible. They came loose from the marble with four loud pops, the sound of suction cups forcibly pried from a smooth surface.

The bobbins of the miniature tape recorder were still revolving slowly. Paul pressed the stop button and the machine ceased to record. He slipped the still-attached receiver into his inside jacket pocket.

After briefly poking his head into the hall to make sure he was alone, Paul unscrewed the ear-piece of the telephone. Snuggled next to the plastic and hooked into the main wire was a small disk, about the same size as a stack of four quarters. It was a miniaturized transmitter, more commonly known as a bug. Paul plucked it from the handset and replaced the earpiece. He slipped out of the booth and walked outside, passing the marines at the front door. He headed for the parking lot, where he found his rented BMW without too much difficulty.

Making sure he was unobserved, Paul opened

the front passenger door on the left, closing it behind him as he got in. He opened the glove compartment and extracted a Walkman and headphones. Placing the headphones over his ears, Paul tugged the miniature recorder from his pocket and pressed the tiny eject button. The slender machine revealed a hidden compartment and burped out the cassette it contained. Paul inserted the tape in the Walkman and pressed PLAY.

He listened to a woman calling a babysitter at home to check on her children. An Englishman's voice followed, informing his wife or girlfriend that is was "nothing interesting, just another diplobore," and that he'd be home in a couple of hours.

The next and last voice was that of an older man, speaking in clipped Afrikaans. He was clearly upset, his tones cracking and distressed. He asked the operator to place the call for him, Johannesburg 628–8117.

A man answered, also speaking Afrikaans. "Yes?"

"This is Father."

There was a pause. "Yes, Father, go ahead."

"There is trouble. I am at a reception at the American Embassy in Pretoria. I have been handed a written warning that Elizabeth and you are in peril. I do not know the author's identity. I do not dare attempt to find out for fear of drawing attention, although it seems quite obvious that I was invited here so that I could be given this caution. I don't know whether it is a hoax, but we must play it safe and assume that it is genuine. I suggest that you place yourself in immediate seclusion. Meet me in two weeks, on June seventh, at the main entrance to the Johannesburg Stock Exchange, at noon exactly. My advice is that you talk to and see no one until then. Meanwhile, I will try and investigate what is going on."

"You must be careful, Father."

"You must be even more careful. The integrity of Elizabeth can not be compromised. Hide yourself well."

"Good-bye, Father." The conversation ended with a click as Falkenhaus hung up.

Paul removed the headphones and absent-mindedly tapped a drumbeat with them on the dash. He knew from Falkenhaus's *Who's Who* biography that the former diplomat was childless. "Father" was therefore a code name. It would be rather a fitting choice for a former Treasurer. The man at the other end of the line from Falkenhaus had to be the incumbent Treasurer. Paul felt sure of it. The chase was on. Excitedly, he rewound the tape.

On a small notepad Paul jotted down the number Falkenhaus had asked the operator to dial, as well as the date and location of the arranged meeting in two weeks time. He would be there, watching. For now, he would concentrate on the phone number and on Falkenhaus.

Paul strolled back to the embassy and returned to the reception. Fortner and Feldberg were still chatting as if nothing were wrong. That made sense, given Falkenhaus's startled reaction. The note must have seemed strange but meaningless to them. Paul maneuvered through the crowd to Beth, who was conversing animatedly with an Asian couple.

"Oh, Paul, I'd like to introduce you to Mr. and Mrs. Kim. Mr. Kim is the Japanese ambassador." She turned toward the couple. "This is Mr. Paul Jenssen." The couple smiled and bowed, as did Paul. They spoke for a few minutes, and then became quiet as the fourteen-piece orchestra struck up "New York, New York" in honor of the new ambassador's hometown. Couples commenced dancing on the polished floor. Paul tapped Beth on the shoulder gently. "May I have this dance?"

"But of course." She turned to the two Japanese. "Please excuse us. We need a little exercise." The pair drifted to the dance floor and proceeded to execute a respectable fox-trot. The Kims watched, smiling.

Beth whispered in his ear as the band switched to a slower tune. "Did you finish your errands?"

He smiled. "All work done for the night. Nothing to do now but play."

"You don't seem to do too much of that."

His smile grew slightly distant. "I'm sorry if I seem a stick-in-the-mud. I wasn't always so into my work."

They twirled gently to the music, her head resting lightly on his shoulder, her fair hair shiny and striking in the light against his black jacket. She spoke without lifting her head. "Paul,

I know about your wife. Pa told me. I apologize for reminding you of it, but I wanted to let you know I'm very sorry."

He was quiet for a while and then hugged her gently. "It's really okay. I miss Christine a lot, but it's something I can deal with now. It used to be a lot harder. She was ... ah ... a very big part of my life. It's tough to have somebody you love yanked away suddenly and permanently, but after the shock and the ache, you develop a kind of unconscious ability to remember and cherish, without feeling so sad. It's like that now for me. And thank you. It's very sweet of you to say."

The lilt of the violins vibrated through the thick air. The din of people talking had yielded to the music, and those who weren't dancing mostly sat nearby and watched. The lights dimmed. Paul and Beth moved naturally in unison, their steps relaxed and easy. He guided her with the gentlest touch of his hand around her waist, as if he were afraid she was a porcelain doll which might shatter with too much pressure.

They circled slowly, a perfect synchronic movement, fluid and graceful. Oblivious to the other dancers, they swayed gently, rapturously, each attuned to the other.

Gradually, the crowd thinned. Beth and Paul walked through the hallway and exited the building. Paul and the marine sergeant exchanged glances but did not acknowledge each other.

Paul drove quickly back to Sandton, making the trip in a little over half an hour. They made light conversation in an effort to cut the palpable tension.

The car pulled into the drive, Paul first getting out to unlock the big gate. Jamie the collie once again went wild and threw himself on the doors of the sedan, hysterical with elation, barking furiously.

The evening air felt like warm velvet, heavy but not oppressive. The huge full moon of South Africa cast a magical, mauvish light on the grounds. High above, harmless bats flitted noiselessly across the lunar searchlight, mercilessly chasing down their insect prey.

Paul and Beth meandered toward the house, the white gravel of the drive crunching beneath their feet. Beth's satin dress swished gently as she walked, catching the ghostly moonlight in its pale folds. The clack of their shoes sounded absurdly loud in the evening stillness as they climbed the front porch steps.

Inside, at the foot of the staircase, they stopped. She took his hand. "Thank you for a wonderful evening, Paul." She bent forward to plant a peck on his cheek, but at that precise moment he turned slightly; their lips met in an unplanned kiss.

Surprised, he held her to him. She did not resist, but met him with a sudden wave of passion, as if something long-suppressed and ignored were being untapped.

Then, remembering that this was his host's daughter, Paul pulled back. They gazed at each other in the shadowy moonlight, both confused and excited at this new development.

"Paul, this is really very wonderful, but I get the feeling you're uptight because you're a friend of Pa's."

He said, "It's a little strange wondering what your father would say if he knew that his honored house guest was. . . . Please excuse me. I think I should turn in." Feelings of guilt, images of Christine, this lissome woman, all floated in his head.

She patted his arm and they climbed the stairs. Awkwardly they wished each other good night and retired.

Paul lay awake. His mind refused to be still. His feelings toward Beth were more than just a casual crush. He hadn't felt this way since Christine. And it was exactly that, a sort of half-hearted guilt about these feelings, that he was somehow being unfaithful to her memory, that was causing him this turmoil. He knew in his heart that Christine would have wished him happiness, as he would have for her. And yet the pang persisted.

The pool of moonlight streaming through the window caught the edge of his bedroom door as it silently edged open. Paul, facing the other direction, failed to notice.

A figure glided inside and loomed over his bed. A slight creak of the floorboard betrayed the visitor. Paul whirled.

It was Beth. Without speaking, she let her robe

fall and, lifting one corner of the sheet, slipped into his bed.

Gently, lovingly, they delighted in exploring each other's body. Her kisses were deep and impassioned, his tentative and amazed, like a man drunk on a fine wine after long thirst and deprivation.

They lay together on the quilt covering his bed and became lost in each other and in the rapture of the moment. Their great unsatisfied need, long unrequited, was at last fulfilled. Despite the urgency of the moment, he took his time, almost playfully drawing her out until, in a thunderous explosion punctuated by their unconscious and uncontrollable cries, they collapsed into each other's arms, cradling each other tightly and breathing deeply.

Pleased and satiated, they replayed the evening's pleasures in their minds, dwelling on its magical elements. Beth snuggled her silky head into the crook of his arm and delicately traced complicated nothings on his chest. They did not speak.

Gradually, the pleasant mental images became fuzzy and involuntary. The sweet air billowed the white linen curtains, creating a cool gentle breeze in the room. They drew closer together and, smiling, drifted into happy sleep.

It all began with a pebble. The bright afternoon sun shone down on the funeral procession, glinting off the dark glasses of the mourners and the brass handles of the flower-strewn coffin.

The casket resembled a wedding cake, its size smaller than usual due to the young age of its occupant. It was constructed of cream-colored wood, set off by pale blue filigree. On top of the coffin was draped the black, green, and gold flag of the powerful African National Congress. Possession of the flag in itself constituted a crime. However, the dozens of police, both black and white, lining the funeral route knew better than to enforce the law on this point; the hatred in the air was palpable. The least provocation would set off the thousands of blacks streaming after the casket like a match to gasoline.

The last few months had proved particularly trying for the South African police. Forty-plus years of apartheid had finally culminated in the sort of tension which ignites massive and virtually universal unrest at the slightest perceived affront. The helmeted policemen already wore their heavy plastic face guards; they knew that the odds were good they would need them.

This funeral was even more strained than usual. The child, a nine-year-old black girl, had been found the previous morning on a parched soccer field not far from the main police station in the all-black city of Soweto. Soweto was not really a name, but an acronym for South Western Townships. The girl's skin was covered with welts, indicating systematic beating all over her body. Both of her arms were broken, and several teeth were missing. She wore no clothes, and an inch-deep gash stretched from her navel to her genitals. She had most probably died from either shock or loss of blood.

The chief constable had issued a bland statement to the effect that the perpetrators were being sought and would be duly apprehended. This did nothing to allay intense suspicion of the local police.

The evening of the corpse's discovery had seen an eerie calm settle over the massive sprawling slum. The dusk brought a tangible restiveness, a whispering augur of violence floating uneasily on the breeze.

Now, on the day of the funeral, expectation hung heavily in the air. The marchers padded sullenly along the dusty shack-lined avenue, their expressions stony as they passed the well-armored policemen who dotted the roadside every ten yards or so. The marchers at the head of the procession, who bore the coffin, had already reached the cemetery. The grim parade was almost over. There was as yet no physical confrontation.

But then ... the pebble. It flew from among the last of the mourners, and it struck a policeman on his shoulder. A young man, perhaps sixteen or seventeen, quickly lowered his arm. But he had been spotted. Three officers, including the one hit, rushed at the crowd as if to pry the boy loose. Their riot sticks were raised. Chaos ensued.

The image of the attacking police raised a roar of hitherto suppressed fury from the crowd. They ceased marching and whirled to face the police, who suddenly realized that they had a problem. They stepped backward. The crowd surged at them. They were surrounded in seconds.

The lines of police hesitated. The marchers were going berserk. To attempt to free their three comrades would be to risk the fury of the crowd. Yet it was unthinkable that they simply abandon the three to the mercy of the mob. They decided to fire canisters of tear gas. The pellets belching clouds of acrid smoke landed amid the mass of black faces, scattering them.

Instantly, a hail of Molotov cocktails, rocks, bottles, and rotten fruit rained down on the dozens of policemen. Several officers were injured. The police opened fire. The shriek of bullets whizzing through the smoke and dust caused many in the crowd to scream in terror. Yet most did not flee, but continued their primitive barrage. The dozens of dead and bleeding injured lay untended in the dust.

Eventually, there ensued a standoff. The police ceased firing, and the crowd ran out of bottle bombs. The mourners at the far front of the procession quickly concluded their burial ceremony and returned home. The riot had ended as abruptly as it had begun. Dusk fell on Soweto.

Yet the three captured policemen were nowhere to be seen. They had been hustled away to a small plot of land behind a patched shack roofed with industrial corrugated tin.

They had the misfortune to be black.

Had they been white, they would not have been subjected to the fate they were about to meet.

Being black, however, their captors regarded them differently. As traitors, not as oppressors. Cooperators with the enemy. Collaborators.

In wartime, the enemy is taken prisoner. But traitors are executed.

The blacks of Soweto reserve a special method of execution for those whom they judge to have betrayed their own people. It is called "the necklace." That is not to say that shootings, stabbings, and even hangings do not happen. On the contrary, they occur with grim regularity. But the necklace is the technique of choice.

The unfortunate victim is held upright by the captors. He or she is tied to a wooden pole no higher than his or her shoulders, wrists bound behind the back. Invariably this requires at least four men to accomplish, as the victim is fully aware of his or her imminent fate and is struggling wildly, often simultaneously offering financial deals of the greatest profitability in exchange for freedom. These offers are never taken seriously.

Once the victim is securely attached to the stake, an old rubber tire is placed around his neck. It is heavy, but it is a weight that will not long be borne.

Gasoline is then carefully poured into the inner rim of the tire, until it sloshes around the entire inner circumference. The odor from the petrol, practically next to the victim's nose, is almost overwhelming.

Someone lights a match. The other captors step back a few paces. Nobody wants to get singed.

The match is tossed at the tire.

Sometimes it goes out while flying toward its target. Sometimes it misses its target altogether. No matter. Another match is lit and tossed, and another if necessary. There are always enough matches.

The tire bursts into flames, a golden halo of fire around the neck of the traitor. His or her screams last only a short period of time before unconsciousness sets in, shortly followed by death. The circle of spectators is silent, utterly absorbed.

Soon there is only an untidy pile of blackened bone and scraps of charred clothing. The crowd turns, and walks quietly away. There are no cheers and shouts of satisfaction after the execution; only a solemn dispersion.

The three captured policemen were led to slender but sturdy wooden stakes driven hastily into the dusty earth. They were spaced about twelve feet apart. They had gone quietly with their abductors, not wishing to make matters worse. They thought they were to be held hostage, for money or for food.

Until they saw the stakes.

They knew what the stakes were for.

They began to shriek.

The two dozen men who had hustled the officers away from the confusion of the riot expeditiously tied them to the stakes. Two of them were weeping, the third desperately offering a reward of amnesty and several thousand rand for his liberty. Their captors wordlessly finished trussing the officers to their poles and solemnly placed tires over their heads. Mindless of the screams and sobbing, the captors carefully poured gasoline into the tires and the crowd stepped back. The three men evoked in several minds images of Jesus at Calvary, but these thoughts were not shared. Jesus may have been crucified with two thieves, but he was no traitor like these unfortunates.

Three slender youths stepped forward. Each held a book of matches. They each carefully lit a match, cupping the tiny flames in their bony brown hands. But the warm wind extinguished them. It was blowing strong tonight. The young men continued striking the matches, only to have them die in the breeze.

One of the policemen summoned the strength of will to shout, "It is a sign from God."

This drew laughs and jeers from the crowd. "Don't you worry, sir, we're not done yet," a malevolent voice called from the circle of spectators.

Someone produced an old broomstick the sweeping end of which was matted with dust and debris. Gasoline was poured on the filthy brush and then lit. The broomstick was transformed into a long torch. All hope evaporated for the prisoners.

The youths who had tried before with the matches approached the doomed officers. One of them carried the blazing broom aloft like a trophy. He chose the policeman in the middle. Standing as far back as possible, the boy slowly lowered the brush. The victim's eyes watched in hypnotized terror as the flame approached. He screamed "No!" and his face was instantly swimming in flames.

The executioner passed the torch to one of his two comrades. Striding purposefully to the officer on the left, the boy quickly set the man ablaze. He clearly did not relish his task.

The last of the young trio was crueler. He accepted the burning broom and strolled teasingly to the remaining victim. The doomed man closed his eyes and began mumbling a prayer, beads of sweat glistening on his forehead in the glow from the two nearby fires.

"Pray hard, you Judas. You're off to Hell." The policeman's eyelids flew open and a train whistle of a scream pierced the night. The youth waved the flaming brand in the night air like a majorette twirling a baton, and then dropped the burning brush to the tire. The man screamed in agony, and then all was quiet. Only the sounds of the sad moan of the wind and the crackle of the three fires punctuated the stillness.

The assembled men watched the fires until they dwindled to fuzzy masses of semi-charred clothing and carbonized bone, and then the crowd disbanded into the warm blustery night to tell their wives what they had done.

8

Beth was wakened by a sound in the hall. Her cloudy eyes focused on the door handle: It was turning. She moved a hand to wake Paul, but he was gone. The door swung open, and there stood Paul, his powerful body oddly incongruous with the matronly apron which barely covered his nakedness. In his arms he carried a large wooden tray, on which steamed a large breakfast of coffee, fried eggs, fragrant smoked bacon, fresh orange juice, a bowl of strawberries with a pitcher of thick cream, and a large slab of the white-iced coffee cake Beth had baked the previous morning. The Johannesburg *Times* was carefully folded under the old silver coffee jug.

"Ta-dah." Paul carefully placed the tray on the end of the bed and walked around to the window at the left. He parted the curtains; a flood of sunlight transformed the room. He opened the window. The singing of birds reveling in the morning light floated in. He then disappeared downstairs again, returning in several seconds with two prop-up trays upon which to eat breakfast in bed.

Beth grinned, shaking her head. "And he's a cook too. Where did you find those breakfast trays? We haven't used those for years. This all looks so good. And strawberries too. You've thought of everything."

Paul opened the collapsible breakfast trays and placed one of them above Beth's waist. She yanked one of the extra pillows which had fallen to the floor and propped herself higher in bed. He then removed a silver cover from one of the chafing dishes to reveal two eggs and a generous portion of bacon. "It may not be as grand as your South African breakfasts, but it's doing pretty well by American standards. I hope you like your eggs this way. Watch for eggshell." He placed the plate and a glass of juice on her tray.

"Thanks, they look scrumptious." She patted the bed beside her. "C'm'on, the chef has to eat too."

Paul removed the apron and slid under the covers beside her, tweaking her waist gently. He then opened his own tray, and after he served himself, they set to work on the food.

Between bites, they kissed, caressed, and nudged each other in the distinctive puppy way that new lovers do. They basked in the glow of newfound intimacy long missing.

After finishing, they placed the trays and dishes on the wooden floor beside the bed. They lay together for a long while, her cheek resting on his broad chest, his left hand gently cupping her firm breast. She dozed. Finally, he whispered into her ear, "Hey, Beth. Psst. Psst."

One eye flickered open. "Do you think I'm a cat? 'Psst' is for cats, not girlfriends."

"Sorry. Can I call you Kitty?"

"If I can call you Spot."

"No deal. You have to call me Tiger."

"Why, I could only call you Tiger if you acted like a tiger. Do you act like a tiger?"

"Sometimes. Would you like to see?"

"Well, you know, I think I'd better. Nicknames should be accurate."

Paul placed his lips on Beth's neck and slowly growled. She started to laugh breathlessly. "Oh, Tiger, you'd better stop. I'm ticklish."

"Grrr." He continued to nuzzle her until they dissolved into long kisses. They entwined themselves, drinking in each other's smell, intoxicated with passion. They made love slowly, taking great joy in each wonderful sensation, riding a wave of ecstasy higher and higher until, astonishing themselves, they climaxed in a frenzy of uninhibited pleasure.

They remained motionless and quiet, savoring the moment. Paul finally put his mouth to her ear and whispered, "Good morning."

"Yes, it is." She hesitated and then added, "I hope I haven't presumed too much."

He looked at her sharply. "How so?"

She waved a hand at the bed. "This. You were sending such mixed signals last night. I came and listened by your door and heard you tossing."

A small smile played around his lips. "You're

pretty sharp, aren't you?" He caressed her hair. "I think I just needed you to show me the way, and I guess my feelings toward you made me feel—"

She interrupted, placing a finger on his lips. "Listen, Paul, I understand. You're not replacing Christine, or even being untrue to her. Do you really think she wouldn't want you to go on with your life? I'll bet she would."

They held each other for a while, before Paul pulled back the covers. "I have to get up. I have work to do."

She wrapped her arms around his neck. "You can't. I won't let you. You have to join me on my day off from work."

"Are you challenging me to a wrestling match, oh lovely one?" He tickled her gently on her flat stomach. She began to laugh and struggle.

"All right, stop. You can go."

He leaned forward to kiss her and then took the remains of breakfast downstairs.

Beth picked up the newspaper. She perused the front page and muttered, "Oh, how awful." She called to him. "Paul, did you see the headlines? There were terrible riots yesterday in Soweto and Durban." He did not answer; he was already in the kitchen.

In an hour Paul was showered and ready. Calling good-bye to Beth, he emerged through the front door into the late morning glare of another cloudless day. He opened the gate, hopped into the rented sedan, and eased it into the lane. Getting out to close the gate, he observed the dark green Jaguar several hundred feet down the road. He offered no indication of being aware of it.

Driving slowly, he watched through his rear-view mirror as the Jaguar pulled into the lane and began tailing him at the same speed. Paul headed for the highway leading back to Johannesburg. The suburban roads of Sandton were quiet; most of the town's inhabitants were long departed for work.

The road curved to the right ahead, immediately preceding the highway entrance ramp. The curved section was hidden by a large grove of tall cypress trees. Paul gauged the line of vision of his pursuer and, at the instant he disappeared from view, pressed his gas pedal to the floor. The BMW shot forward, taking the curve narrowly on the inside. Seeing a gap in the trees, Paul veered off the asphalt and backed into the cavity. He waited, his heart beating rapidly.

Twenty seconds later, the Jaguar passed by. Its velocity was increasing, its driver obviously perplexed at his quarry's failure to reappear ahead.

Waiting until the Jaguar had rounded the curve and disappeared, Paul raced the car back onto the road, heading in the direction from which he had come. He drove as rapidly as possible without attracting notice. He had shaken off his trackers.

After consulting a street map, Paul continued past the splendid homes of the suburb. They were set well back from the roads, many with long drives and most with sophisticated security. These were the monuments to the incalculable wealth far beneath South Africa's soil.

He drove several miles until he reached Sandton's eastern edge, across town from where Pieter Danniken's house was located. Like that area, this quarter could not boast of the most opulent residences, yet they too were more than comfortable, home to the wealthy but not super rich.

Paul peered up at the street signs and slowed the car to a crawl as he turned onto Eyck Street. He watched for the street numbers: 37, 35, and there it was, number 33. He passed it and continued down the quiet lane. The street was devoid of people, its residents either at work in the city or sequestered within their secluded and walled-off dwellings.

At the corner, Eyck Street came to an end, forming a T with Van Houten Street. Paul curved left. He was glad he had rented the BMW; anyone watching would get the impression that he was house hunting. A less expensive car might have raised questions about his presence in the exclusive neighborhood.

A small church drew into view on the left. The subject of next Sunday's sermon was visible, written in Afrikaans on the black and white sign hanging on the entrance. The Dutch Reformed Church pastor knew the composition of his audience well enough to know that the English translation of his message was not only unnecessary, but unwelcome.

The church's driveway to the left of the building was empty. Paul turned off Van Houten onto it and rolled softly over the gravel past the church until a parking lot appeared in back. It too was free of cars. He stopped the car and got out, pocketing the tape recorder and cassette he'd used at the embassy and which were resting in the glove compartment. The sunny warmth of late morning combined with the buzz of flower-crazed bees and the smell of fresh-cut grass to give a languid summery feel to the air.

Paul strolled back along the driveway toward Van Houten Street. A woman driving an Audi sped by, late for an appointment at her beauty salon. She did not see him. He walked along Van Houten, retracing his car's route, and then turned right again onto Eyck. The sparkling homes rested almost arrogantly behind the iron and brick fences, nestled like giant candies among a plethora of rose blossoms.

He arrived at the iron-barred gate of number 33, a spacious manor house built along the lines of a French squire's country retreat. A mailbox in front displayed on its side the carefully painted inscription E. FALKENHAUS. On the edge of the granite wall adjoining the gate hung a brass plate containing a white button. Paul adjusted his tie and pressed it.

Immediately, a cascade of wild barks echoed from inside the house. These grew louder until their source, two massive rottweilers, shot around the right side of the house and raced to the gate. They leapt up, their front paws splayed out against the bars as they adopted a threatened two-legged stance. Their white fangs shone vividly against the pink tongues, which salivated hungrily just inside their massive, powerful jaws.

An elderly woman materialized at the front door. She wore a pale blue linen dress of the style known as "garden party," favored by wealthy women in warm climates around the world. Sleeveless, hanging an inch below the knee, its simplicity conveyed an immediate image of aristocratic coolness and privilege.

The woman picked her way carefully but firmly down the slight incline of the front lawn toward the gate. She looked Paul in the eye through the iron slats for several seconds before saying only "Ja?" Her Afrikaans was curt, her tone a sort of cross between polite curiosity and unconcealable suspicion.

"Mrs. Falkenhaus?"

"Yes, I am Anna Falkenhaus."

"My name is Paul Jenssen. I am sorry not to have phoned first, but I'd like to speak with your husband, on a personal matter, if I may."

"Mr. Falkenhaus is relaxing in his garden. Is it important that you speak with him now?"

"I'm afraid it is."

"Very well. You may come in." She opened the gate and sent a couple of badly aimed kicks in the direction of the two dogs. "Bodo, Jani, be quiet! Shh. Ignore them. They won't hurt you if you just walk slowly behind me."

Paul looked dubiously at the still snarling

beasts. He cautiously stepped through the space, muttering "Nice doggies" under his breath. The dogs walked, flanking him on each side, growling ominously.

Mrs. Falkenhaus led him around the house to the back. A beautiful lawn studded with lounge chairs bordered on a large, orderly garden. The bright red and blue stripes of a man's shirt were partially visible, bobbing behind a sizable patch of sweet corn. She pointed. "There. You can try to talk to him, but I can't guarantee he'll want to. He's very serious about his gardening."

"Thank you." Paul crossed the lush lawn and approached the garden. The man's face was invisible, his body hunched double, his face poking among the tomato plants.

Paul cleared his throat. "Mr. Falkenhaus."

The contorted figure straightened itself. The lined and aristocratic face of Ernst Falkenhaus stared at Paul. "Yes, who are you?"

"Mr. Falkenhaus, my name is Paul Jenssen. I'd like to speak with you privately concerning a matter of importance."

The elderly Afrikaner raised his eyebrows and placed his hands on his hips. "Okay. What would you like to talk about?" His expression was questioning without being rude.

"It's about the Treasurer."

The effect on the old man's face was electric. His eyes widened in alarm. Wordlessly, he started off toward the back of the house. Paul followed several feet behind. They traversed the lawn and entered the large residence through a glassed-in patio. Inside, they turned left, entering what was obviously the former diplomat's study. It was lined with books and globes, and its windows looked out onto the backyard and the garden. Although the garden was hidden by a curtain which kept out the bright midday sun, the windows were open, allowing a breeze to cool the room.

Falkenhaus pointed mutely to an armchair and seated himself behind the antique Venetian desk sheathed in black enamel and adorned with touches of gold leaf. He picked up a pencil from the blotter and tapped with it several times. His hand was shaking visibly, although whether from age or shock Paul could not decide.

"Where did you hear of the Treasurer?" The man's voice trembled slightly.

"Mr. Falkenhaus, that's really not important right now. What is important is that you tell me about him and what he represents."

"Why in God's name would I do that?"

"Because you'd be stupid not to. I already know what he protects and what his duties are. I know that he's in Johannesburg and that you were most likely his predecessor. I know a great deal more. But because I'm writing a book about this, I want it to be accurate. You have the choice of either risking inaccuracies on my part, or of making sure that what I write includes the *Broederbond*'s side of the story. Either way, it becomes public knowledge. I assure you, without your cooperation, it may be very one-sided indeed. You should also know that, should something happen to me, what I have learned will be automatically released to the American media." Paul placed what he hoped was a confident smile on his face and prayed his bluff would work.

Falkenhaus opened a desk drawer and withdrew a packet of cigarettes and a gold lighter. He fumbled with a cigarette, fitting it into an ivory mouthpiece, and then lit it shakily. He puffed it, sucking hard on the filter. "I will consider discussing this matter with you. I shall require a week to think about it. I must also have your word that you will not break the story until after the fifteenth of next month. I will ring you up on May thirty-first to let you know my decision. Are we agreed?"

Paul hesitated, wishing he knew what would happen on the fifteenth. "Agreed."

The old man nodded. "Now, what is your telephone number?"

From the corner of his eye Paul detected a sudden movement. A shadow flickered behind the white curtains. Its shape was long and narrow. It stopped abruptly at the sound of their voices, carried outside through the open window.

The shadow was unmistakable. Silently gesturing *get down,* Paul threw himself on the ground, landing against the wall directly beneath the window. He lay on his side.

Falkenhaus, startled and uncomprehending, turned to watch Paul press himself to the wall. "What the—"

The diplomat's speech was chopped in midsentence as a spray of gunfire exploded into the room. The sound was surprisingly muffled, due to the effective silencer attached to the business end of the weapon. His neck burst in a fountain of blood as a dum-dum bullet opened like a flower in his throat. The invisible assassin's Uzi submachine gun peppered the room for thirty seconds with a hail of death. Glass and papers flew wildly as the elegant study instantly became a scene of chaos and destruction. Paul crouched, shielding his eyes, the bullets flying inches above his head. A shower of glass splinters poured over him.

The killer stopped. The deadly shadow disappeared. Falkenhaus lay on his back, his face hidden by the overturned chair on which he had been sitting. Paul sprang up and cast around the shambles for a weapon. His eyes came to rest on the brass poker standing in front of the fireplace. Carefully making no noise, Paul grasped the weapon and flattened himself against the wall behind the closed study door. He was bleeding in several places where shards of glass had fallen, but was otherwise unscathed.

The dull thud of heavy cushioned footsteps grew louder, though muffled through the wooden door. He hefted the heavy poker so that he held it like a bat, over his left shoulder.

The doorknob turned. Cautiously, the killer opened the door; it swung inward toward Paul.

The unmistakable shape of the tip of a semi-automatic weapon appeared. The rest of the lethal weapon soon followed, a large fist tightly clenching its lean form. The killer had spotted

Falkenhaus across the room. He headed toward him. He wore khaki-colored clothing, his skull covered by a nylon stocking.

When the man was three feet into the room, Paul swung the heavy rod in a silent powerful stroke. The end of the poker connected with the man's left collarbone, which shattered with a gruesome crunch. The man collapsed where he stood, his weapon tumbling onto the floor.

Paul dropped the poker and wiped it clean of fingerprints. He then bent over the unconscious assassin and removed the ski mask. He rolled the man over. The man was white, about forty, with high cheekbones and thin, pinched lips. The face was somehow familiar, but no name came to mind. He searched the man's body for identification, but there was nothing but a few one-rand coins and a pair of reflector sunglasses. Meditating for a minute on the man's features, Paul slipped the glasses over the closed eyes. It was . . . the man from Johannesburg, the man behind the newspaper in the car.

He remembered Mrs. Falkenhaus. He ran outside. The backyard was deserted. Racing around the side of the house, he found the old woman. She was by the property's main gate. Her petite body lay stretched out on the grass, faceup, as if she had suddenly been overcome by fatigue and simply plopped down for a nap. Two bright red stains on her abdomen marred the light blue of her frock. One arm was arched unnaturally under her, creating the impression that she had a bad itch on her lower back.

172

Close by lay one of the rottweilers. The enormous skull dangled semi-detached from the body; one of the bullets had entered the dog's fearsome mouth and blossomed under his tongue, the shrapnel ripping out the jugular vein and vocal cords. He had died without a sound. Paul glimpsed the body of the other rottweiler under a rosebush several feet away.

The gate was ajar. The killer evidently had begun his rain of death almost immediately after the dead woman had admitted him.

Paul dragged the bodies of Mrs. Falkenhaus and the rottweiler which lay at her feet off to the side, out of direct line of vision through the bars of the gate. He then closed the heavy iron door. It would not do to have a curious neighbor drop by to investigate while he was still on the grounds.

He returned around the house to the back, searching for anything he might have dropped which would later reveal his presence. There was nothing.

He entered the hellish scene of the study once again. The carnage was extraordinary. In the center of the room, the killer lay in the same position, still unconscious and still wearing the sunglasses. Paul knelt by the body and pressed his index and middle fingers firmly under the man's jaw. The pulse was regular. He would probably awaken shortly.

Paul was troubled by the killer's lack of identification. There must be something. He unlaced and removed the man's tennis shoes. They were soled with thick rubber crepe, yielding the wearer an advantage in stealth.

The sneakers were manufactured by an international shoe company and so provided no clue. Paul did not bother to replace them on the man's feet.

He then opened the man's mouth to inspect the dental work. The fillings were poorly done, almost sloppy. It was doubtful that the work was done in a Western country.

Lifting the torso, Paul removed the beige turtleneck and drew a startled breath. It was there, imprinted on the skin just below the left armpit. Undeniable. The tiny red tattoo of a bear claw. The mark of the KGB. He let the man's body fall back to the floor.

But why? The Soviets must know he'd resigned from the CIA two years ago. If they meant to avenge themselves for the humiliation of the defection coup he'd pulled off three years ago, they'd have tried something long ago. So why this now?

Elizabeth? That made sense. But how could they know so soon after his discovery of Verwoerd's letters? If the child's death on the airplane was no accident, then the KGB had to have learned of his discovery before he left England. Only two people had known: Arthur Jones and Dean McWhirter. One of them was leaking information to the KGB. Knowingly or unknowingly, personally or indirectly.

The house was quiet. Paul was grateful for the pains the killer had taken to muffle his attack.

He would have a look around the study—it would be his last chance. But first he would have to attend to the unconscious Russian executioner.

The elegant desk was a portrait of chaos. Bullet holes perforated its polished veneer. The gray telephone sat jumbled on the floor, its handset wrapped around one of the legs of Falkenhaus's chair. Paul disconnected the cord from the far wall and detached the other end from the base of the telephone, leaving him holding a twenty-foot length of plastic-coated wire.

He walked back to the killer and flipped him facedown. Grasping one end of the wire, he entwined it around the man's wrists, which he held together until they were securely fastened. He then passed it under the man's stomach and around his waist several times, drawing it steadily lower on his body until he was trussing the man's ankles. Paul triple-knotted the cord. The killer would be unable to free himself.

Able now to search without fear of interruption, Paul commenced sifting through the swamp of papers which lay in disarray on the desk. They were innocuous: notes on stock investments, a few unimportant letters from relatives and friends, a bank statement, a dog-eared desk calendar.

On the floor, a sprinkling of pens and pencils lay scattered haphazardly. A box of paper clips had spilled; its contents slowly hardened in a puddle of glue from a bottle which had been blown in half.

Paul noticed the glossy corner of a piece of

paper protruding from Falkenhaus's shirt pocket. He reached down and extracted it. It was a photograph. The bottom third was in tatters where the schrapnel from the dum-dum had mutilated it, and the resulting wound had cast a dark wine stain over what remained. But the image was still visible, and it made Paul gasp.

What he saw was a picture of himself, taken with a telephoto lens as he walked out of the building housing the U.S. Consulate in Johannesburg.

Paul flipped the ragged photo. On the back, scarcely legible, was some scribbling in Afrikaans, the blue ink turned black by the blood. He translated:

Paul Jenssen.
When approaches, pretend Treas.
My code: FATHER
Rosebank 41–12–17

Paul instantly began assessing the implications of this find. There was only one: The *Broederbond* had planted bugs in Pieter Danniken's house. His strenuous opposition to apartheid made him a logical target for eavesdropping. Therefore, the two conversations in Pieter's study had been completely overheard.

Following this line of thought, Falkenhaus's shaken reaction to Paul's anonymous note at the embassy party had been a brilliant charade. He must have suspected he'd be recorded when he made a dash to the phone booth. That would also explain why the number he'd called was out of service—Paul had tried dialing it earlier that morning. They must have disconnected it after Falkenhaus put through his phony warning. There was to have been no meeting at the Stock Exchange, or maybe there would have been something, but for Paul's benefit only, another red herring to waste his time.

Falkenhaus must have been *Broederbond,* Paul reasoned, for him to go along with the deception. Given his former high rank with the government, that was not particularly surprising. It was also possible that he had held the office of Treasurer. But nothing in Falkenhaus's notes ruled out Fortner or Feldberg as possibilities. If they were both *Broederbonders,* which was also likely given their biographies, then they would certainly have cooperated with whomever was masterminding the plan. They would have feigned puzzlement, appearing exactly as they did.

The best thing about Falkenhaus's jotted notes was their confirmation of both the Elizabeth fund's continued existence and the strong probability of a Treasurer. It also offered him a clue to follow, a name and telephone number which he'd bet would lead to the brain behind the sham. Possibly even the Treasurer himself.

Paul considered the question of his own position. The local police would be mystified by the scene they found at the Falkenhaus home, unless the *Broederbond* clued them in. Yet the *Broederbond* could have arrested him the instant they learned of his mission in South Africa via the bug in Pieter's study. They had not done so. Instead, they had developed an elaborate scheme to set him on the wrong track. They apparently either feared that he still worked for the CIA or that his arrest or disappearance would only attract attention. It was reasonable to assume that whichever was the case, it still held true. Besides, they'd have no way of knowing that he had found Falkenhaus's notes.

Paul pocketed the tattered photo. Glancing around carefully to make sure he'd left no clue to his identity, he walked out of the house and around to the front. The street was still silent and deserted, except that several hundred feet down the road a gray Peugeot sat parked by the curb. There was no question that the Russian was the same man who had followed him from the Johannesburg library.

He glanced in both directions. Nobody. The gate swung open heavily and, walking quickly but not running in case anyone was watching, he strode to the corner and turned left onto Van Houten Street. He proceeded to the church. The whole neighborhood was like a ghost town—a real bedroom community.

His car was still the lot's sole occupant. Paul hopped in and hurriedly rolled out of the driveway onto the quiet road. He swerved left, heading away from the bloodbath on Eyck Street. The nightmare had begun.

The four ancient men waited patiently. The flickering candlelight cast hundreds of shadows between the folds of their pale wrinkled skins. The darkness of the house, in its total absence of windows, lent the illusion of night, but in fact it was a few minutes after nine in the morning.

They were unaccustomed to meeting during the sunlit hours. It left them too open, too vulnerable. Theirs was an assembly which required the secrecy provided by the shroud of darkness. There was too much at stake not to be careful.

The door opened. The figure that entered shouldered the invisible mantle of power which renders those who wear it distinct and recognizable. The four men, the Executive Council of the *Broederbond,* rose in greeting.

"My Brothers." The right hand gestured at them regally, almost papal in the secure knowledge of authority.

"Honored Treasurer."

The latecomer sat. The other four followed suit. Their joints labored under the burden of time, but in their eyes shone a gleam which contrasted with their advanced age. It was the expression of the zealot, of the obsessed, of the paranoid. Their mission was noble; all else was immaterial and irrelevant.

As always, the candle holder sat on the table next to the open Bible and the old silver dagger. They were links to the distant past, bridges spanning time, cementing a people with their cultural roots.

The five hurried through a recitation of the Twenty-third Psalm, yet despite the sense of urgency, the invocation was not perfunctory.

These were the tones of the true believers, of those confident of their favor in the eyes of the Lord. They meant what they prayed.

In the usual manner, their leader, the late-comer, commenced, "Let us begin."

"We shall follow," the other four intoned.

"As we are all aware, the thirty-six hours since we last convened have seen an undeniable further deterioration in the delicate social fabric which binds this blessed nation. The riots yesterday were the worst ever. I would not presume to speak for the Executive Council. However, I suggest that its members now discuss the pros and cons of issuing the formal notice of evacuation, and whether or not to stick to the June fifth date as tentatively planned last meeting."

One of the men placed his silvered head in his hands. After several moments he lifted it and gazed at the company, his eyes suddenly tired. "How the thought of leaving this land weighs on my soul, I can not adequately express in words. The land of my boyhood, and my father's. I have never left the borders of this country, and have no wish to do so now. I do not think I will live long in exile. Yet before any personal consideration, the cause of our Brotherhood must endure supreme. The time to retreat is upon us. We must not be blind to the dangers which unwise delay may hold. I have watched the waves of unrest come and go over the years, but this one is not a wave, it is an avalanche, and I fear it is inexorable. The notice must go out on June fifth. We are fools if we waver any longer."

The man to the speaker's left had pressed his fleshy wrinkled lips tightly together throughout the speech, his jaw clenching in anger. Now he burst forth in a passionate tirade. "That, with apologies to my dear Brother, is the way of the coward. We began our fund years ago as an escape hatch, but we never seriously considered using it. This is no time to start.

"I am not blind," he continued. "I am aware that the violence has escalated. Yes, people are being killed. But flee? To do so now would be the act of old ladies, of toothless lions. Are we so bereft of resources, so afraid of battle, that we must depart the field without engagement? People are always going to be killed; the rest of the world will always protest our way of life here. But to abandon our homeland in the face of a fight is virtually sacrilege, and I cannot stomach such cowardice."

The first speaker coughed, while the other three watched intently. "With respect to my dear Brother, I must express my profound disagreement. To flee before doing battle with an enemy of superior force is not cowardice, but merely wisdom. The blacks of this country, in their current state of mind, ultimately constitute an enemy of superior force. They are *not* going to back down. Good God, can't you tell? I am not panicking prematurely; I don't deny what my own eyes tell me. This country hovers on the brink of civil war. If we go into exile now, we shall still manage to salvage most, if not all, of what we have worked so long and hard to attain.

To remain here to do protracted battle in a war which, after great destruction and internecine killing, we shall unquestionably lose, is sheer madness. My Brothers, the time is now. We have long prayed that this day would never come. Now that it has, we cannot shirk our duty. The notice must be issued at the earliest possible occasion."

The Treasurer said nothing, observing the conflict. The other two members of the Executive Council shifted uncomfortably in their wooden chairs. They were being forced to take a stand, a decision which would affect the entire nation. Their eyes studiously avoided those of their more outspoken colleagues.

At length, the man who had lashed out against the idea of leaving cleared his throat. "My Brothers," he addressed the two. "We are all aware of the agonizing decision which is asked of us. We cannot wait for events to happen. We must create the events and choose our own battlefield. I sincerely hope that you will agree that to leave now is wrong, and that to stay and fight is the only option with honor. But whatever you decide, you must do so now. We must reach a course of action. A life of exile, or massive retaliation and crackdown. Which will it be?"

One of the undecided men lifted his eyes and gazed at the other. "This is the hardest choice I have ever had to make. I do not wish to go down in history as one of the shadowy men behind the scenes who plunged South Africa into the bloodbath of civil war. But worse, I do not want to carry to my grave the fear that I voted to yield up our motherland out of fear. I am not convinced that the unrest, though far worse than it has ever been, will continue. Better, I think, to take a risk than to surrender by not playing at all. I vote that the notice be withheld. If the army is required to put down the uprising, so be it. If it is war they want, it is war they get. God protect us."

All eyes focused on the uncommitted member of the Executive Council. Outside, a child shrieked with joy, oblivious to the momentous decision making inside the cottage. Silence from the assembled, waiting.

The man at last gave a deep sigh, as a man would who has decided to sell his soul to the devil because he needs the money so badly. He spoke, averting his eyes from the others. "May God forgive me, but I vote for the notice. Better exile than to lose everything." The tight-lipped member who had spoken first against exile slammed a fist into his thigh.

The Treasurer coughed dryly. "My Brothers," he said, "as I'm sure you are aware, this leaves the Executive Council in the unusual position of a split vote."

The man who had been last to vote glanced around, bewildered. "But we must come to a decision on this. We can't just let it sit."

"Quite correct." The Treasurer turned to nod in his direction. "As I was about to say, according to the bylaws of the Council, in the event of a tie, the policy is to drop the issue until the subsequent meeting, and the one after that, if necessary, until a majority is achieved."

"But we can't delay this decision any longer," the same man interrupted again.

"No, we can't. But if you recall, there is a clause in the bylaws which permits the Treasurer, although not a member, to cast a tiebreaking vote on any issue which affects the fund. Correct?"

There were assents all around.

"Does this body then agree to accept my vote as binding on its course of action?"

The four members of the Council nodded, a couple of them reluctantly, as if they had planned to dispute the Treasurer's right to vote should it be against them.

"Then so be it. I vote unhesitatingly for the issuance of the notice of evacuation on June fifth. All members of the *Broederbond* to be out of the country by June fifteenth. Our noble order has far more important duties than to become embroiled in a civil war. We are leaving."

The first of the pro—civil war men looked as if he would explode.

The Treasurer continued, eyes gazing down at the granite flagstones on the floor. "I am sure that we are first and foremost respectful of the will of the majority. All of us will uphold the decision taken here today to the best of our ability. Am I correct?" The eyes of the Treasurer and the malcontent locked icily for several long seconds before the latter's will seemed to give way.

"I will support the Executive Council on its decision. You have my word." The man's voice was cracked, almost breaking. The end of an era was at hand.

His fellow voter slowly bobbed his head. "And mine."

"Very good. This body will issue the notice to all section leaders on the morning of June fifth. The entire Brotherhood must be notified by midnight the same day. Any further questions?"

There were none.

"Then let us pray." The Treasurer spoke the Thirty-fourth Psalm alone.

Upon finishing, the members of the Council murmured, "Amen."

"This meeting is concluded. Good day, my Brothers."

"Good day, honored Treasurer."

The Republic of South Africa produces approximately seven hundred tons of gold annually, which amounts to half of the world's total output. The process by which this staggering chunk of wealth is transformed from ugly gray ore into gleaming bars of pure yellow metal is fascinating and relies heavily on basic chemistry.

The dull rock which contains the gold is first brought from South Africa's rich gold mines to a plant above ground. There it is pounded until its consistency resembles that of talcum powder. To this is added water, which turns the powder into a sort of grayish soup.

This liquid is then mixed with cyanide, which

dissolves the gold from the other solid substances with which it is mixed. After these waste products are strained out by means of rotary filters, the remaining gold-bearing solution is subjected to additional chemical treatments. As a result, the gold is precipitated out of the solution. It is subsequently smelted and molded into bars of bullion, each about seventy pounds in weight and eighty-eight percent pure.

Soon afterward, the bullion is transferred to the Central Rand Refinery, built in 1921 in the town of Germiston, not far from Johannesburg. This is the largest and most carefully protected refinery in the world. There the bars are subjected to final purification, known as Miller chlorination. This process was invented in 1868 by an Australian who for the first time successfully filtered chlorine gas through molten gold of eighty-eight percent purity. The chlorine binds to the roughly twelve percent impurities, forming metallic chlorides, which are skimmed off the surface to which they rise.

The remaining material is between 99.6 and 99.9 percent pure. This is remolded into bars, each of which weighs approximately 27.5 pounds. Normally these are stamped with the weight, the name of the refinery, and the name of the bank or depository to which the bullion is being transferred. Normally, but not always.

On a sunny autumn day in May, for example, some 900 new bars of 99.9 percent pure gold, totaling 396,000 ounces, sat in the vault at Germiston bearing no visible stamps at all. They sat piled upon each other, as if Midas had wandered into a brick foundry. Collectively, at four hundred U.S. dollars an ounce, their worth was a little less than one hundred sixty million dollars. They waited in their steel safe in unmarked anonymity.

At eight o'clock in the evening of that day, three large armored vans, each capable of carrying more than ten thousand pounds, arrived at the main transferral dock of the Central Rand Refinery. Several minutes later, the nine hundred bars of unmarked gold were conveyed by forklift to the waiting vans, onto which they were quickly but carefully loaded.

The sealed vans drove the few miles to nearby Rand Airport. They stopped at an isolated corner of the small airfield. One hundred feet above them, four army helicopters hovered, their spotlights illuminating the vans, the whir of their rotors surprisingly quiet. Each helicopter was armed with a GA1 twenty-millimeter automatic cannon, a lightweight and versatile weapon appropriate for helicopters. It is highly favored by the South African army, for whom it is produced on a large scale. The cannon has several important advantages, including remote control firing, easy stripping and maintenance, unusually low recoil, and most significant, superb accuracy.

The armored trucks were relieved of their cargo, which was then placed immediately in the hold of a waiting army transport plane. The gold was then covered with several hundred burlap bags, upon which were stenciled the words RICE—EMERGENCY AID. Had they been opened, the sacks would indeed have been found to contain short–grain Chinese rice. The only marking on the plane's flanks was the huge emblem of the International Red Cross, a simple crimson cross.

Without ceremony, upon completion of the loading, the huge plane taxied to the runway and roared into the sky. As it gained altitude, heading almost due north, the dense cargo in its unheated hold became gradually colder. Twenty-five thousand pounds of gold chilled under a quilt of white rice.

Shortly before dawn, the plane began to descend. The pale bluish glow preceding sunrise silhouetted the vast plain of bloated cumulus clouds which stretched to the horizon in all directions. As it plunged through this layer, the transport's pilot depressed the transmitter and spoke into his microphone. "Red Cross One Eight Two Two requesting clearance to land at Niamey." Although he came from a small town not far from Pretoria, one of the pilot's attractions to his employers was his ability to entirely mask his South African accent. At that moment, anyone listening in on his radio frequency would probably have thought him to be American.

The radio crackled with static. After the elapse of several long seconds, an almost garbled African voice sputtered a gruff permission to land, providing virtually unintelligible instructions for the approach. Not that the pilot needed them—this airport, which was surely one of the world's ten quietest belonging to a capital city, was long familiar to him.

The plane continued to drop. Below, the first light of day etched in ghostly gray the endless expanse of flat plateau which fills the bulk of Niger, a destitute nation frequently confused with oil-rich Nigeria, which lies to the south. It sits roughly halfway between South Africa and Europe. Away to the left, the snaky outline of the Niger River provided the only variation to the unbroken flatland. All other waterways in Niger were dry to their beds by May: Most of the impoverished nation's half million square miles are part of the Sahara Desert.

Here and there farms and plowed fields dotted the arid landscape. To the north, the buildings of the capital, Niamey, flickered into view. The airport, hardly more than a long strip of concrete in a sea of scrub, appeared as the plane prepared to touch down.

Once on the ground, the transport rolled to a hangar, beside which were parked three smaller planes, also transports. Their powerful engines would enable each of them to carry their eight-thousand-pound shares of the treasure. They were painted a mottled dark green color, which would render them invisible in a forest. A contingent of about a dozen men, all armed with pistols or submachine guns, stood sprinkled between them.

With hardly so much as a greeting, the just-arrived transport was relieved of its gold, which was divided in three and loaded onto the smaller ones. While the now empty pseudo–Red Cross plane refueled prior to its immediate return to South Africa, the other three zipped into the air at five-minute intervals and disappeared.

Their flights north were uneventful. They passed quietly over Algeria, the Mediterranean, and northern Italy. To the air traffic controllers whose jurisdictions they entered, they identified themselves as property of the Hertzenberg Mining Company, a Swiss corporation which actually existed but in truth possessed no assets. It had been created for just this purpose.

Some five hours later, they were winging through Austrian airspace, carefully skirting the eastern end of Switzerland. They flew at so low an altitude that they barely skimmed the peaks of the summits of the soaring and snow-capped Tyrol, the Austrian Alps. In so doing they also failed to appear as little green blips on the radar screens of the Austrian Border Police.

Sandwiched between Austria and Switzerland lies a curious minuscule freak of a country. Liechtenstein is the final vestige of the once mighty Holy Roman Empire. Although its foreign affairs and defense are handled by the Swiss, it is a sovereign nation. It is ruled by a hereditary prince and a low-key parliament. Interestingly, there are no customs inspections on traffic between Liechtenstein and Switzerland.

Some two miles north of the capital city, or more accurately capital town of Vaduz, lay a good-sized forest. It was private property and was bordered by a high electronic security fence.

In the center of this forest, a small runway, just wide and long enough to accommodate a small transport plane, had been inserted among the pine trees like a splinter. A tiny asphalt tarmac was attached to one end of it. The entire structure was kept covered by a series of retractable rolling tables, onto which were stacked hundreds of four-inch-thick stainless steel barrels. From each of these barrels arose a single pine tree, of the same variety as the earthbound pines in the forest, and whose height was more or less equivalent to the surrounding trees. From the air, it was impossible to detect anything other than pine trees while the barrel-laden rollers covered the asphalt.

A narrow road, also covered with tree-bearing rollers, connected the airstrip with the large private estate at the edge of the forest.

By the mere flick of a small black lever, a man in a small cottage in nearby Vaduz could cause the rollers to retract sideways, like a smile reveals teeth. Considering the difficulty and frequency of his duties, the man was well paid.

The pilot of the first of the three planes announced into his microphone his estimated time of arrival of fifteen minutes. The transmission was immediately acknowledged by one word: "Understood." The planes were now near Bludenz and rapidly approaching the Austrian-Liechtenstein border.

The man in Vaduz who had said "Understood" arose from his shortwave radio set and walked to a small aluminum panel set into the wall in his kitchen just above his refrigerator. He opened the panel and tugged gently down on the lone switch inside. He closed the panel.

The hydraulics beneath the rollers on the airstrip, tarmac, and connecting road purred softly as the camouflaging trees parted and revealed their secret.

Unnoticed, the plane slipped into the teacup-sized principality of Liechtenstein and returned to earth. The late morning sun shone dully on the plane's dark green skin. It rolled to a stop and turned quickly onto the tarmac to allow the other two to land. They were all parked side by side within ten minutes.

An unremarkable green van hummed along the private road from the estate. Its very average exterior concealed a vastly powerful motor endowed with a strength which its original manufacturer would not have believed possible. It met the first plane as it was just pulling off of the airstrip, and parked on the tarmac alongside it. From its rear popped eight men, who immediately began to transfer the precious cargo to the van's steel-lined interior. As the two other transports landed they were each relieved of their three-hundred-bar shipments.

Another vehicle, painted the same color, now arrived. It was shaped differently, like an oil or milk truck, and in fact its tank was filled with highly flammable airplane fuel. Its driver alighted and placed the nozzles of three hoses, which protruded from the tank's side, into the respective gas tanks of each of the three airplanes. In less than thirty minutes, they were refueled and, newly lightened, they returned to the air. They vanished in the direction of Austria, to the east.

The two trucks rolled slowly back toward the estate. In a short time they arrived at its impressive *schloss*, a fourteenth-century castle complete with turrets and crenellated battlements. The fuel truck driver flicked on his citizens' band radio and said the word "Complete" into his transmitter.

The man in Vaduz, who was waiting for this, rose again from his stool and walked to the panel in his kitchen, where he now pushed the black lever up. The trees in the forest moved back into place. The gap was closed.

For the fourth time in less than a day, the gold was moved, this time from the van to a compact but extremely sturdy utility truck with a fifteen-ton capacity. The truck was a rental, obtained several days in advance from a firm in Lucerne, about an hour's ride south of Zurich. It was absolutely undistinguished in appearance.

From the estate's long drive, the truck turned onto a modest avenue. This road after several miles quietly crossed the Swiss border into the town of Buchs, whose surrounding Alps provided a beautiful backdrop to the quaint village. From there, the truck turned north onto the Swiss N13 highway toward St. Gallen, arriving around lunchtime, a meal for which the driver did not stop.

From St. Gallen the truck turned west, passing through the industrial and cultural center of Winterthur, prior to arriving at the outskirts of Zurich. Slowly, methodically, he made his way to the city's center. The driver was confident of his direction; he had made this trip before, many times.

The truck veered onto Bleicherweg, a broad avenue leading directly to the no-traffic Bahnhofstrasse. At their junction set the Parade-Platz, a large square which was home to a number of the world's most powerful and secretive banks. At Parade-Platz could be found the building housing the headquarters and central vaults of the United Bank of Switzerland. The driver hopped out. He locked his door, although he knew there was no need. For he was aware that in cars parked around the square, in office windows overlooking it, and even lounging on the sidewalk, were at least a dozen men armed with a cornucopia of firepower. It was so much less obvious this way than with an armored truck.

The driver walked into the bank. In less than a minute, an electric garage door opened fifty feet to the right. The driver returned through the bank's front door to his vehicle and slowly drove the small distance to the garage, whose portal closed behind him.

Inside, the driver was met by a nervous, dapper man in his fifties, who hovered around the truck like a bumblebee. He clenched and unclenched his hands, saying nothing. He knew better than to speak to the taciturn driver;

experience had taught him that the response, if any, would be monosyllabic, even snubbing.

The driver silently handed him a single sheet of paper, upon which was written 900 x 12.5 kg./ 99.9%. *Deposit into account of Elizabeth Limited.*

The bank executive nodded and snapped his fingers. A half dozen guards converged on the rear of the truck and began to unload the gold onto a powerful forklift.

The executive reached forward and selected three gold bars at random. One of the guards carried them to a closet-sized laboratory adjoining the garage. The driver and the executive followed.

They found a bookish young man wearing a white lab coat. He weighed each of the bars. The liquid readout of the electronic scale read 12.5000 kilograms. The technician nodded and placed each bar behind a high-penetration X-ray machine. He clicked the shutter, and several minutes later bobbed his head in approval at the photographs—the bars were uniform. This test was a counter against those swindlers who thought to place, inside a shell of gold, a core of some cheaper metal such as silver or copper.

Lastly, the young man put the gold through chemical analysis. Using a small, diamond-tipped industrial saw, he shaved an infinitesimal amount from each of the three bars. These shavings he placed on a glass dish which he inserted into a futuristic box which resembled an oven. He turned it on; it began to gurgle.

A computer printout hooked up to the analyzer spat out a sheet of paper. The technician tore it from the sheaf and examined it. The analysis was short. "Gold, ninety-nine point nine two six percent. Trace elements [silver, lead, copper], point zero seven four percent." He held it out to the bank executive. "They're pure gold, sir." He looked over the executive's shoulder at the piece of paper the driver had given him. He sighed when he saw the words. Nine hundred bars, and each would have to be tested. Good customer or not, at almost a hundred and eighty thousand dollars a bar, the bank took no chances. But the driver only had to stay for a random test.

The executive and the driver returned to the garage. The guards had just finished moving the gold. One of the guards approached him. "Eight hundred ninety-seven, sir, plus the three you took make nine hundred even." The executive withdrew a silver pen from his breast pocket and signed and dated the paper the driver had handed him. He gave it back to the driver and turned toward the door leading into the bank. The driver placed a hand on his shoulder to stop him.

"Yes?"

"Tell the people who will need to know that this will be the last deposit into Elizabeth. From now on, there will be withdrawals. The owners of the account expect the bank's complete cooperation and assistance."

The driver then jumped back into his cab,

backed the truck out of the garage, and melted into the city.

The banker hurried inside, flushed with worry. He had some bad news for his superiors. He hoped they wouldn't hold the messenger to blame.

9

Paul drove back toward the center of Sandton as quickly as he could without attracting the attention of the omniscient Sandton police. At all costs, they must now be avoided.

It was just after eleven o'clock. The weather was warm and sunny, clashing surrealistically with the bloodiness he had just witnessed. Paul wondered how long it would take the police to realize that the man he'd left trussed up like a Thanksgiving turkey was a KGB assassin. He would telephone them anonymously in a few minutes. He wasn't worried about the Russian talking: If the Soviets were after him, as Paul assumed, the last thing the killer would do would be to reveal the name of his intended victim. The KGB would send down a "hit man for the hit man" for breaking silence. Paul supposed it was remotely possible that the killer was after Falkenhaus, but it was just too coincidental that Paul should be there at that moment, especially in light of the other attempts. No, unquestionably, the Soviets wanted him dead, reason unknown.

Paul arrived back at the enormous Sandton City Mall. Its sidewalks were thronged with housewives with little more to do than idly browse through its many shops. He found a public telephone near the main entrance and quickly stepped into it. He dialed the police. To the gruff sergeant who answered, Paul announced, "There has been a murder at thirty-three Eyck Street, in Sandton. The murderer is lying tied up in the study." He hung up. That should cause something of a sensation, he thought.

He consulted the photograph he'd discovered in Falkenhaus's office and dialed the seven-digit Rosebank number shown on its back side.

It rang twice, and then a woman's voice answered "Van Fester Residence" in Afrikaans. She sounded like a maid or housekeeper.

"Yes, is Mr. van Fester in please?" Paul had no idea what he would say if the master came to the phone.

"No, sir, Mr. and Mrs. van Fester won't be back for at least another hour and a half. Would you like to leave a message?"

Paul assumed his most dulcet tones, genially taking the woman into his confidence. "No, that's really all right. You see, my wife just baked a large batch of Mr. van Fester's favorite cookies, and she wanted me to run them over to him. I'd like to just drop them by in a half hour if that's okay."

"Oh, well, I'm sure he'd like that very much,

sir." She giggled. "He sure do like his sweets, though, that's the truth."

"Fine. I'll be by soon." Then, as if as an afterthought, Paul added, "You know, I don't think I'm exactly sure of the address. What is it again, please?"

"It's twelve Jacaranda Court, Rosebank."

"Thank you. I'll see you in a bit." He hung up.

Paul hopped back in his car and in five minutes was at the Danniken house. After cleaning his face and arm where the glass had cut him, he penned a carefully worded two-page note to Beth and placed it on the table in the kitchen where she wouldn't miss it. From the crockery cupboard he removed a worthless, slightly chipped dinner plate. Then, following a hunch, he climbed the stairs to his room and packed a small bag of toiletries and a change of clothes. He then walked down to the front door and closed it behind him.

Outside, the steady noon heat had raised the temperature in his car to an uncomfortable level. After airing it for a minute, Paul stepped in and headed toward Sandton's commercial section, about a mile from the crowded mall. He checked his rearview mirror frequently; he was not being followed.

The shopping area came into view. The main street was crammed with pricey clothing stores, exotic food shops, jewelers, gift stores, and beauty salons. Paul spotted an upscale bakery called L'Eclair d'Or and parked the BMW out front.

Inside, most of the items for sale were either pseudo-French pastries or ineffectual attempts to duplicate French baguettes and country loaves. But he found what he was looking for. In one corner of the glass display case, on the lowest shelf, a platter of chocolate chip cookies sat, neglected and not especially enticing. But they were the only cookies for sale. Paul ordered two pounds of them.

The salesgirl boxed them and tied the package with string. He paid for the cookies and returned to his car. There he slit the string and transferred the cookies to the old plate he'd taken from the Danniken kitchen. He draped a paper napkin from the box over the top of them; the whole presentation was believable as a homemade gift.

Once again, consulting his map, Paul drove the few miles to the adjoining suburb of Rosebank. The streets were immaculate, the grand homes reflective of the considerable wealth of the town's inhabitants.

He entered a verdant section of Rosebank. The houses were undoubtedly the suburb's largest, its self-evident "millionaires' row." In the midst of the arboreal opulence Paul found Jacaranda Court, a dead end from which receded the long, intimidating drives of three grand estates. Number twelve was the middle one.

A state-of-the-art brushed steel gate blocked entry into the drive. Next to it, embedded in the ten-foot granite wall, a black plastic intercom connected visitors to the mansion far up the drive. Atop the wall, curved steel barbed wire provided discouragement for would-be intruders. Two cameras, one on each wall on either side of the gate, emphasized the rigorous security measures the van Festers had installed. Wishing himself luck, Paul pressed the speak button on the intercom and said, "Hello."

A momentary wait followed. Then the two cameras rotated so that their lenses were focused on Paul. He looked up obligingly, tempted to place his forefingers at either corner of his mouth and stick out his tongue, but refrained from doing so.

The voice of the woman he'd spoken to, the maid, emanated from the speaker. "Yes?"

"Hi, it's Louis de Ries. I called about the cookies." Paul tendered the plate toward the cameras.

The gate clicked and swung open. Paul returned to his car and rolled the BMW gently through the gate. The long drive stretched out of view. The address was well named; Jacaranda trees provided a shadowy canopy that augmented the impression of vast wealth and power.

The drive meandered for a half mile. After a final curve, it opened on a spectacularly palatial English garden. The beautiful grounds sprouted meticulously sculpted topiary and regal fountains, the spray of which formed tiny rainbows in the glittering sun. Among the hedges stalked peacocks. Several of the males were strutting ponderously, tails open and extended in an extraordinary display of lapis, turquoise, indigo, and emerald. The drab females continued to root for grubs in the lush grass, seemingly unimpressed with the finery of the other sex.

The crushed gravel of the drive concluded in an elaborate oval. At its far end loomed the stately columns enclosing the mansion's main entrance. Paul parked in front of the enormous white pillars and mounted the dignified staircase constructed of the same pale stone. On either side lounged an imperious lion, its stone forepaws extended in regal repose.

A young black woman appeared at the front door as Paul reached the top of the staircase. She was clad in a maid's uniform of black, with white apron and frilly white cap.

"Mr. de Ries?" She greeted him in heavily accented Afrikaans. Like most blacks in South Africa, she had learned the language as a required course in school. Prior to that she only spoke in one of the local Nguni dialects used by a majority of the country's blacks.

"Hi." Paul wagged a finger at her and pointed at the plate in his hand. "Now, I know these will be tempting, but you're going to have to be strong."

She giggled and moved forward as if to take them.

"I'd like to leave a note with these if possible. Then we could hide them someplace where he'd be bound to find them. I bet he'd be surprised to see them in his study—could we leave them there?" Paul gave the maid a conspiratorial grin. "I'm sure he'd be pleased."

Still tittering with humor at the prospect, she nodded and bade him follow. Inside, the mansion was as awe-inspiring as its exterior. Rising from marble mosaic floors, the walls were hung with stunning Flemish and Burgundian tapestries, their colors somewhat faded but still remarkably clear after more than three hundred years. Paul wanted badly to admire them at his leisure, but the time was not right.

They passed a half dozen salons, several of the doors to which were ajar. Paul glimpsed frescoed ceilings capping gilt and mirrored walls. He felt like Maria from *The Sound of Music,* entering the von Trapp family mansion for the first time. The house was like a museum.

The maid led him up a grand alabaster staircase at the end of the sumptuously decorated hallway. The bevels of the posts in the balustrade were edged in gold. A staircase for a monarch.

They turned right at the top of the staircase and proceeded down another long hall, lined with closed, gold-handled doors. Opening one of these, the maid ushered Paul into a dim, comfortable room out of character with the rest of the mansion. It was very much a man's room, a study somewhat similar to that of Pieter Danniken's. Heavy wood and leather furniture sat squatly on a threadbare Oriental rug. An enormous map of South Africa covered the entire left wall.

And then, with a gasp, it hit him.

The picture.

On the wall behind the solid oak desk, directly above a window looking out on the mansion's grand drive, a large oil painting dominated the room. It portrayed a hellish scene. The flames were astoundingly realistic. From the midst of them, a single bizarre bird seemed to writhe in agony, its body fuel for the blaze. The gray and green feathers of its plumage contrasted strikingly with the vivid oranges and reds of the fire which was consuming it. Its two heads were entwined, the beaks agape in the throes of death. It was a double-headed phoenix.

Paul had seen the scene once before. The wax seals of Hendrik Verwoerd's two letters he had bought from Arthur Jones both bore the same eerie image of a bird with two heads being devoured by flames. He knew he was looking at the symbol of the *Broederbond*. How appropriate that they had chosen the phoenix as their mascot. The mythological bird consumed itself in fire every five hundred years and then instantly arose reborn from the ashes to live another half millennium. If the purpose of Elizabeth was to give rebirth to an exiled people, the phoenix was the perfect emblem.

Walking past the maid, Paul placed the cookies on the desk. "Now, I need a pen and a sheet of paper." He seated himself behind the desk as if it were the most natural thing in the world. He removed a pen from the marble desk set and tore a blank page from a notepad lying on the blotter, then placed the tip of the pen in his mouth as if deep in thought.

The woman looked at him doubtfully for a few seconds, and then, apparently deciding Paul was harmless, said, "Sah, when you finish, just call me and I show you out. I have to tend to the washing." She let herself out of the study.

Instantly, Paul began examining the contents of the desk's four drawers. One contained supplies—paper clips, staples, Scotch tape, sealing wax, and such. Another held a box of stationery. Its heading ran JAN VAN FESTER.

The third drawer yielded two items of interest. One was a four-inch cylindrical steel spike signet, rather like a Chinese chop. At one flat end, a bas-relief of the double-headed phoenix dying a fiery death was engraved.

The other important article was a faded sepia photograph. It showed three men gazing straight at the camera. They stood side by side on a grassy knoll or mountaintop, the horses saddled and waiting in the background. Their expressions were those of confident men, self-assured and indomitable. On the back of the photograph, in ink smudged from many years of fingerprints, a barely legible inscription read: *Photo taken by Roelof du Plessis. From left: J. Vorster, H. Verwoerd, J. van Fester. Drakensberg Range. 7 January 1939.*

Paul stared at the photograph: two of apartheid's most ardent proponents, President Hendrik Verwoerd and his successor John Vorster. How strange to see them so young. Yet they both had that air of determination, the same proud angle at which they held their heads that would be so visible to the world years later.

The third man wore a slightly different expression. It was not that he was smiling, but there was an insouciance, a smugness, the face of someone who is holding a trump card or who knows the answer to a riddle but pretends not to.

Van Fester was therefore a man connected to the very inner core of the Afrikaner ruling elite. Yet Paul had never heard of him. Was it possible that the mysterious master of this fabulous estate was the Treasurer of the *Broederbond*? Certainly the last initial was correct, but the "Jan" did not correspond with the first initial *E*. And what other high office carried with it the guardianship of the secret society's eerie seal? The symbol of the mythical bird obviously held huge significance for the *Broederbond*. Why else would a man hang a painting of it in such a prominent position in his private study? Paul sensed that van Fester was a man who enjoyed an immense quantity of power.

He replaced the photograph and shut the drawer. He tugged on the last one; it was locked. He paused to listen for approaching footsteps, but there was no sound.

Paul removed a paper clip from a porcelain dish next to the dark green blotter. Bending down, he inserted one pointed end of the clip into the keyhole of the drawer and delicately probed the lock. He silently gave thanks for one of the first courses attended by all new CIA operatives: "Doors and Safes."

Paul felt the tiny bolt turn. He pulled the drawer open. Inside was a Mauser pistol and a single unsealed manila envelope. He pocketed the gun and lifted the flap of the envelope. Out slid a notebook, luxuriously bound in black leather. On its cover was stenciled in gold a single word: ELIZABETH.

The crunching sound of a car rolling down the drive grew in a gentle crescendo. Paul watched through the window with horror as a navy blue Mercedes limousine materialized from the trees and banked to a stop before the columns in front. A white driver in dark blue livery immediately got out to open the doors for an elderly couple. A slender white-haired man helped his wife to her feet and then squinted at Paul's parked BMW. He gestured to the driver before grasping his wife's elbow and commencing a slow ascent up the front steps. Meanwhile the driver sauntered over to the car and began examining it.

Paul grabbed the notebook and raced into the hall. It was deserted. Making as little sound as possible, he sprinted down the staircase and headed toward the back of the house.

He heard the click of the front door opening echo through the empty halls as he entered the kitchen. Somewhere off to the right he could hear the maid singing to herself as she folded laundry.

A door. An exit. Paul could see it through the pantry. The maid was oblivious to him. He slipped across the kitchen and through the cool dark room whose cabinets contained enough canned food for a siege. He opened the door a crack.

Asleep and basking in the afternoon sun not ten feet away were two muscular rottweilers. Obviously, the *Broederbond* pet of choice. They were attached by metal chains to a concrete block some fifty feet away at the edge of the broad back lawn. They did not open their eyes.

There appeared to be approximately thirty feet of slack in the chain. That meant that, if he tried to run for it, he'd have to make it twenty feet to be home free.

He noiselessly shut the thin steel door behind him and was a yard into his escape when from somewhere in the bowels of the mansion came a roar of anger. It had to be the old man.

The dogs snapped awake as if they'd been switched on electronically. They stared at the intruder uncomprehendingly and then roared to their feet.

Paul ran.

In a frantic tangle of black and tawny fur, the snarling animals were yanked when their chains reached the limit of slack. Restrained at the collar, standing on hind legs, the vicious rottweilers were practically throttled as they struggled against the unyielding chains. They bayed with fury as their quarry vanished around the side of the house.

Paul never looked back. He raced onto the front lawn and spied the uniformed driver examining the BMW's license plate. He was facing away from Paul.

The man never heard a thing. The slice of Paul's right hand to the man's neck knocked him to the gravel, instantly unconscious. Paul jumped in the car and inserted the key. He revved the motor and with a spray of gravel roared past the limousine toward the front gate. The weight-sensitive trigger at the end of the drive responded to the car and the steel portal swung open. He gunned the accelerator and the car shot through the aperture. He was free.

It would now be only a matter of minutes before the police were hunting for a green BMW.

Paul drove quickly back to the Sandton business district and parked next to a phone booth in front of a hardware store. Still holding the book, he hurried to the phone and dialed the U.S. Consulate in Johannesburg.

In a few seconds, Pat Ryan came on the line. "Hello, doll. What's shaking?"

"Pat, I'm in a serious bind."

"What's wrong? Are you hurt?" Her voice was tense.

"No, but I think in a short while some very important people whose toes I just stepped on are going to sic the South African police after me."

"Oh, Christ, Paul, what the hell did you do?" She sounded somewhat relieved.

"I invaded the privacy of the *Broederbond*. Do you know about them?"

"Of course. They're like the Mafia here,

except better organized. They run the whole country."

"Yes, well, I think I may have nosed a little too much into their business, and I didn't have time to cover it up. Pat, I can't go to a hotel— they'd find me right away. I need a place to stay. Do you have a couch I can crash on? It shouldn't be for long."

"Paul, did you ... ah ... commit any sort of crime, or do anything you'd be ashamed to tell your mother about?"

"No. Yes. What I mean is, I swiped a book, which I haven't even had time to look at yet, from the desk of someone who I think is an important figure in the *Broederbond*. It's not a crime, in the sense that I'd never be officially arrested for it—the police would dream up some other charge. But yes, Mom, I did take something that doesn't belong to me."

"What's so important about the book?"

"I suspect it holds some big *Broederbond* secrets. I haven't had time to look at it yet."

"And that's all you've done? You haven't robbed a bank or shot someone or exhibited yourself in public?"

"That's all I've done."

"Okay. Here's my address." She issued him directions to her rented cottage in nearby Randburg. "There's an extra key under one of the begonia pots by the mailbox out front. Are you allergic to cats?"

"No."

"Good, then Hortense won't bother you."

"Gee, Pat, *that's* a pretty name."

"Don't knock it. It was my grandmother's. Anyway, the couch in the living room is a roll-out, so make yourself at home, and Paul, help yourself to whatever's in the fridge. I'll be home around five-thirty."

"Thanks, I'd better get moving. See you when you get home." He hung up and returned to his car.

Following her instructions, he arrived in the suburb of Randburg in ten minutes. The houses were matchboxes compared to the mansions of Sandton and Rosebank, but nevertheless they were well kept with carefully trimmed hedges and rosebushes everywhere.

Paul easily found the house. It was a pleasant pink stucco villa with an attached garage. Over the door to the garage hung an old-fashioned Pennsylvania Dutch hex sign, an import from Pat's hometown of Lancaster. The walls of the house trailed streams of lush ivy, providing a colorful contrast to the pale coral of the stucco.

Paul hopped out of the car and opened the garage. It was spacious enough to accommodate two cars. The BMW fitted snugly on the right side adjacent to the locked connecting door into the house. He turned the ringer of the car phone to its top volume and rolled down the right front window so it would be audible from inside the house. Grabbing the black leather book and his small suitcase, he walked outside and shut the garage door behind him.

Out front he spotted the half dozen pots filled

with magenta begonias, clustered like bodyguards around the mailbox. After rooting among them for a few seconds, he discovered a brass house key sandwiched between one of the pots and its water dish.

Inside, the house was much as he expected to find it—pale blue wall-to-wall carpeting, walls dotted with reprints of art exhibit posters from the twenties, a small army of framed photographs of family and friends huddled in clumps on most of the available surfaces, several dozen houseplants, a crocheted throw hanging lopsidedly over the couch, and a large fish tank. Pre—old maid clutter.

The fish tank provided the room with its only surprise. Peering at its inhabitants, Paul realized that it was filled with sea anemones and clown fish, the only marine creature able to navigate through the anemones' swarm of deadly tentacles without being stung. The weird headless animals looked like bushes of parti-colored snakes, pink and purple and white, writhing gently in the water as the brilliant orange, black, and white clowns calmly wriggled in their midst.

Paul stood watching them for a minute until he heard a tentative "Urrow?" Looking down, his eyes met those of an obese Siamese cat. It looked up at him inquisitively, as if it didn't care who he was but only whether or not he'd brought dinner. Realizing that a meal was not forthcoming, it waddled off mournfully in the direction of the kitchen.

Paul sat on the couch and opened the book

labeled ELIZABETH. The first page showed no writing, but another chilling drawing of the two-headed phoenix.

He turned the next page and gaped in amazement. It was a ledger. The first entry was listed as March 8, 1952. To the right of it was written *525.000 ons fyngoud.* More than half a million ounces, or about thirty thousand pounds, of pure gold. He quickly calculated the value to be just over two hundred million dollars at the current market price.

Beneath this entry were some thirty others, all consisting of a date and a quantity of gold. Beginning with the second listing, a third column appeared. Paul immediately recognized it as a running total, in ounces. He flipped the page. Pages two and three were similarly inscribed. He kept turning.

The last entry, on the eleventh page, was dated May 27. Yesterday. It showed an amount of 396,000 ounces of gold, worth about one hundred sixty million American dollars. The figure at the right, the last running total, made Paul gasp again. In the same bold handwriting as the rest of the book was scrawled *One hundred twenty million, three thousand, five hundred ounces.* This was the secret hoard of the *Broederbond.* The Treasurer was custodian of a fortune's worth—approximately forty-eight billion American dollars.

The rest of the book was blank except for the three names penciled into the inside back cover. The first two, *Anton Richtmeister* and *Richard*

Neuhaus, were crossed out. The writing appeared old and faded. Beneath them, the third, *Gerhard Neuhaus*, was scribbled in a different handwriting and looked relatively recent. After each of the three names appeared the word *Zurich*. Paul recognized none of the men.

The piercing beep of the car phone broke the quiet. He raced to the door to the garage and unbolted it. The open window of the BMW lay just on the other side. Reaching in, he snatched the telephone from the console.

"Hello?"

"Paul? It's Beth. What's going on? What's all this mystery for?" She sounded frightened.

"Are you calling from—"

"Yes. I just got home and found your note, so I went out again in search of a pay phone. Paul, why can't I talk to you from the house?"

"Because, darling, something happened today which indicates that the *Broederbond* has bugged your house, or at least your father's study. It isn't terribly surprising considering how much he flaunts his dislike for what they represent. Did you see any cars parked in front of your house?"

"No, Paul, I didn't, and I wasn't followed, and will you please tell me what is going on?"

"Darling, I can't. What you don't know can only protect you. Please trust me. I just don't want to get you mixed up in all this."

"I already am." She sounded grumpy.

"Please try and understand that I couldn't bear it if something happened to you because of what I'm doing. That's already happened to me once in my life, and I won't allow it again."

"Well, how long are you going to be away?"

"I'm not sure. I'm following up some strong leads I discovered today. But listen to me, Beth. I want you to go about your day as if everything is perfectly normal. Do just as I've told you and keep calm. You and Pieter are totally safe. Are you going to be alone, or is there a friend who could come over and stay with you?"

"Pa's due back this evening from Durban. Are you sure the house is bugged? He's going to be furious."

"You're probably right. Whatever you do, don't tell him out loud. Write it out, then burn the paper. They may sift through your garbage. We don't want to tip them off that we know they're listening."

"How will I contact you?"

"Same as you are now. If you can get to a public phone without being followed, try me on the car phone. If I don't answer, try later. Let's set aside this time, four o'clock each day, as the regular time you're going to call me. But if I don't answer, don't worry. I may not be able to. Just try later. Don't disappear to the pay phone too much or it will attract attention."

She was quiet for a bit, and then softly said, "Paul, I miss you. Last night was so . . . special."

"Beth, darling, I promise you, when this is over, you and I are going to be spending a whole lot of time together. I care for you a lot more than I think you know."

"Paul, I want to tell Pa about us."

He laughed softly. "I hope he doesn't decide to come after me too. But if you think it's okay, fine."

"Please be careful if you can."

"Thank you. I will. You're my incentive. I'll talk to you tomorrow." He blew a loud kiss to her and replaced the phone in the car.

Paul returned to the house and spent the next ninety minutes examining the ledger and considering his precarious situation. His thoughts were interrupted by the sound of an automobile pulling into the driveway. He silently crept to the door. Looking through the keyhole, he saw Pat Ryan hoist a bag of groceries from her car and carry them toward the front.

He opened the front door as she was inserting her key. She looked surprised.

"Wow. I knew you were here, but it's still weird to see someone else let you into your own house. Here." She handed him the groceries and bustled inside.

"It's no palace, but it's home. I hope you'll be comfortable."

"Pat, if it were a barnyard I'd still be grateful. This is far more than I have any right to ask of you, and I truly thank you. I really needed it."

"No prob. Hey. I picked up two T-bones for dinner. I hope you're not one those mineral-water food sissies into health or something."

"Real food for real people."

"That's what I like to hear. A carnivore after my own heart. None of that bean curd or organic lentil burger shit in this house." She popped two large potatoes into the oven.

He helped her unpack the groceries and put them away. "Pat, I can't go out shopping or anything where I might be spotted by the police, but if you've got anything that needs fixing around the house, I'd be more than happy to give it a try. I'd also like to cover those groceries."

She started to object, but he interrupted. "Pat, respectfully, shut up. I may be taking advantage of your limitless kindness by invading your home, but I'm not a sponge." He slipped a couple of hundred dollars worth of rand into her hand and closed her fingers into a fist around the money. "Not another word."

"Thanks, Paul. You don't have to do that, but thank you anyway." She disappeared into her bedroom and reappeared momentarily, her ample frame crammed into a pair of jeans and a large University of Minnesota sweatshirt.

"Okay, sport, it's chow time. We're going to partake of the quintessential American dinner: steak, baked potato, salad, and for dessert Chef Pat will be serving the excessively rich and gooey Mississippi mud cake she labored over yesterday. If you'll set the table, dinner should be ready in a little while."

While he was laying out the plates and silverware, she casually asked as she prepared their dinner, "So, Paul, does it look like you'll have to sneak out of the country, or am I on the wrong track?"

He chuckled. "Curiosity can be dangerous,

Patricia." He paused. "Although I'm holding a bargaining chip, which I swiped from one very rich, very powerful South African, I need to stay hidden. We'll just have to see what happens."

She turned back to the Formica counter, deep in thought. The steaks bubbled and spat fragrantly. She watched them broil with the careful eye of an experienced cook. As she turned them, the telephone in the kitchen rang. Still prodding the meat with a fork, she answered it. "Hello?"

She recognized the scratchy sound of a long-distance call. "Mr. Paul Jenssen, please," a man's voice requested. She thought he might be foreign, but his English was excellent.

"Could you hold on a moment, please? I've got something on the stove." She put the phone on the counter and motioned furiously to Paul. "It's a man calling from overseas for you!" she whispered.

After conferring briefly with Paul, she told the caller he'd reached a wrong number.

"Is this not the home of Patricia Ryan?"

She affirmed that it was she.

"Miss Ryan, let me put it this way. If in the near future you *should* encounter a man named Paul Jenssen, would you be so good as to let him know that I tried to reach him? My identity is unimportant, but I am in possession of something which I am quite sure is of great value to him. It concerns the *Broederbond*. I am in Europe now, but will be in Johannesburg tomorrow. I will be waiting in the parking lot of the Kyalami Racetrack in Midrand at eleven o'clock tomorrow night. If he is interested, he may meet me there, alone. I shall leave if I see that he arrives accompanied."

"Okay, but I'm telling you, there's no one here by that name." She replaced the phone and related the conversation to Paul.

With an effort, they kept the conversation light. The food was delicious, but neither enjoyed it completely. The phone call had put a damper on the evening. They finished and washed up, after which they moved to the living room to watch television.

At ten o'clock, Pat retired for the night, claiming exhaustion. Paul unfolded the couch, and soon the house was still. But though he could hear her snoring softly behind her bedroom door, Paul dozed only fitfully, keeping one ear cocked. He did not fall into deep sleep until five the next morning. His last thought before he sank into oblivion was that he could always take refuge in the U.S. Embassy, because at least the Americans weren't after him.

The limousine lurched abruptly to a halt. A marine, white-gloved and polished, leaned forward stiffly like an egret to open the rear right-hand door, while the driver scurried to get the one on the left. The car's two passengers, both clad conservatively in navy blue suits, stretched their legs under the portico of the south entrance to the White House, and then allowed themselves to be escorted inside. They passed through an X-ray machine and then were analyzed by a device capable of detecting high concentrations of nitrogen, an element found both in dynamite and in the infinitely more dangerous and moldable explosive known as plastique.

Walking down the long, carpeted corridor several feet behind the staffer who was their temporary guardian, the two men hardly spoke. Neither the director of the CIA nor his lieutenant looked forward with anticipation to this meeting. It was not likely to be pleasant. Director William Sullivan and Assistant Director Jim Bell knew this president too well to be optimistic.

The escort led the men to a plush, wood-paneled anteroom. A secretary sat at a desk laden with telephones. From the walls, portraits of presidents past gazed condescendingly at those who sought audience with the current one. A Gilbert Stuart rendering of George Washington numbered among them. The CIA director and assistant director were asked to be seated on one of the several leather couches filling the anteroom. The staffer stayed standing.

At five o'clock, the huge old grandfather clock which had been added during the Kennedy Administration solemnly chimed. Three minutes later, the secretary signaled to the staffer, who informed the intelligence men that he would now take them in. Following him, they entered the ovate cream and navy sanctum of the most powerful man in the world.

At his desk, the president of the United States looked up from a sheaf of papers, dropped them, and rose to greet his guests. His wavy hair, mousy gone gray, was combed casually, emphasizing his boyish, patrician appearance.

The president shook the spies' hands. "Bill, Jim, good to see you. Sit, please."

Off to the right of the president's desk, two men sat on a striped damasked sofa, and they both also rose for the newcomers. They were immediately recognizable as George Williams, the president's youthful chief advisor, and Harold Bainbridge, his gruff chief of staff.

The visitors sat in two plush Chippendale armchairs which had been strategically placed across the desk from the president seconds before the CIA men's entrance. Two goblets and a crystal ewer containing ice water perched on a glass table situated between Sullivan and Bell. The junior man filled the glasses, sure that they would be needed to moisten two dry, nervous throats.

"Well, what can I do for you gentlemen? I assume it isn't good news because neither one of you is your usual cheery self. Right?"

Bell looked over at Williams, who had pressed his hands together to his lips. The director nodded slightly, signaling Bell to begin. "Mr. President, at the time you were briefed by the Agency following your election, do you recall anything about the file known as Operation Lodestone?"

The president squinted his eyes and rubbed a nonexistent itch at the end of his nose. "Ah, let me see, that was one of those World War II foreign policy files or something, wasn't it?"

Bell said, "Good memory, sir. It was the practical implementation of a specific policy of the U.S. government toward South Africa. Specifically, prior to the outbreak of World War II, there was great uncertainty about whether South Africa would enter the war, or would stay neutral. Many of the strong minority of South Africans favoring neutrality were in actuality quite sympathetic to Hitler. A fair number even wanted the country to enter the war on the side of the Axis. As you may be aware, much of the white population is made up of Afrikaners, or Boers farmers descended from German and Dutch ancestry, so that explains much of the pro-Hitler sentiment."

The president nodded somewhat impatiently. "Yes, go on."

"President Roosevelt felt strongly that South African neutrality would be a grave blow to the war effort. He feared the possibility of German ships able to freely use the country's ports to refuel. He wanted the manpower of the South African army to lend some much-needed support in Europe and North Africa, where events were not going at all well for the Allies. In addition, he also wanted the treasure trove of minerals and wealth sitting buried in South Africa's mines to help finance the war effort. It became obvious to him that the country's immediate entry into the war on the Allied side was absolutely critical."

The president tapped a forefinger on the burnished walnut desk. "I assume the history lesson is essential, Jim."

"Yes, sir. It's almost over. In accordance with President Roosevelt's wishes, a project code-named Lodestone was initiated. The operation's aim was to help persuade South Africa to join the Allied war effort."

The five-foot-three frame of the CIA director twitched in his chair. He knew what was coming.

George Williams shrugged. "Well, there's nothing particularly wrong with that. Governments try to influence the decisions of other governments every day."

Bell turned to him. "Yes, that's true. Except in this case, the implications were deemed so grave that the project was taken to another level. The vocal minority of South Africans who favored either neutrality or joining the Axis powers consisted almost entirely of Afrikaners. They were represented politically by the National Party, which had never managed to attain power." Bell looked sideways at Sullivan, who still sat looking down at his folded palms. "President Roosevelt authorized a secret proposal to the leader of the National Party. A deal."

The president's interest revived. "What sort of deal?"

"An exchange. A promise of major covert political and financial assistance to the National Party following the eventual conclusion of the war, in return for a commitment not to oppose South Africa's joining the Allies. A secret agreement."

The large form of Chief of Staff Bainbridge swelled in his tight suit jacket as he leaned forward. "I still don't see why that's so bad. It's nothing new for us to be friendly to opposition political parties in foreign countries or even to offer them help."

"The problem, Harry, is that there's more to it than that. The United States essentially went behind the back of an ally, the then-current South African government, comprised almost entirely of English settlers, not Afrikaners. In addition, our ally, Great Britain, would have been outraged, because Afrikaners are the historic enemies of the English, and we would have been abetting them at the expense of the English-descended government of South Africa. If word got out, it would send a message to the world that the U.S. could not be trusted as a reliable ally."

"Well, I guess that's so. But why is this so critical all of a sudden?" The president seemed perplexed.

"Sir, the implications are a lot worse. In a nutshell, the National Party bears solitary responsibility for implementing the laws of apartheid. If it ever came out that the United States was the primary force behind their accession to power in 1948, there would be race riots around the nation. In the eyes of the world, we would be the ultimate hypocrites, vocally condemning apartheid, but really responsible for it."

"Bill, why wasn't I told of this before?"

The CIA director swiveled his round head like an owl to return the president's baleful glare. "Mr. President, as you were made aware at the time of your briefing, there are certain intelligence matters about which you are not informed in detail, so that if confronted publicly, you will not be placed in the awkward position of having to lie. This was one of those situations. The events which Jim just described were not supplied to you before because potentially they might have embarrassed you."

"Well, if it was secret, who's alive now that could break the story?"

"Unfortunately, sir," Sullivan continued, "until today we thought no one. But only a short time ago, the U.S. government received a telegram, directed to me, threatening to expose the U.S. role in bringing apartheid into being unless a large sum of money is placed in a Cayman Islands numbered account. The author of the telegram is a former agent of ours named Paul Jenssen. He resigned two years ago with a grudge against the Agency. He makes it quite clear that he intends to hold the U.S. government up for blackmail." He reached into his briefcase, withdrew a single sheet of pale blue paper, and pushed it across the desk to the president. "I think, sir, if you read this, you'll have a more accurate concept of the parameters of this problem."

The president adjusted his simple horn-rimmed reading glasses on his nose and looked down at the papers. It was a top-priority telegram, for immediate delivery. It ran:

JOHANNESBURG, MAY 28. TO WILLIAM SULLIVAN, DIRECTOR, CENTRAL IN-

TELLIGENCE AGENCY, LANGLEY, VIRGINIA, USA. ARRANGE FOR SAM TO DEPOSIT $100M INTO ACCT #300122 AT CAYMAN ISLANDS INTERNATIONAL TRUST COMPANY ON GRAND CAYMAN ISLAND STOP DEPOSIT SUM BY MIDNIGHT MAY 31 EST STOP ALTERNATIVE EXPOSURE OF 1939 MARRAKECH ACCORD STOP MALAN'S ULTIMATE BUSINESS TRANSACTION AND WEXFORD'S CONTRACT STOP NO FURTHER COMMUNICATIONS STOP CONSIDER PAYMENT SETTLEMENT FOR AGENCY-CAUSED PERSONAL LOSSES STOP JENSSEN STOP END OF MESSAGE.

The president snapped his head up, furious. "And I suppose that *M* means—"

Bell interrupted. "Millions, sir. He's blackmailing us for one hundred million."

"Well, how can he prove it?"

"That's the problem, sir," the assistant director continued. "It was always the Agency's understanding that the agreement was oral, and therefore that no record would ever come to light to embarrass the United States. But after this telegram arrived we went back and checked the project file.

"On March 31, 1939, Bayard Wexford, a senior policy advisor to Cordell Hull, Roosevelt's secretary of state, quietly slipped out of Washington for Marrakech, Morocco. His secret mission was

227

to finalize the agreement which had been previously proposed to Daniel Malan, leader of the National Party. The deal was simple and straightforward: Get the Afrikaners to tone down resistance to South Africa's joining the Allied war effort in exchange for the promise of secret political and financial support after the war's end. Malan had agreed in principle to the terms of the understanding, but kept stalling, apparently hoping for more concessions. Wexford's job was to meet with Malan and to extract a decision from him.

"We know that Wexford made it to Marrakech by April 4. He was spotted leaving the airport by an agent assigned to make sure he arrived in time to meet Malan. We also know that he met with Malan because three days later, back in South Africa, Malan called on the U.S. ambassador and asked him to give Roosevelt a letter. The letter was essentially a thank-you expressing pleasure at their secret agreement, and it made mention of having met with Wexford.

"The truth is, however, that after his meeting with Daniel Malan, Bayard Wexford disappeared off the face of the earth. He vanished. Malan was the last person known to have seen Wexford alive." Bell paused for quick sip of water and continued. "The difficulty, sir, isn't really his disappearance, so much as the fact that Bayard Wexford was carrying on his person secret contracts which put the oral Roosevelt-Malan agreement on paper. Wexford knew that he was only authorized to sign them if it looked like

Malan would scuttle the agreement without something on paper.

"When Bayard Wexford failed to show up, the intelligence community in Washington became extremely edgy. The prospect of those contracts emerging at such a critical period of the war was frightening. There was a big fear that they might so enrage the South African government that it might elect for neutrality and say to hell with the Allies. Needless to say, the British would also have had a fit. But Malan's letter to Roosevelt provided some reassurance and soon, very quietly, the vocal Afrikaner protests against joining the Allied side just faded away. Malan fulfilled his half of the bargain. South Africa declared war on Germany on September 6, 1939. Wexford was given up for dead and was forgotten."

The president placed his elbows on his desk, arms pointing up, and then lowered his face so that his eye sockets rested on the palms of his upturned hands. Bell stopped talking. The others were silent.

After a pause, the president looked up and quietly said, "You're about to tell me that, after the war ended, the U.S. then followed up with its side of the bargain and proceeded to help these people, this National Party, to take power and institute apartheid. Therefore we are responsible in no small part for the existence of apartheid in South Africa. Is that what you're about to tell me?"

Sullivan cut in and commented dryly, "That's

exactly what he's about to tell you, Mr. President. That one line in the telegram we received yesterday sets out our position quite clearly. 'Wexford contract.' He's telling us he's got the secret papers Bayard Wexford carried as a last resort. If he made them public we'd be unable to credibly deny our involvement."

The president massaged the bridge of his nose. "What the hell am I supposed to do about it? We obviously just can't print a hundred million dollars. Why are you people telling me?" He was extremely angry.

Sullivan smiled warily. "Sir, if this does come out, and we are sincerely doing all we can to ensure that it doesn't, inevitably the United States will become entangled in a scandal of such proportions that the Iran-Contra affair will resemble a picnic by comparison. We are advising you and your top aides of these events because, in a worst-case scenario, you will need at least a modicum of preparation to face the onslaught. In the meantime, we'll try and locate Jenssen."

A pregnant silence descended on the group. Each knew what would happen to Jenssen when and if they found him.

Sullivan and Bell rose to leave. The chief of staff pressed a button on the telephone to the right of the sofa, and immediately the young staffer reappeared to show out the visitors from Langley.

Once in the limousine on their way back to Virginia, Sullivan musingly turned to Bell.

"Wasn't that funny? All of them thinking, 'They're going to kill this guy, they're going to take him out.' But too afraid too ask."

His assistant looked out his window, speaking distantly, as if to himself. "But they're right."

The director bobbed his bald head like a polished marble attached to a spring. "That's true. Oh, we'll ask him to return the contract, of course. Might as well give that a shot. But I've no doubt he's turned. No choice but to take him out. Have someone sent over to Johannesburg tonight, would you?" He glanced at his watch. Only two more hours until "People's Court," his very favorite television program.

"So what are we going to do about it?" Colonel Lubichoff turned to stride across the smoke-filled office of his colleague Colonel Vasylich for the one hundred and eighty-fourth time that afternoon. It was not quite one o'clock in Moscow.

"Will you please stop that awful pacing? You're behaving like a caged bear."

Lubichoff threw his plump frame into a vinyl upholstered armchair, from one corner of which the foam rubber stuffing was peeping out inelegantly. Everything and everybody in the Soviet Union, including the amenities of the KGB in the Lubyanka, was on a shoestring budget. He ran his fingers through his curly black hair and pulled at it gently as was his wont. By now it looked like a mound of burnt spaghetti. He was fast approaching a state of panic.

Colonel Vasylich allowed his eyes to drift once again through the sketchy details of the preliminary report lying on his battered and splintery desk. It had arrived ten minutes ago. He grunted with disgust at the entirely unsatisfactory lack of solid facts and inhaled deeply from his cigarette. Many of those who knew him said he lived most when he smoked.

Vladimir Lubichoff clapped a hand to his mouth, remembering his boss's anger. His colleague Georgi Vasylich thought he resembled at that moment a forgetful girl he had known in high school, not a full colonel in the KGB. But then Vladimir had more brains in his ass than the girl had had in her head.

Vasylich gazed distractedly at his colleague. "Okay. We know Kyushin's in the custody of the Johannesburg police, who think he's some kind of crazed psychotic murderer. He'll know if he opens his mouth and says one word they'll realize he's a Russian. In which case, he knows he'd be KGB dead meat."

Lubichoff asked, "What if they do figure out who he is and decide to make a big incident over it? Not inconceivable, is it? For once, somebody else is the international asshole instead of South Africa."

Vasylich shrugged. "You know, the thing that really gets me is that the cops supposedly found him tied up right next to the dead guy, whoever the hell he was." He consulted the report. "Falkenhaus. Never heard of him. So who tied him up, and what the fuck was he doing there in the first place?"

Lubichoff was alternating between biting his nails and examining them. "I wish there was some way we could get in there to talk to him. God, what a nightmare."

Vasylich savored another lungful of smoke and tilted back his head. He blew three smoke rings. "I don't think there's much chance of that opportunity coming our way."

Lubichoff looked sharply at his partner. "You realize that we have only two options on Kyushin, don't you? We're either going to have to spring him, or we're going to have to kill him. And to be frank, I don't hold out a great deal of hope for the two of us taking on the whole prison, much less getting him and us out of the country. Why the hell did the stupid ass have to get himself caught? We can't have him sitting the rest of his life in a dungeon. He'll begin to get ideas like trading the truth for immunity and asylum. I don't think we have any alternative. And on top of that we still have to nail Perseus." As an afterthought he added, "Maybe he was the one that bagged Kyushin."

Vasylich did not respond for several seconds. When he did it was in the firm voice of resolve which Colonel Lubichoff knew meant his partner had come to a decision. Addressing him in the familiar patronymic form, he announced, "Vladimir Antonivich, we're going to have to go down there ourselves, immediately. If we can deal with Kyushin before the shit hits the fan and then snuff that bastard Perseus, everything will be okay. If not, we're screwed anyway. Might as well give it a shot."

Colonel Lubichoff bounded out of his chair, excited at the prospect of salvaging his career. "Georgi, you're right. We'll leave immediately." He sat down again, considering the plan. "We'll have to sneak in. What do you think? Austrians? Germans?"

Vasylich shook his head. "No, hold on a minute. We don't have time to apply for visas." He hefted a large paperback entitled *Visas* and opened it. The pages were in alphabetical order by country. He flipped to "South Africa." "It says the only countries whose citizens do not require visas are Botswana, Ireland, Lesotho, Swaziland, Switzerland, and the UK. I think the UK, don't you? We both speak fluent English, so we'll say we're from London. Okay?"

Lubichoff nodded. "Litkoff is a creep, but at least he works fast. I'll tell him I need the passports ready within an hour."

Vasylich closed the book and picked up his telephone. He pressed the intercom button to his secretary in the outside office.

The door to the office swung open. A green-eyed blonde of voluptuous charms appeared in the threshold. "Da?" Her tone, although perfectly correct, sounded sexy and exciting. It always did. "Yelena, I need two round-trip tickets: Moscow-Zurich-Moscow and two Zurich-Johannesburg-Zurich. Leave the returns open. Book the departures for anytime . . ." he consulted his watch, "after two-thirty today. Colonel Lubichoff will supply you with the names for the reservations in a few minutes."

"Yes, Comrade Colonel."

"Then call my wife and Mrs. Lubichoff and tell them to pack us suitcases. Plan on a week's change of clothing, warm climate. The suitcases need to be at the airport in time for whatever flight you put us on. If it's very tight, send different cars to each of our apartments immediately to pick up the suitcases, which should be ready by then, and then drive the bags to the airport."

"Yes, sir."

"Get me and the colonel vouchers for cash, and then the maximum allowance in South African rand. Also for one week. If that jerk in the bursar's office gives you any trouble, call me right away."

"Yes, sir."

"That's all."

"Yes, Comrade Colonel."

The secretary wheeled around smartly and left the office. Both men watched her posterior until it disappeared.

Smiling for the first time that morning, Colonel Lubichoff looked at Colonel Vasylich and pointed out the door.

"Did you ever—"

Colonel Vasylich made a noise like a parrot choking. "You're out of your mind. My wife can smell lust before the idea's even occurred to me."

An hour later, at two o'clock, the two KGB colonels climbed into the backseat of an unmarked government car in the underground garage of the Lubyanka. They wore elegant Western suits and conservative striped ties. The car headed northwest, covering the sixteen miles to Moscow's Sheremetyevo Airport in just under thirty minutes. There, using their Soviet VIP passports, they proceeded to the head of the queue and quickly checked in. They then ambled off to the departures lounge.

At two-forty, a flight attendant announced the boarding of Aeroflot Flight 608 to Zurich. The colonels joined the rest of the passengers, mostly affluent Swiss tourists, and at three o'clock the aging Ilyushin Il-62M jetliner barreled into the ether.

The KGB men used the time to bounce off each other various possible solutions to their problems. Their conversation was interrupted halfway through the three-and-a-half-hour flight when a stewardess tapped Colonel Vasylich on his shoulder.

"Comrade, the copilot just received this message by radio from your office. It is apparently quite urgent." She extended a piece of paper to him.

The note read, *Perseus located (95% sure). Staying at home of Patricia Ryan, Randburg, Tel. (011) 704–8812.* Vasylich smiled and passed it to Lubichoff.

Three and a half hours later, at four-thirty in the afternoon local time, the plane touched down at Zurich's Kloten Airport. Making their way quickly to the SwissAir counter, the men checked in for their six o'clock connection to Johannesburg, using the names printed in their new British documents. They then proceeded to a pay phone. Colonel Lubichoff, who in addition to his English also spoke French and Hungarian with virtually no trace of a Russian accent, placed an overseas call to the exchange in South Africa.

A woman answered and after a pause told him he'd dialed a wrong number. He could tell from the way she'd paused that she was lying. After leaving a message for the man she claimed was not there, he hung up and the two colonels walked to their gate.

By six-fifteen the plane was airborne. The trip was long and exhausting, but neither man slept. Both were extremely nervous about the moment of truth: South African immigration. If their phony passports did not hold up and they were arrested for illegally attempting entry into the country on false identification, Bareshkov would undoubtedly order them killed. The embarrassment of a public trial would be too humiliating for the Soviet intelligence service to bear. "The dignity and reputation of the KGB supersedes the personal well-being of its employees"—the cardinal rule impressed on each agent at the beginning of his or her training.

The Boeing 747 jumbo jet landed at midmorning for a quick refueling stop in Nairobi, and once again took to the air. With each minute the two colonels grew increasingly jittery. As usual, Vasylich smoked; Lubichoff fidgeted.

At just after four in the afternoon, the 747 began its final approach to Johannesburg. Colonels Vasylich and Lubichoff had by now carefully hidden their Soviet passports in a concealed slit in Colonel Lubichoff's imitation leather toiletry case. The stewardesses distributed landing cards for South African customs, and for theirs the colonels used the information appearing on their day-old British passports. These looked remarkably real and were imaginatively filled with entry and exit stamps from several countries.

The plane's wheels kissed the runway, bounced, and then stayed down as the huge engines thrust into reverse. The jet taxied to the SwissAir terminal, and in a few moments the passengers were following the Afrikaans and English signs to the baggage claim. Although the carousel spat out Colonel Vasylich's suitcase almost immediately, Colonel Lubichoff's was among the last to arrive. Finally, luggage in hand, they approached the long line waiting for immigration. The queue advanced excruciatingly slowly. It required all of Colonel Lubichoff's self-control to refrain from fidgeting like a madman. Colonel Vasylich smoked nonstop and was thankful that this was not America, where, he had heard, smoking was banned practically everywhere.

At last they were at the head of the line. A guard motioned them to two separate counters.

Colonel Lubichoff was, to his great surprise

and pleasure, treated to a cursory glance from the official, who then stamped an entry into his passport and wave him through. Gathering his documents, he could scarcely contain a whoop of elation as he sailed past toward customs.

Colonel Vasylich, meanwhile, stood calmly and smoked while the policeman thumbed through his passport.

"What is the purpose of your visit?"

"Vacation. Tourism."

"Mmm. And how long do you plan to be in South Africa?"

"Oh, a couple of weeks, I think."

"Mmm." Growing bored, the policeman turned to an empty page and pressed an entry stamp onto it. He returned the passport to Vasylich and jerked his thumb behind him. Vasylich was clear.

Customs was much easier. The two men walked unhindered through the green "nothing to declare" door and found themselves in the main terminal of Jan Smuts Airport.

Discreetly, Colonel Lubichoff offered a sweaty hand to his partner. "We made it."

They shook hands. The killers from Moscow had arrived. It was time to go hunting.

Gary Bahre was employed by the U.S. government. His title was deputy commercial attaché and he worked in the politico-economic section's wing of offices at the U.S. Consulate in Johannesburg.

This was a cover.

Like most overseas-based operatives of the CIA, Bahre was assigned to a diplomatic mission, simply because it was the easiest and safest way to conduct the serious business of spying. Easy because diplomatic personnel are seldom denied the right of entry by the prospective country; safe because, if later caught spying by that country, the agent's worst punishment would be deportation. The beauty of diplomatic immunity.

As the "resident" for Johannesburg, Gary Bahre reported directly to the chief of station, who was based at the embassy in Pretoria. At the age of thirty, Bahre was extremely young for the job and was proud of the fact. He was ambitious and had no intention of staying put in Johannesburg for long. Bahre was aiming for an administrative position at Langley, where the action was. He hated languishing in what he regarded as a remote backwater.

What really irritated him about the overseas assignment was how unglamorous it had turned out to be. The job consisted almost entirely of information gathering, but very little information assessing. As luck would have it, his attending one of the few glittering occasions of diplomatic life, the new ambassador's welcome reception yesterday, had been dashed when the chief of station called a staff meeting at the same time. Bahre had had to travel to Pretoria, and the party had ended long before the bureaucratic powwow. When somebody had grumbled, the chief explained that nothing interesting happened at embassy functions. Which was bullshit, and everyone knew it. The chief was a jackass who liked to throw his weight around and show his staff who was boss. Agent Bahre had resolved that when his soon-to-happen meteoric rise placed him in a high enough position, he would ensure that the chief was demoted and made resident in Ouagadougou. What goes around, comes around.

It was now late afternoon. He looked lethargically out of his office window at the brick wall of another building. It filled the view. Another perk of high office, he mused bitterly. If he were station chief he'd rate a terrific office overlooking the embassy's fountain-filled garden.

Reminded of his boss, he thought again of the unusual phone call he'd received from him this morning. The jerk wanted him to keep his eyes open for a former Agency operative named Paul Jenssen, believed to be in South Africa, but wouldn't tell him why. Typical. The lazy asshole kept his job by getting his bright staff to do all the work, for which he claimed all the credit.

Bahre decided to read the *Herald Tribune*'s sports page in the men's room. That should kill another half hour or so. He left his office, walked down the hall, and let himself into the bathroom, the newspaper folded and concealed inside his jacket. Impressions were everything in government service.

After a half hour of leisurely perusal while seated comfortably in one of the two stalls, he ambled back toward his office. The corridor was lined with tiny rooms occupied by bureaucrats conducting the business of the U.S. government. He waved or smiled at those who looked up as he strolled by.

He looked in as he passed the office of Pat Ryan, the consulate's political advisor. Her door was ajar, and she did not see him. She was engrossed in a telephone conversation. He continued past, but stopped, his curiosity piqued.

". . . and Paul, help yourself to whatever's in the fridge. I'll be home around five-thirty."

To the best of Bahre's knowledge, Pat Ryan was unmarried. He'd never heard a word to the contrary. He seemed to remember hearing she'd been divorced, but decades ago; nothing since then. And now, if she wasn't married, it sounded like she was shacking up with someone. More power to her at her age, he thought.

Then he froze. She had just used the name "Paul." Of course it was a common name, but given the circumstances, what if . . .

She ended her conversation and hung up. Bahre quickly returned to his office and thought for a minute. Then, lifting his telephone, he pressed the button to his outside line and dialed the consulate's main number.

The receptionist answered, and he told her to let Pat Ryan know that if she wasn't too busy, Mr. Jenssen would like to speak with her for one more quick moment. She put him on hold. The line clicked. Pat said, "Paul, I'm glad you called back. I forgot to ask you if you like steak."

Bahre softly replaced the handset and smiled. He had found a trump card.

He removed his navy wool-polyester-blend suit jacket and walked to the elevators. "I'll be back in a few minutes. I'm just going to grab some gum," he informed the receptionist.

"I have some, would you like a stick?" the woman offered.

"No, no thanks. I also want to grab a paper." The elevator arrived and he descended to the lobby.

Outside, Bahre walked to the public telephone at the corner. He slipped inside and dialed "O." The operator who answered put through his call to the United States and took down his credit card billing information.

The hollow hum of the transatlantic call was followed by the faint sound of a ring, eight thousand miles away. A man's voice answered curtly. "Lewis."

"John, it's Gary Bahre."

"The Bahremeister! How you doing, guy?"

"Good, John. I'm still in Johannesburg, unfortunately."

"Hey, could be worse, right?"

"Right. John, did you ever hear of a guy named Paul Jenssen?"

There was silence at the other end.

"I think he used to be with the Company," Bahre added.

"I know who he is. I was just trying to figure out how you'd heard of him."

"Easy. The troglodyte I report to put out an alert on him this morning."

"What time is it over there now?"

"About three-thirty."

"What did . . . Who's your station chief?"

"Vandermeullen. Ralph Vandermeullen."

"What did Vandermeullen say Jenssen was wanted for?"

"He didn't. And wouldn't. It's hush-hush house. So tell me who he is."

"He's someone who I think is suddenly very in-demand here at Langley for reasons known only to God and a couple of high muckety-mucks. Why do you want to know about him?"

"I think I may have found him."

"Where?" Lewis became excited.

"Here, in Johannesburg. I just don't want Vandermeullen to claim all the glory. I'd like to get out of this place soon, John."

"Gotcha. Do you know where Jenssen is, exactly?"

"I think so. I'm ninety-five percent sure he's staying with a woman who works right here at the consulate, in the political section. Her name is Pat Ryan. Tonight I'm going to find out for sure."

"Tell you what. You'll be a star if you've found this guy. When you're positive he's there, I'll pass on the word that you found him, and your station chief will have to give you credit."

"John, so help me, when I get out of here I'm going to buy you the best steak in Washington."

Lewis laughed. "You're on."

"I'll call you tomorrow to let you know if it's Jenssen. And thanks again." Bahre hung up and returned to his office. He immediately picked up his telephone and dialed a number in the capital city of Pretoria.

"Yah?" The voice was raspy, the result of a thirty-year three-pack-a-day cigarette habit. The static caused by the man's mobile phone exacerbated the effect. His accent was Flatbush Brooklynese.

"Bernie? It's Gary Bahre, in Jo'burg."

"Hey, what's shakin'?" The scratchy words were garbled. His mouth was filled with pizza. The man always seemed to be either smoking or eating.

"Bernie, are you working on anything right now?"

"Nope. Just sittin' here in da van, scratchin' my ass and tryin' to figya out da meanin' of life."

"Great, Bernie. Would you mind driving the van down to Jo'burg for a while? I just want to monitor a house for a little bit."

"Hey, boss, dat's what I'm here for, right? Am I right?"

"You're right, Bernie."

"Damn straight. Uh, address?"

"It's . . . hold on." Bahre flipped through his consular directory. "It's eighty-seven Roos Street, in Randburg."

"I'm on my way. How long do I listen?"

"Can you manage two hours?"

"Is a pig's ass pink?"

"Thanks, Bernie. Call me at home when you're done. You have my number?"

"I got everybody's number."

"Oh, and Bernie, would you mind keeping this just between you and me? I want to show Ralph what you find, but in case I'm wrong, I don't want him to know I barked up the wrong tree. Okay?"

"You got it, chiefie. Ciao." He hung up.

Agent Gary Bahre leaned back in his chair and allowed an expression of unadulterated self-satisfaction to steal over his face. His star was rising. He could feel it.

Bernard-Antonio Pasquarella, more familiarly known to his colleagues as Bernie, finished stuffing the last crust of pizza into his mouth and wiped his tomato-stained lips with a dingy sleeve.

His daily afternoon snack always consisted of pizza. He had sniffed out the one establishment in Pretoria serving a passable product. "The other places is shitholes. Dey ain't got no right to call demselves a pizzaria. What a load o' horseshit." Bernard-Antonio Pasquarella had failed to capitalize on his overseas assignment by learning about exciting and unfamiliar cuisines. "You won't catch *me* puttin' any o' dat curry shit in *my* mout'" fairly accurately summed up Pasquarella's attitude toward exotic food.

Placing the wrappings and grease-stained paper remains of his feast on the passenger seat to his left, Pasquarella turned the van's ignition key and slowly rolled the vehicle out of the parking lot located behind the U.S. Embassy. He drove the short distance to the freeway and in forty-five minutes was creeping up Roos Street in Randburg, checking the houses for street numbers.

He found number eighty-seven. No one seemed to be home; there was no car in the driveway. Nevertheless, Pasquarella quietly pulled the van to the opposite curb twenty yards further down the street and killed the motor. From the exterior, the vehicle appeared to be one of the sort favored by repairmen of televisions, dishwashers, and other amenities of modern life.

The street itself was still quiet, its owners for the most part not yet returned from work in the city.

Pasquarella stood up inside the van and walked to the compartment in the back. Its sides were lined with computer monitors, television screens, speakers, a radar scope, and several other prime intelligence-gathering devices. He placed himself in a seat bolted to the floor before one of the television screens and carefully adjusted the heavy plastic dial resembling a steering wheel, which rose from the metal ledge next to it. As he turned the wheel, the camera fitted under the van's five-inch false top revolved correspondingly. The outer edge of the artificial ceiling, constructed of specially blown industrial glass, permitted the camera an unhampered view while simultaneously appearing opaque from the outside.

The unpretentious walls and grounds of Patricia Ryan's house appeared cloudily on Pasquarella's screen. He adjusted a small inner dial in the steering wheel's center and the fuzzy image on the screen locked rapidly into focus.

Attached to the left of the camera was a two-foot-long cylinder resembling a poster tube. The wheel in the van also controlled its aim, and one of its beveled ends was now also aimed at the Ryan residence. It was an ultrasensitive eavesdropping gun, capable of clearly picking up conversations up to a quarter mile away.

Pasquarella pressed a button on a nearby computer keyboard marked AUDIO. Instantly, the electrical hum of the speakers crackled to life. There was no sound or other indication of someone inside the house, but that meant nothing. He looked at his watch. It was five-fifteen. Slumping back lazily in his chair, he began munching a bag of cheese doodles he'd bought several weeks ago at the American commissary and had sagaciously stowed in the van. In his murky mind, Pasquarella likened himself to a squirrel storing walnuts for future need.

At half past five, a red Volkswagen Beetle pulled into the driveway. A short robust middle-aged woman got out and carried a bag of groceries to the house. On his screen, he watched as she fumbled for her keys and let herself in.

"Wow, I knew you were here, but it's still weird to see someone let you into your own house. Here." Pasquarella listened to the woman speak to someone inside, to whom she passed the groceries. The door closed behind her. The spools of a tape recorder attached by cable to the listening gun revolved smoothly to Pasquarella's left, registering every sound.

After listening for several hours, he returned to the front of the van and pressed the buttons on the mobile phone.

In a minute Gary Bahre answered.

"Hey, it's Bernie. I been watchin' dat house here in Randburg for a coupla hours. You want me to stay longer?"

"Bernie, who's in the house, did you hear that?"

"Sounds like two people. If they's more, they's ain't talkin'. One's a lady, named Pat Ryan."

"Yes, yes. And the other?" Bahre prompted impatiently.

"The other's a guy named Paul Jennings or Jenssen. I didn't hear too clear. Somebody called for him too. I got it all."

"Bernie, you are beautiful, buddy. You sure it recorded properly?"

"Hey, do I seem incompetent or something?"

"Can you drop it by? My house is only about ten minutes away, if it's not a problem."

"Shit, what's ten minutes?"

"Great, it's in Honeydew, the next town to the west. Eleven Gold Street."

"I'm leavin' right now. See ya' in ten minutes."

A quarter of an hour later, Gary Bahre was thanking Bernie Pasquarella profusely and pressing a bag of Chips Ahoy cookies on him for the ride home to Pretoria. Pasquarella did not decline.

Seated in his favorite armchair in his cramped convenience apartment, Bahre listened to the cassette Pasquarella had left off. There was no longer room for doubt, Jenssen was hiding out in Pat Ryan's apartment. It was like a gift from heaven.

Jenssen's phone call from Europe was a weird twist. Someone else had figured out Jenssen's whereabouts and wanted to meet him to discuss the *Broederbond*. This really might turn out to be Bahre's ticket to Langley.

He picked up his telephone and dialed the United States. John Lewis answered on the first ring.

"John, it's clinched. He's there. It's Jenssen, absolutely."

"Gar, that's great detective work."

"Also, John, he's got some sort of thing going connected to the *Broederbond*. Some guy called him from Europe and wants to meet him tomorrow night at eleven o'clock at the Kyalami Racetrack parking lot in Midrand."

"Where's that?"

"About twenty minutes from Jo'burg. Jenssen sounded pretty intrigued. My guess is he shows up."

"Anything else?"

"That's about it."

"Gar, hold off if you can on telling your boss, until I let you know. I'll make sure the right people hear about this."

"Thank you, John. You have no idea what that means to me. I'm dying out here."

"Oh, I think I've got a pretty fair idea. I'll talk to you soon, Gar." He clicked off.

For the second time that morning, John Lewis walked from his first-floor office in the CIA's main administration building to one of the pay phones in the lobby. He also dialed the same London number, and within seconds the same stiff voice at MI 5 answered "Crowley."

"Hi, guess who? It's definitely him. Confirmed just now."

"Splendid work. I should think you'll find a little something extra in your acocunt next week."

"Thanks. Also, I'm informed that Jenssen received a phone call from person or persons unknown who tracked him down and want to meet him tomorrow night at the Kyalami Racetrack parking lot in Midrand. That's it."

"Kyalami? How do you spell that?"

"I have no idea."

"No matter. Keep up the good work, Lewis. Ta."

Having ensured a further supplement to his income, John Lewis then went off to tell his superiors of the new development in Johannesburg.

The assistant agricultural officer in the Soviet Embassy in London thanked Alistair Crowley for the second time that afternoon and replaced the telephone. He hurriedly descended to the embassy's basement and handed a short message to the telegraph operator. This was rapidly encoded and then transmitted to the Lubyanka in Moscow, marked URGENT for Colonel Georgi Vasylich.

Ten minutes later, in Colonel Vasylich's office, his assistant, Major Joseph Bashin, received the decoded message and laughed. After having received word of Perseus's whereabouts some two hours ago, the major had transmitted the information, as well as two suggestions for suitably discreet meeting places near Johannesburg, to his boss on board the Aeroflot flight to Zurich. Major Bashin was gratified to learn that Colonel Vasylich had made use of Bashin's proposition of Kyalami, although such knowledge was acquired indirectly. It was one of the rewards of having plants in London and Washington. Especially since his colonel was so stingy with praise for his underlings.

The man parked his blue government sedan in the visitors' area at Andrews Air Force Base in Camp Springs, Maryland. He effortlessly slung over his shoulder his two pieces of luggage, a nylon gym bag, and a small violin-shaped case, and carried them inside to the squat concrete building. His large body was packed tightly into a khaki summer suit. He looked like a midlevel executive in a big company who spent his lunch hour working out.

Inside, he was greeted by an unsmiling corporal who led him to a spartanly furnished waiting room littered with old issues of *Stars and Stripes*.

The man reflected that the army's billions certainly weren't going toward interior decorating.

He waited only five minutes before the door swung open and an air force colonel entered and offered his hand. "Mr. Ellison? I'm Stephen Digby. Just got in from Norfolk. I'll be piloting your plane. If you'll follow me, we can get started right away."

The colonel led the civilian down a flight of stairs to a back door, leading to the vast asphalt plain of the military base. A jeep was parked at the door and the men climbed in.

Digby drove to a huge hangar at the far side of the base. Its exterior walls were plastered with AUTHORIZED PERSONNEL ONLY signs. Two armed M.P.s guarded the entrance. Digby flashed his I.D. and gestured to Ellison. "He's my passenger. He's expected." The guards waved them in.

Sitting in the hangar was an F-15E Eagle. Its sleek aerodynamic form allowed it to attain a speed of approximately sixteen hundred miles per hour. Its fuel tanks permitted uninterrupted flying of 5.25 hours. Its weapons bay and wings had been divested of bombs and missiles to reduce weight, thereby allowing an increase in speed.

"You'd better use the john now if you need to, 'cause we won't be able to stop at a Howard Johnson's on the way." Digby winked.

"I'm fine."

The men climbed the mobile staircase into the two seats in the nose of the plane, the military officer seating himself in front, Ellison just behind him. The luggage was stowed in a small compartment under Ellison's seat.

Digby handed a helmet to his passenger and placed one on his own head. He explained how the parachutes worked in the remote event of a premature exit and demonstrated the use of the oxygen masks which would be needed throughout the flight.

"The G-forces will feel like someone's sitting on your chest for a minute or two, but I guess you know that from all those flight simulation classes you took last year. Just relax and stay calm. They'll let up when we start gaining altitude."

Ellison gave a thumbs-up, displaying confidence while secretly petrified. The two men strapped themselves in securely. A corporal stood at the top of the mobile staircase and ran through the commencement checklist with the pilot. To every question, the colonel replied, "Check."

The corporal lowered the transparent top of the cockpit. It resembled a thick lid for a Tupperware bowl. The corporal descended the stairs, saluted, and rolled the steel structure away from the plane.

Digby switched on the drive and the powerful jet rolled out of the hangar. He followed the yellow fluorescent hand flares waved by the corporal, although the evening light was still sufficient.

Once he had cleared the hangar, Digby flicked

on the ignition switch. Instantly the thunderous boom of the Pratt and Whitney turbo-fan engines obliterated all other noise. The pilot revved each engine, meticulously ensuring that the plane was in perfect working order.

Ellison sat back hard against his chair and wondered how he'd ended up in this line of work. He had always feared flying; this should be a new level of terror. He hoped the parachutes weren't all tangled up.

The jet followed the series of blue and yellow lights set into the asphalt. It taxied to the end of the runway, turned, and screamed into the sky. It vanished in seconds, swallowed in the deep blue-violet troposphere. Ellison philosophically reasoned that at least death would come quickly.

The F-15 quickly ascended to fifty-five thousand feet. Ellison leaned forward and watched the radium-illuminated arrow on the altimeter spin unfalteringly clockwise until he became somewhat nauseated at the thought of flying so high. He sat back and attempted to relax.

Approximately twelve miles below, the silvery waters of the North Atlantic lapped the densely populated eastern shore of Maryland. The fighter banked toward the southeast, and the display on the digital speedometer rose rapidly until it came to rest at Mach 2.46, almost two and a half times the speed of sound.

They were over Bermuda in forty minutes. From there, the jet continued on the same southeast heading, flying parallel to the chunk of

South American coast encompassing, in order, Guyana, Suriname, French Guiana, and finally the whole northeast Brazilian littoral. Shortly afterward, about two hundred miles south of the equator, the plane was at a point exactly halfway between South America and Africa. Roughly nine hundred miles of water stood between the jet and each of the two continents.

After a journey of almost three hours, the F-15 began to dip sharply. The pilot spoke tersely into his microphone and received instructions on his approach to land. The vast South Atlantic Ocean, and nothing else, sprawled below, hidden by the early morning darkness.

Dimly, Ellison glimpsed a string of lights several miles ahead. The engines slowed and in a minute the pilot was kicking on the reverse thrust as the plane rolled to a stop on the desolate island, almost a thousand miles of barren ocean separating it from the nearest land.

A ramp was rolled to the plane. Digby popped open the cockpit hatch and they descended to the tarmac, where an officer wearing the uniform of a Royal Air Force colonel was just alighting from his jeep. He saluted and shook their hands. "Welcome to Ascension Island, gentlemen. I am Colonel Smithers. Colonel Digby, if you don't mind waiting for just a moment until we get your passenger onto his connection, I'll show you to the base. We'll find you some breakfast and a bed so you'll be rested for your return to the States." Then, turning to Ellison, whose name he did not know, he added, "Sir, as Washington requested, we'll have you airborne as soon as possible. The plane just arrived about twenty minutes ago and should be refueled momentarily. Are those all of your bags?"

Ellison nodded sleepily. It was three A.M. local time, and the moist, chilly ocean wind was bracing after the warmth of the jet cockpit. He hefted his luggage into the jeep and the three men climbed in.

The Englishman drove to the other end of the runway on which the fighter had just landed. Two jeeps and a fuel truck encircled a Gates Learjet 55LR sporting the Brazilian flag on its sides. The words BRECKENRIDGE ENTERPRISES INTERNATIONAL were painted in black on its hull. It sat sedately while a half dozen RAF mechanics tended to its engines and customized, extra-large fuel tanks. A long hose snaked from the fuel truck to the side of the aircraft. The pilot sat on the ramp steps chewing a stick of gum, his black leather jacket buttoned to the top. The whole scene was bathed in the ghostly greenish light emitted from the incandescent beams attached to the fuel truck and the jeeps.

Smithers pointed at the plane and smiled at Ellison, who hoisted his two bags from the jeep and carried them up the ramp to where the pilot was squatting.

"You the guy fer Swaziland?" The pilot's accent was Deep South, probably Alabama or Mississippi.

"I'm the guy."

The pilot jerked a thumb toward the plane's

cabin. "Make y'self comf'table. We'll get this motha in the ayer jus' as soon as these limeys stop swarmin' aroun' like a bunch o' chickens with their hades cut off." He masticated his Wrigley's noisily.

Ellison lugged his two bags past the pilot and entered the cabin. The plane's interior was plush by any standard. There were only four chairs, recliners lovingly handmade of buttery leather, allowing a maximum of space in which to stretch out and relax. A mahogany bar filled one corner, while a small kitchenette occupied another. The walls were covered in pale blue silk, with Japanese watercolors of various flora emphasizing the subdued elegance.

Outside, the RAF staff concluded the refueling and the pilot flicked his chewing gum into the night. He would love to have smoked, but because of the airplane fuel, it was not permitted. He stood up and stretched. Then, stepping into the plane, he retracted the collapsible stairs and sealed the door shut. Poking his head into the cabin, he asked, "Y'all set?"

Ellison nodded, strapping himself in tightly. At least, he thought, this is a real plane, not like that death trap he'd just escaped.

The pilot drew the curtain dividing the passenger quarters from the anteway and walked into the cockpit in the front. His co-pilot, a fellow southerner in his early thirties, was still dozing in his chair. The pilot wiggled a finger into the sleeping man's earlobe. The co-pilot jumped awake, startled, as the pilot grinned and said, "Welcome to reality."

The plane's engines screamed as the aircraft raced down the asphalt strip and climbed skyward, leaving the rocky English outpost far below. It straightened on a southeasterly heading, following almost the same direction as the F-15 had flown from Andrews to Ascension. The ocean lay vast and invisible beneath them, a great black sea of nothing.

In a couple of hours the first amber ropes of dawn appeared across the horizon ahead. Ellison woke, bleary-eyed, cotton-mouthed, and exhausted, and lumbered over to the kitchen. Examining the contents of the refrigerator, he helped himself to a large glass of orange juice before walking up to the cockpit.

The pilot heard him first and swiveled in his seat. "Howdy. We jus' passed over the island of St. Helena, did ya' see it? Ya' look like ya' jus' come off a bender. Hey, this here's my co-pilot, Jerry. Jerry, this is Mr. . . . ah . . ."

"Jones," Ellison muttered.

Jerry rose. "Well, Mr. Jones, if ya'd like some breakfuss I can rustle up some aigs or some French toast or whatever ya' feel like eatin'."

"No, thanks. I'm not really hungry. How long until we get to Swaziland?"

The pilot looked at his watch. "Let's see, we should be over South Africa in 'bout fo' mo' hours, so, say, five hours or so till we 'rive."

"Thanks. Why the hell are you guys so chipper? It's, like, six in the morning or something."

The southerners smiled. Jerry said, "I guess we're pretty psyched up. It's our fust time to Africa. Usually all we do is fly Mr. Breckenridge around Brazil. São Paulo, Rio, Brasília. Sometimes up to Caracas. His business doesn't take him out o' South America that often."

Ellison asked, "What's his business?"

"He's into everything. Timber and mining in Brazil, oil in Venezuela, emeralds in Colombia. He's one busy dude. But, uh, as I was sayin', this trip is real unusual. His secretary jus' called us up yesterday and told us to hightail it over to Ascension Island, pick up a fella, and head on down to Swaziland." Jerry smiled sheepishly and added, "Y'know, I had to look 'em both up in an atlas—never heard of 'em befo'." He looked down at his flight plan, attached to a clipboard. "The leg we're on now is 'bout thirty-two hundred miles. On a normal Learjet 55LR that's at the stretched end of fuel range, but Mr. Breckenridge, he had an extra nine hundred miles range worth o' fuel tank installed, so we don' have to stop."

Ellison nodded distractedly and returned to the cabin. The Agency, he reflected, had really done their homework on this job. The problem of how to smuggle him into South Africa was certainly complicated. The fastest method, the fighter, couldn't be used to enter the country for obvious reasons, but it could take him nearby. The answer: Ascension. The isolated island had three big advantages: It was close enough to South America that a normal plane could travel there from eastern Brazil in three hours to meet him; it was also perfectly situated so that the same normal plane, after refueling, could make the trip between Ascension and southern Africa in seven hours; and finally the British would allow the fighter to land and drop him off without asking awkward questions. The elves at Langley must have worked pretty goddamned fast to get Breckenridge to lend them his personal plane in time to meet him at the rendezvous.

As for the thimble-sized nation of Swaziland, the penultimate destination also held several advantages: Americans were allowed entry without a visa; it bordered South Africa, located fairly close to Johannesburg; and most important, Swazi citizens didn't need visas for South Africa. White Swazis could expect to be waved through without question.

Ellison patted his breast pocket. The brand-new red passport whose cover bore the gilt words KINGDOM OF SWAZILAND was safely tucked away. His photograph graced its inside cover, floating above a new and completely fictitious biography. It looked pretty good. He decided he'd keep the passport after this job was over, just for laughs.

He would enter the country on his new American diplomatic passport which, being diplomatic, would enable him to smuggle into the country without being searched the custom-adjusted M21 rifle lying snugly in the violin-shaped case. They'd probably think he was with the New York Symphony or something. Twenty minutes later he'd be driving a rented car across the Swazi/South African border as Mr. Nevile Wallace, residing at 10 Mhlanhla Road, Mbabane, Swaziland. By late afternoon he'd be in Johannesburg. That would leave plenty of time to rest up before surprising this goddamn traitor Jenssen during his eleven o'clock meeting.

The rifle was his prized possession. Basically the same as the standard 7.62mm M21, the official sniping rifle of the U.S. Army, Ellison's weapon had been altered in a few critical areas. The trigger was an individually molded attachment, curving slightly to the right, an attribute Ellison's index finger found more comfortable. A laser spot device had been added to the sight, whose cross hairs and stadia marks were illuminated in brilliant radium green. Unlike the standard-issue rifle, whose stock was of epoxy-coated walnut, Ellison had ordered the stock on his weapon made of layers upon layers of glass fiber, which along with a customized featherweight action reduced total weight by almost two pounds. The killer was extremely proud of his toy. He referred to it as "Emma." His pride and joy.

From his nylon bag, Ellison withdrew a manila file he hadn't had time to examine in the frantic rush to leave. It contained a thorough detailed description of one Paul Winthrop Jenssen, including background, character analysis, strength and weaknesses, personal and sexual history, as well as two recent photographs taken at close range.

Ellison memorized everything and replaced the folder. He would burn it later. As one of only a handful of men kept on retainer by the Central Intelligence Agency for "odd jobs," Ellison was a fanatic about tying up loose ends. His job, which consisted mainly of eliminating people deemed potentially dangerous to national security, demanded it.

In cases like this, where the target was a former trusted government employee turned "irretrievable," Ellison had no pity. He was repulsed. Blackmailing the U.S. government was the same as blackmailing all Americans, and Ellison was looking forward to sending this blackmailer to meet his maker. He would surprise Jenssen at his meeting, demand the document from him, and then, whether Jenssen handed it over or not, would blow his fucking head off.

The assassin from Washington leaned back in his chair and clamped his eyelids shut determinedly, trying unsuccessfully to sleep. His stomach flew into his throat every time the plane dropped a few feet. He fantasized wistfully about air travel without turbulence. Air pockets frightened the bejabbers out of him. Next time he'd take a boat.

10

The Valrand mine is the world's single biggest producer of crude gold ore. Located 26 miles southeast of Johannesburg, it measures almost two miles at its widest and 1.5 miles at its deepest. From the depths of its bountiful soils are extracted annually some 1.2 million ounces of pure gold.

Under normal circumstances, security at the mine is fairly rigorous. As an important source of income for members of the Afrikaner community as well as for the government, it is a logical target for sabotage by the ANC and by other antigovernment groups.

The entire perimeter of the mine was sheathed with fifteen-foot barbed wire fencing. Through the fence flowed four hundred volts of electricity, enough to stun but not kill a man. A closed-circuit television system was serviced by rotating cameras positioned on wooden poles just inside the fence every twenty yards. In addition, a twenty-foot trench, some ten feet across, encircled the fence on the outside. To complete the protection, all greenery and undergrowth within fifty yards of the trench had been cleared. At night, huge klieg lights illuminated the whole eerie landscape. For all practical purposes, the mine was impenetrable.

But during this last week, security had been strengthened even more. Stationed at intervals at the outside edge of the deep trench were several dozen curiously shaped vehicles. They were not quite tanks, but were every bit as lethal. They were military in appearance, but ungainly, as if a tank had mated with a Thunderbird convertible. This was the Crotale 4000 mobile weapons system.

Mounted on a heavy base were four cone-tipped surface-to-air missiles, each containing sufficient explosive material to destroy in midflight any airborne object within a range of eight miles. The missiles were capable of reaching a maximum speed of Mach 2.3, or 2.3 times the speed of sound, in less than three seconds. They had proved in exhaustive testing to possess an eighty percent probability of eliminating a target flying at 550 miles per hour, once it entered maximum range.

The means of ensuring the destruction of approaching aircraft could be found nestled between the four missiles. This was a convex plate, shaped like a large fruit bowl on its side, from the middle of which rose an antenna. It was a radar dish, capable of tracking one target and guiding two missiles simultaneously. Immediately after firing, the tracking beam of the radar would latch onto the missile, using an infrared locational system. A radio receiver on the fired missile would allow the transmitter, attached to the radar, to broadcast guidance signals so that the missile could adjust its trajectory toward the target.

The weapon was the joint effort of two French companies: MATRA, which manufactured the missiles, and Thomsen-CSF, which produced everything else. South Africa, which received fourteen firing units in the early 1970s, named the weapon "the Cactus."

Two other measures had been implemented to eliminate the mine's vulnerability. One of these was the installation of an Israeli-made RAJ101 Ground Radar Jammer. Hidden on a grassy hillock a half mile from the edge of the mine, the device was able to detect offensive radar and jam it. It worked in all directions at a range of more than twenty miles. It was a product of the Rafael Armament Development Authority in Haifa and was a favorite with the Israeli army.

The other defensive measure sat parked at regular intervals around the edge of the mine, between the Cactus antiaircraft vehicles. These were the Elands, light armored cars fitted with sixty-millimeter mortar guns and 7.62-millimeter machine guns. They were an excellent deterrent to ground attack. The minitanks were manufactured by the Sandock-Austral Berperk Company of Boksburg, South Africa, and had been a bulwark of South African army operations in Angola in the 1980s.

The explanation for the increase in military protection was to be found deep in the heart of the mine.

Two days earlier, at eleven o'clock on an almost moonless night, a silent convoy of four army trucks had slowly wound its way up the dirt road leading to the mine. The first, second, and last trucks were filled with crack marksmen from the South African army. Each carried a loaded Uzi submachine gun.

The third truck was shaped differently than the other three. It was almost cubical. While the others were painted in military camouflage, this one was gray metal, a sort of dark slate color. In fact, it was pure lead.

The convoy entered the perimeter of the mine and ground to a halt. The soldiers jumped from the transport vehicles and surrounded the boxy truck, their weapons cocked.

Four of them opened the truck's rear doors, struggling with the dead weight of the heavy load. From inside, they removed a bread-box-sized cylindrical steel object weighing roughly three hundred pounds. The other soldiers formed a phalanx around the bearers, guarding the precious cargo.

They approached the entrance to the mine shaft. The soldiers clambered into several railed cars and, activated by some unseen switch, the dusty vehicles slowly disappeared into the mine.

The interior grew gradually warmer and

moister. From somewhere much farther down, the sound of water dripping floated up to the soldiers.

The cars descended steadily. Half a mile. Three quarters. One mile.

As unexpectedly as they had begun, the cars halted. In the sulfuric light of one of the wall lanterns, they appeared to have stopped at some sort of platform.

The passengers alighted and ever so carefully lifted the weighty and valuable cylinder onto the landing.

Just ahead, marked in fluorescent orange, was a small door, almost a cupboard, in the dark gray rock. It swung open on silent hinges, and the men deposited their burden inside.

One of the soldiers then bent forward and pulled a five-foot collapsible antenna from the side of the object.

The sweating men closed the door and hopped back inside the mine shuttle. As deliberately as they had come, the soldiers were transported from the mine's humid depths to the surface above. They restarted their trucks, and in a few minutes the convoy had vanished.

In each of the forty-seven major gold mines in South Africa, the identical sequence of events took place that night, witnessed only by a few hundred specially selected soldiers and a few hundred entirely trustworthy guards.

In the very center of each mine, primed and deadly, was an atomic bomb. Each was placed so as to guarantee maximum destruction of the mine and maximum radiation distribution to the gold ore each contained. Detonation would render a mine useless for at least decades.

With steel antennae scoping up from their sides like clams of Armageddon, they waited. The signal would come. From the north.

Beth Danniken stood at the kitchen sink preparing her dinner. Into a bowl she spooned a scoop of cottage cheese and then began washing lettuce and cucumber for a salad. Lying inconveniently at her feet, the collie stared up piteously and imploring, refusing to believe that her supper of vegetables would be unpalatable to him. She leaned down and offered him a leaf of lettuce. He sniffed it, eyed it disdainfully, and then returned his begging gaze to his mistress.

The dark of evening necessitated that she switch on the overhead light. It was bright but scarcely cheery. To alleviate her loneliness she turned on the radio at the far corner of the white Formica counter.

The station began blaring an old Elvis Presley tune. Caught up in the song, she dropped the head of lettuce she was holding and began dancing around the kitchen. She held one fist to her mouth as though it were a microphone. The collie watched, intrigued.

"... You ain' nothin' but a houn' dawg ..." she warbled at him.

He leapt to his feet and tried to join in her frolicking, jumping up to lick her face and barking loudly. She was forced to interrupt herself.

"Jamie, *down! Down!*" The collie reluctantly dropped to his feet and lay down, abashed. Beth returned to the sink to finish preparing her salad.

She was just chopping the last bit of carrot when the light suddenly flickered, and then failed. The radio's broadcast of Elvis Presley's accusing words ceased simultaneously. The house was suddenly dark and silent.

Beth groped her way to one of the drawers under the counter. Opening it, she fumbled for and found a flashlight and flicked it on. The arc of white light eerily turned the collie's eyes red as it caught them peering inquisitively at its source. Beth carefully edged her way out of the kitchen, walking slowly down the hall toward the front. The door leading downstairs to the cellar where the circuit breakers were located was situated just under the staircase leading to the second floor.

As she turned the handle of the cellar door, she heard a noise, an unidentifiable scraping rasp, on the front door. The combination of darkness, stillness, and the weird beam from the flashlight made her suddenly nervous. She snapped her fingers, and Jamie trotted out from the kitchen to join her.

Beth inched cautiously toward the front door, telling herself that the noise was probably a squirrel or a cat. She reached the door, gathered her resolve, and swung it open, holding out her flashlight like a sword.

The man in the doorway did not move, but merely said, "Miss Danniken?"

"Yes, who are you?" She was shaking.

"I'm with the Bureau of State Security. I would appreciate your accompanying me to headquarters. You are wanted for questioning."

Her heart was racing. "Questioning? What about?"

"Please, ma'am, you'll hear soon enough."

Beth summoned up a measure of control. "I want to see some identification first."

The man reached into his inside jacket pocket and withdrew a wallet. He opened and proffered it to Beth, who aimed the flashlight at it. The plastic card bore a photograph of the man, under the heading BUREAU OF STATE SECURITY. His name was imprinted to the right of the picture.

"Can't this wait until morning?"

"I'm afraid not, ma'am. It's quite urgent."

"Very well. I'll just leave my father a note; he's due back late tonight. I'll just be a moment. Sorry about the flashlight; the electricity seems to have blown a fuse." Beth walked back to the kitchen, found a pen and paper, and scribbled her father a message. She yanked a thumbtack from the bulletin board on the side of the refrigerator and returned to the policeman at the front door.

"Will this take long?"

"It shouldn't, ma'am; just a few questions, really, but they're very important."

Beth tacked the note to the outside of the front door, just above the handle so her father

271

wouldn't miss it. Still using the flashlight, she and the policeman descended the porch steps to his standard-issue government car.

She turned to him. "How did you open the gate?"

He held the passenger door open for her and nonchalantly said, "I used a pass key."

She climbed in, muttering, "I certainly hope this is important enough to merit not waiting until tomorrow." She extinguished the flashlight.

He got in behind the wheel, locked both doors automatically by pressing a lever on his armrest, and said, "I assure you, ma'am, it's most important."

A thick blanket of clouds covered the sky, blocking the silvery light of the nearly full moon. Thus, Beth did not see that the man, in spite of his serious, somber tone, was smiling.

Pieter Danniken concluded his speech on the inherent immorality of apartheid and stepped down from the podium. The audience cheered and applauded wildly. It was well sprinkled with members of the foreign press, a preventative measure against Danniken's being imprisoned. A half dozen uniformed policemen stood around the perimeter of the lecture hall, frowning with disapproval. Another half dozen plainclothesmen mixed with the crowd and pretended to praise the professor's liberal message.

After the last speaker had ended the forum, Danniken gathered his notes and exited the auditorium via the stage entrance in back. He walked across the jammed parking lot toward his old woody wagon, the late afternoon sun drawing beads of perspiration on his wrinkled forehead. It had been a long day; he'd caught a midmorning flight, and he was tired. He removed his checked tweed blazer and loosened his tie.

The trip to Durban in the southeastern province of Natal had been an unequivocal success. He had spoken out convincingly for both realistic white acknowledgment of the dramatic and irreversible changes under way in South Africa, and for a special effort at moderation in the coming inevitable black assumption of power. The latter, he suggested, might take as its model the birth of neighboring Zimbabwe. Due to President Robert Mugabe's relatively moderate policies toward whites, the country which previously had been white-ruled Rhodesia managed to avoid the complete and total exodus of white professionals, businessmen, and landowners that was feared would follow the death of apartheid. It was an example well worth studying.

Danniken had declined the customary tea with the hosting faculty from the multiracial University of Natal, begging off on the grounds of a long six-hour drive back to Johannesburg. The next flight back to Johannesburg would have been after dark, and Danniken had a phobia about flying at night.

It was now just after four, and he decided to get a snack and eat it on the way.

He followed the bilingual signs toward the campus gate on King George Avenue. The university grounds swarmed with students lounging outdoors, enjoying the sea air and sunshine. They talked earnestly and enthusiastically, debating the nation's rapidly deteriorating political situation.

Leaving the campus, he headed north toward the Western Freeway, the N3 national highway connecting Durban to Johannesburg. A half mile or so from the entrance ramp, he pulled over into a small arcade of shops and found a combination grocery shop and delicatessen. He stopped only long enough to purchase strong coffee, a couple of ham and Swiss cheese sandwiches, and a slice of *butterkuchen*, a rich German cake whose main flavoring was butter.

Returning to the road as he munched a sandwich, Danniken reflected excitedly upon the transformation the country was experiencing. Reluctantly or stoically, the whites were losing control. Only God knew what the political circumstances would be like in another year or so.

He nosed his rented car onto the freeway. It was jammed, clearly illustrating South Africa's position as one of the most densely motorized countries in the world. This despite an embargo by the Middle East oil-producing nations which necessitated petroleum importation by clandestine means and pushed gasoline prices up to $3.50 a gallon.

Once out of Durban, the pace on the freeway quickened as the traffic thinned. Danniken accelerated. It was more than three hundred miles to Johannesburg.

The sun gradually drifted lower in the western sky, to Danniken's left. The yellow light of day changed to orange, then salmon, lavender, mauve, and finally the deep blue of evening. The cars racing northwest to Johannesburg had switched on their headlights. Danniken rubbed his eyes and wished he were home, or anywhere but on a highway.

Shortly after nightfall, the traffic began slowing. The red of rear brake lights formed a half-mile ribbon in front of him. There must have been an accident. He sighed. This would add another half hour to his trip.

The cars inched forward, a bumper-to-bumper parade of irritated drivers. Slowly, the flashing red and blue lights of the police came into sight. There seemed to be a lot of them.

The reason for the delay was suddenly apparent. There was no accident or rubbernecking. Danniken watched as the police walked from car to car, requesting and inspecting identity papers. It was a roadblock.

An officer approached him. He rolled down his window cautiously.

"Papers, please."

Danniken reached into his breast pocket and extracted his wallet. He flipped it open to the official identity card which every South African, black or white, is required to carry at all times. He extended it to the policeman, who aimed a flashlight at it. "What's the roadblock for?"

The cop ignored him. "Professor Danniken, your residence is in . . . ?"

"Sandton."

"I'm afraid I'm going to have to ask you to drive over to the side of the road. There are some people conducting an inquiry in Johannesburg who would like to speak with you. You're to be brought to the city as soon as possible."

Danniken began to splutter, then saw that it was useless. "Shall I follow you?"

"No. We'll have someone drive your car back for you. You'll get to Johannesburg much faster in one of our cars." The policeman held up a hand to halt traffic in the adjacent lane and motioned Danniken over to the side through the resulting passage. He then accepted Danniken's car keys and helped him carry the heavy briefcase over to the police car parked twenty yards ahead. A young cop waited, bored, in the front seat.

The professor's escort rapped the driver's window sharply with his knuckles. The man started.

"This is Professor Pieter Danniken. Get him to town right away. You know where to take him."

"Yes, sir." The driver got out to help Danniken into the backseat, then climbed back in. He switched on the siren and in seconds was gone, speeding the last fifty miles into the city.

As he looked back through the rear windshield, Danniken saw the dozen or so policemen climbing into their cars. The blockades were being removed. The roadblock was over. They had been waiting for him.

11

Paul woke late, at ten. Pat was long gone. The eternal South African sunshine was blocked by the living room curtains, which were still drawn. He stretched and rose stiffly, his back sore from the concave roll-away bed.

On the kitchen counter, he found a note in Pat's blunt, choppy hand. *See ya later, call if you need anything. O.J. and eggs in the fridge. Try and stay out of trouble. -P.* He poured himself a glass of orange juice and sat down to examine the copy of the Johannesburg *Times* which lay unread on the table.

The front page headlines mostly described the escalating nationwide rioting. References to an "impending police response" warned of the possibility of a severe crackdown or a return to martial law. Paul reasoned that the situation must be really bad for the censored South African papers to be reporting such violence.

At the bottom of the front page, a small insert announced, PROFESSOR DANNIKEN AND DAUGHTER KIDNAPPED IN SEPARATE INCIDENTS. PAGE

3. Paul gazed uncomprehendingly at the blurb. Kidnapped? *What?*

He flipped the sheet frantically. At the top of the third page, his disbelieving eyes scanned the article.

LIBERAL ART HISTORIAN AND DAUGH-TER ABDUCTED SEPARATELY. May 29—Police sources reported today that Professor Pieter Danniken, a world-renowned art authority on Impressionism, disappeared yesterday evening while en route from a speaking engagement in Durban to his home in suburban Johannesburg. He is believed to have been kidnapped.

In what seems certain to be a related incident, Danniken's daughter, Beth, was also abducted yesterday evening, apparently from the Dannikens' home. The telephone lines outside the house were discovered snipped.

Although no ransom note has been received, the police sources added that a cryptic telephone call was received at police headquarters in Sandton at ten-thirty last night. The caller, who refused to identify himself, said, 'Pieter Danniken and his daughter have been taken into custody until the stolen property is returned. No harm will come to them if what has been taken is restored to its rightful owner. The stolen property must not be duplicated. It must be in its owner's hands in forty-eight hours or the Dannikens will be executed. No further communications will be issued.'

Police are loath to speculate on the meaning of the message's enigmatic references to 'stolen property.' The identity of the message's target is now being investigated. The Dannikens have no near relatives, and it is suspected that the message may have been meant for someone emotionally linked with either or both of the kidnapped, perhaps a boyfriend of Beth Danniken's. Police are currently searching for an American male, a family friend, known to be residing as a guest in the Danniken household for at least two days, who has suddenly vanished.

Paul's heart was pounding furiously. This was impossible. Pieter and Beth knew nothing.

Then he reconsidered. If the house was bugged, the *Broederbond* would know that Paul both considered Pieter a dear friend and was romantically attached to Beth. Falling in love with Beth, he corrected himself. If they so much as touched her ... He could not think about it or he'd go crazy.

He ran to the garage door and yanked it open. In an instant the car phone was ringing the Danniken house. A deep, unfamiliar voice answered, "Yes?" It was the police. Or the *Broederbond*. What was the difference, really?

Paul hung up and returned to the kitchen. What to do? He had to return the book; there was simply no question. But he'd copy the information first, by hand if necessary, and then return it to van Fester. They might be able to force him into surrendering it, but there would be no way for them to know he'd copied its contents. He'd smuggle it out of the country and publish it once Beth and Pieter were free.

But what if he returned it and they didn't release Beth and Pieter? There would have to be an exchange, a guarantee of their safety. Once Beth and Pieter were safely rid of their captors, he'd return the book.

Paul wondered again about the mysterious caller last evening. He had said he had something of great interest to Paul. How had he known Paul was staying with Pat? Could he have been connected to the kidnappings? Possibly the caller knew the two Dannikens were imprisoned. It would make sense to meet him tonight at Kyalami. He would see what it was all about, and one way or another he'd make sure Beth and Pieter were released by tomorrow. In the meantime, he had to arrange a swap.

The exchange would have to be conducted in such a manner as to ensure that the Dannikens were released in front of a crowd of people, preferably the press. That would prevent a re-kidnapping.

He called Pat at work. She was devouring an eclair and spoke to him between bites.

"Hey, lazybones, did ya just get up? Sorry about the food, ya caught me in the middle of my eleven o'clock snack."

"Pat, do you have a camera here I could use? I need to take about fifteen shots."

"Yeah, there's one in my uppermost dresser drawer. I think it's got film in it. You're welcome to use it. Are you going on safari now?"

"No, I'll explain later. Thanks, I'll see you tonight. Bye."

He entered her bedroom and opened the top drawer of the huge dresser. A compact Olympus 35mm with an automatic flash lay amid a clutter of photographs, lenses, film, and cartridges. The camera's counter was at "one"—the film inside was new.

Paul examined the lenses. One of them was a microphoto attachment, for high-definition close-up photography. He'd had no idea Pat was a camera buff. He screwed the lens into the camera and carried it to the living room.

Paul placed van Fester's book on the kitchen table and carefully focused the camera on the first page. He clicked the shutter and the flash bathed the room fleetingly in white light. Paul proceeded to photograph each page and then, after he finished, took a final photograph of the book labeled ELIZABETH sitting next to that day's newspaper. He wound the film inside the camera, withdrew the cartridge, and replaced it in Pat's bedroom.

Paul consulted the paper he'd taken from Falkenhaus's study and dialed van Fester's number. A gruff baritone voice answered.

Paul spoke quickly, aware that a trace could be completed in less than a minute. "Tomorrow, at noon exactly, the Dannikens will be released in front of the Johannesburg Art Gallery in Joubert Park. There will be people there to make sure this is done. At five minutes past noon, once the Dannikens are safely released, the article taken from your desk will be placed in a secluded spot nearby, sealed in a heavy plastic bag. Directions to the location will be relayed to this phone number within ten minutes, by twelve-fifteen. I am not interested in the book, only the Dannikens' safety. I have no wish to further antagonize you and will abide by this agreement. Good-bye."

"You—"

Paul hung up before the man, whom he presumed was van Fester, could speak. Now came the hard part—waiting until the meeting that night in Midrand.

It was not Viktor Kyushin's day.

He had regained consciousness only an hour ago. One minute he was carrying out what seemed to be a wonderfully successful assassination necessary to the security of the Soviet people; the next he was waking up in bed in a hospital, his body strapped down like Frankenstein. He was unable to turn his head, and his left shoulder throbbed horribly. The lone window in the dreary gray room was striped with steel bars. He wondered if there'd been a third rottweiler he hadn't seen. It was all very wrong.

Kyushin was an involuntary guest of the Johannesburg Police Prison. He was the prime suspect in the gory and bizarre murder of former diplomat Ernst Falkenhaus and his wife, Anna.

He had not yet been charged, however, because, at the time of his arrest, while still unconscious from the poker blow to his neck, he had been found trussed up with a telephone cord. This disturbing fact meant that there had to be someone else to do the trussing. The police were investigating further.

Downstairs, in the hospital lobby, two white-clad doctors with clipboards walked past the tired-looking policeman on duty at the front desk. The doctors were deeply involved in a medical discussion, pointing at one of the chipboards as they headed for the elevator.

In fact, they were only dressed as physicians, and their collective knowledge of anatomy was unquestionably meager. Their white lab coats had disappeared several hours previously from a medical supplies closet at the regular Johannesburg Hospital. This theft was deftly accomplished by Yuri Druchenko, Viktor Kyushin's assistant. He had been ordered to produce the whites after meeting Colonels Lubichoff and Vasylich at the airport and escorting them to their hotel.

The two colonels headed for the elevator. Inside, next to each button, a description of that floor's services was printed. Adjacent to the button for the third floor were the words MAXIMUM SECURITY. Colonel Lubichoff pressed it.

The colonels exited the elevator into a long, wide hall. It was empty except for a single guard outside of a room at the far end. They headed in his direction, heads close together while they conversed in low tones, evidently struggling with a challenging diagnosis.

The guard nodded to them as they approached. They appeared not to notice, and only at the last second, when they arrived at the door he was guarding, did they seem to become aware of his presence.

Colonel Lubichoff pointed a finger at the door and peered myopically at the guard. "How is he?" Druchenko had also produced two pairs of glasses set with bottlecap lenses. They looked bulletproof, and significantly altered the colonels' appearance to one of scientific harmlessness. They were highly effective props.

The guard shrugged. "I don't know. He was still out a half hour ago." He unlocked the door and allowed the bespectacled men to enter. The door clicked shut behind them.

Kyushin lay in bed, apparently dozing. His head lay on the pillow facing away from them, and he did not stir as they entered.

Vasylich motioned to Lubichoff to stay by the door and approached the motionless prisoner. He gazed down at the bound man and softly said, "Kyushin."

The prisoner rolled over as if he'd been slapped, his eyes wide with shock. "Colonel!" He saw Lubichoff by the door. "Colonel Lubichoff! What are you doing here?"

Vasylich turned to his partner and commented, "Isn't that a coincidence? Kyushin wants to know what you and I are doing here, while you and I are dying to find out what he's doing here." He turned back to Kyushin. "What *are* you doing here, comrade?"

"I don't know, sir. I was in the process of eliminating Perseus when something happened—everything went black. But I think I got him." He smiled despite the pain in his shoulder.

Vasylich glanced at Lubichoff again. "Isn't that wonderful, Colonel? Our boy has gone and made us proud. I guess the American we're going to meet tonight must be . . . an imposter, don't you think?"

Lubichoff nodded. "Definitely a fraud."

The smile faded rapidly from Kyushin's face. "You're meeting . . . What do—"

Vasylich leaned forward and patted the bedridden Russian on the head. "Now, don't you go worrying yourself. You need to rest. How do you feel?"

"Terrible. I think my shoulder is broken or something. Can you get me some codeine?"

Vasylich motioned to Lubichoff and leaned forward, as if he were about to confide an important secret. "You know, Viktor, we found out that the South Africans plan to let you sit with the pain until you talk. So we brought you a strong painkiller. You'll have to stay here for a couple of days before we can get you out, but at least the pain will be gone. Does that sound all right?"

Kyushin nodded.

"Good. Well, then, Colonel Lubichoff, will you please administer the codeine?"

Lubichoff withdrew a syringe and a vial from his lab coat. He removed the syringe's plastic tip and plunged the needle into the vial, which contained a clear liquid. He then inserted the needle into Kyushin's left arm and whispered, "This shouldn't take long. You'll be out in no time."

The two colonels watched as the prisoner slowly drifted off to sleep, a smile once again on his lips. He would never know that the liquid inside Colonel Lubichoff's syringe was not codeine, as he supposed, but sodium thiopental, a barbiturate, or sleeping aide. The lethal dose of 2.2 grams which the colonel pumped into his bloodstream took effect within fifteen seconds, causing a permanent, irreversible cessation of brain activity. The Russian's life ended shortly thereafter. It was an entirely painless way to die.

The fraudulent physicians tapped on the door. The guard opened it, and the two men in white ambled into the hall. Colonel Vasylich tapped the guard on the arm. "He's still asleep. He shouldn't be disturbed for at least another hour."

"Okay. I'll make sure he isn't."

The KGB men descended to the lobby and walked outside, where Druchenko was waiting in a rented Audi. They climbed into the backseat and drove off. Only five hours left until the meeting with Perseus.

Vasylich patted Lubichoff on the shoulder. "Sometimes, my dear friend and comrade, certain events in life are regrettable, but unavoidable."

Lubichoff nodded. "This is true, Georgi. Shit happens."

12

The Kyalami Racetrack in Midrand is the site of the annual South African Formula One Grand Prix, held in November, one of twelve races on the International Grand Prix circuit. At that time, Kyalami becomes the scene of virtual pandemonium, when the international press descends on the track to broadcast the race to beery fans worldwide.

After the race is over, the track lies unused, a deserted oval of smooth asphalt. It sits abandoned until next year except for an occasional saloon car event or motorcycle rally. The bleachers stand empty, while the vast parking lot's only visitors are teenage joyriders executing "donuts" in their souped-up jalopies in a weak-minded effort to impress their girlfriends on Saturday nights.

On this evening, a Wednesday, Paul found no one. He had shown up at eight, three hours before the meeting, in order to ensure he was not being set up for a trap. He wore a navy blue windbreaker over a light cotton sweater, having noticed that the temperature had dropped somewhat and the weather had turned gusty. Van Fester's Mauser was tucked securely into one of the windbreaker's pockets.

The huge parking lot looked as if it had been swept with a broom—there was nothing. Separating it from the track, the ticket offices and gates stood boarded up. It was a desolate and lonely place.

Kyalami lay just off the NI national highway linking Johannesburg to Pretoria. The dusty road from the highway to the track was also devoid of life, with the exception of a few scraggly trees and some tall dry grasses. A couple of long-abandoned shacks, their paint peeling and windows shattered, defied gravity by remaining erect.

Paul turned off the road a half mile from the racetrack and parked behind one of the dilapidated buildings. The plum-colored sunset was fading into the rich cobalt of night. The flat landscape was eerie in its desiccated starkness. There was no sound, except for the blustery howl of the winds sweeping down from the Drakensberg and Strydpoort mountains across the prairielike flatness of the eastern Transvaal.

Paul pulled a flashlight from the glove compartment and quietly closed the car door behind him. He headed off on foot in the direction of the track, the rapidly dissipating light just barely enough to see by. He was thankful for the wind, which would have drowned the sound of his car had someone beaten him to the rendezvous.

Ahead, the soaring grandstands of Kyalami loomed like some shadowy Druidic monument. Paul slipped around the edge of the parking lot, looking for somewhere to hide. There was nothing, only flatness.

Finally he warily approached the boarded ticket office. A huge metal garbage bin just in front overflowed with beer cans. The sour odor was offensive, but at least it provided effective cover. The few dim lights illuminating the parking lot created a shadow behind it. Paul squatted down in the darkness and settled in for a long wait.

About an hour later, at nine-fifteen, the headlights of a car passed by on the road adjoining the parking lot. The sedan braked, its driver apparently scanning the area. Mindful of night scopes, army binoculars using infrared light to allow night vision, Paul crouched behind the trash bin. The car turned around, cruised slowly back in the direction from which it had come, and sped off.

The roar of the motor floated to him over the flat asphalt. The combined din of the wind and the engine almost concealed a click, the brief, crisp note of metal meeting metal. The sound of a car door closing. Paul's right hand unconsciously made its way into his jacket pocket, where it grasped the Mauser.

Paul strained to listen. There were no footsteps, there was no crunch of shoes on the dusty lot. Yet that click was undeniable. Someone had jumped out of the car as it sped off. They had relied on the revving motor to mask it, but it had failed to do so completely. Somewhere in the gloom, someone else was waiting.

Nothing happened for almost two hours. At one point, Paul thought he heard the low hum of a motor farther down the road, but he wasn't sure. His legs grew stiff from crouching.

At five minutes to eleven, Paul heard a car approach. Under the greenish streetlights, he saw that it was a medium-sized Volvo. It appeared to be the sedan which had cruised by two hours earlier, but he could not be sure.

The car rolled deliberately across the parking lot, coming to rest beneath one of the lights. The driver killed the engine and gently eased the door open. He stood up and looked around. "Jenssen?" he called out into the night.

Paul remained motionless. He watched as the man idly fidgeted, jiggling the key chain holding the car key between his fingers.

The bushy hair and short plump physique, barely visible in the poor light, seemed somehow familiar, but Paul couldn't remember from where.

Ten minutes passed. Twenty. The man became restless. He craned his head in all directions, squinting into the gloom. "Jenssen?" he shouted out again.

An hour elapsed. The man was clearly irritated. He stamped his foot and slapped the side of the Volvo in irritation. The evening was obviously not going as planned.

Shortly after midnight, Paul suddenly became aware of another shadowy figure, off to the right. It moved slowly toward the car. The glow of a cigarette gilded a pair of high cheekbones and a small, cruel mouth.

Recognition hit Paul instantaneously. He stared in disbelief. Vasylich! And that was Lubichoff by the car! The KGB. The killers from Moscow. It was a trap.

He watched as Vasylich walked to the Volvo.

The two KGB colonels conferred quietly. They were too far for Paul to hear, but it was obvious that they were upset. Lubichoff slammed his fist on the Volvo's hood.

Paul considered whether he could take them both out. He could shoot one, but the other would duck behind the car. Or into it. And a Volvo at full speed could do a lot of damage to a trash can and to the person huddled behind it.

As he deliberated, a third figure suddenly entered the murky scene, also from the right. He was clothed totally in black, and only by squinting could Paul make out the outline of his body. He shouted in English, "Put your hands up!"

The two KGB colonels spun around. They were caught between the car and the unknown newcomer.

Instead of complying, however, Lubichoff spat something in Russian. They dropped to the asphalt and peeled apart in one fluid motion, pistols already drawn.

The explosive report of a gunshot cut through the groan of the wind. A shriek followed a half second later as Vladimir Lubichoff clutched his hemorrhaging abdomen.

Vasylich, ignoring his stricken comrade, rolled onto his stomach and aimed at the sniper. He pulled the trigger, but missed.

The man in black returned the fire. The bullet zinged off the front fender of the sedan, missing Vasylich's skull by several millimeters. Vasylich pressed himself as flat as possible and fired again, this time grazing the sniper's left arm. The man cursed "Son of a bitch," his American accent carrying over the wind.

He fired back at the pinned Russian, his sight fixed on the forehead. He squeezed the trigger.

Vasylich died instantly, soundlessly, as the metal slug bored through his brain and out the back of his cranium.

The man edged slowly over to the car, his rifle still cocked. The lone sound came from Lubichoff, who lay curled in a fetal position moaning in agony.

In the ghostly light, Paul watched as the black-clad sniper rolled Vasylich onto his back and aimed a flashlight into the dead face.

Another curse pierced the night. "Shit! That's ... who the fuck is that?" The killer turned toward the sound of the wailing. "Who are you?"

Receiving no answer from Lubichoff, he kicked him in the side. "Where's Jenssen? Who are you?"

Lubichoff only moaned louder, his plump belly in exquisite pain.

"Answer me. Where's Paul Jenssen? Where's the man you were going to meet here?"

Paul slowly crept around to the back of the killer. The man was oblivious to everything except the wounded Lubichoff, whom he was interrogating without success. He did not notice Paul approaching him, pistol extended.

"Drop it and put your hands in the air," Paul ordered.

Disregarding Paul's words, the man whirled desperately. Before he could aim, Paul fired once. The bullet pierced the man's stomach in almost the same spot Lubichoff had been struck. He collapsed with a gasp.

Paul rushed to the fallen killer and played the flashlight over the contorted face. The eyes were bulging. Paul recognized the man from the CIA.

"*Ellison?* What the . . ." Paul was mystified.

Ellison's eyes focused. His mouth, pinched with pain, now clenched with anger. With difficulty, he managed to say, "You won't get away with it."

"What? With what? What won't I get away with?"

"You . . . traitor. They'll never pay you off."

"Pay me off? For what?"

Ellison's mouth curled into the faintest shell of a smile. "Sudden amnesia? How sad. Quite an actor, aren't you?" He coughed. "The hundred-million hush money on the Marrakech accord. You remember now, don't you, Jenssen? Between Malan and Roosevelt?"

"I don't know what you're talking about."

Ellison coughed again, a long, wracking spasm. With effort, he said, "Suppose you didn't send the telegram either."

"I still don't know what you mean."

"Listen, Jenssen. A word of advice." Ellison's face was deathly white. "It's not good for your health to go blackmailing the director of the CIA. You ... fucked up big-time." He lapsed into silence, his eyes closed. They flew open a few seconds later as if he'd been rudely awakened, and then closed. He gave a shuddery gasp, and ceased to breathe.

Paul stared down at the American killer in astonishment. It was simply too incredible. What telegram?

Paul walked over to Vasylich. The colonel's eyes were wide open, as if he'd swallowed a teaspoon of Tabasco sauce. Not much to be learned there.

Lubichoff, however, was still alive, if barely. Paul moved back to the stricken Russian, feeling like a field doctor on a battlefield of fallen soldiers.

He stared down at the co-architect of Christine's murder. "Lubichoff. Look at me."

At the mention of his name, the colonel's eyelids flickered open. He stared at Paul. "Perseus," he murmured.

"Lubichoff, why are you after me now? I've been retired for more than two years."

The colonel shook his head slightly. His stomach was coated with dark glossy blood.

"What, then?"

The Russian's mouth moved. Paul leaned forward. The whispered words were almost incoherent. "... zabeth. Stop Perseus from ... Treas ..."

He gulped hard with the effort, and gently drifted into death.

Paul sat crouched next to the dead man, thinking of a lovely, wonderful woman. Her killers were dead. A part of him was now free. He looked into the cherubic face, its plump features Buddhalike and inscrutable.

As he stared at the corpse, Paul failed to hear the soft footfall just behind him. The wind gusted noisily, and then he felt a hard, smacking sensation on the back of his head and sank to the ground, his thoughts swirling into the black hole of oblivion.

Paul awoke with a horrible headache to the thrum of motors. His eyes blinked sightlessly several times and then gradually focused on the window. It was night outside. He was in an airplane. He tried to sit up, but discovered he could not, the twine which was laboriously wrapped around the chair holding him firmly in place.

Using his bound feet as leverage, Paul swirled the chair so that he faced away from the window. He saw that he was not alone. Across the G-2's sumptuously appointed cabin sat an elderly man, calmly returning his gaze. In the man's elegantly manicured hand, an ivory cigarette holder sprouted a long, brown cigarette. The hand shook slightly.

"Good evening, Mr. Jenssen. It is a pleasure to finally meet you. I must tell you that, during the last two days, it has not been for lack of effort." The old man's Afrikaans was crisp and concise, the elocution that of an aristocrat. His brilliant blue ascot exactly matched the color of his intelligent, observant eyes.

Paul winced at the pain. His head felt like a balloon stretched to the bursting point. "I'm afraid that—"

The old man clapped his free hand on his knee and gave a cry of dismay. "But of course, how careless of me. Here I am conversing with you, and you haven't the faintest idea of who I am, or where you are. Allow me to introduce myself. My name is Jan van Fester, and you are my . . . guest."

The penetrating blare of her electric alarm clock summoned Pat Ryan reluctantly from dreamy slumber to the grim reality of work. Throwing on a bathrobe, she headed for the kitchen to brew some coffee.

Passing through the living room, she was startled to discover that Paul had not returned. Although immediately worried, she rationalized that he was probably following up a lead. Reassured, she made breakfast, dressed, and headed off to the city. One day closer to the gold watch, she thought.

That evening, however, when she returned home, she became convinced that something had happened to Paul. Caught in the dilemma of his safety versus maintaining secrecy, she decided she would speak with her boss, the consul general, in the morning. After all, from what Paul had intimated, the last people he'd want out looking for him would be the South African police. At all costs he must stay out of their clutches.

Paul stared at the old man, aghast. What had gone wrong? He was unable to respond.

Van Fester smiled gently and took a languid puff. "My wife asked me to convey to you her regrets. She had to go on ahead." He slowly exhaled and then added, "I'll bet you're wondering how you came to be here, my esteemed guest, and more important, what is to become of you. Is that correct?"

Receiving no answer, he said, "Permit me to answer the first part. At two o'clcok yesterday morning, I received a telephone call from the Johannesburg branch of the Bureau of State Security. You are acquainted, I think, with that fine service, which uses the dramatically presumptuous acronym of BOSS. In any event, the branch chief informed me that a man matching your description had been taken into custody by the local constabulary in Midrand. It seems that a gunfight, occurring sometime around midnight, had wakened the night watchman at the Kyalami Racetrack." Van Fester paused for a drag from the ivory holder. He blew the smoke crisply from his mouth, as if ridding himself of something unpleasant.

"The watchman, a surprisingly intrepid soul, watched as you apparently allowed a majority of your pursuers to kill each other off before putting out the third one's lights. As you sat hunched over them conducting what I understand was an impromptu interrogation, the watchman crept up behind you and dealt you an extremely effective blow to the back of your head. I believe he used a tire iron. He then telephoned the local police, who, along with every other law enforcement officer in the country, were on the lookout for you." Jabbing the air with his cigarette for emphasis, he added in a stage whisper, "You removed something of immense value from my desk. Thanks to your cooperation, and with a little help from the pharmacist, I recovered my book yesterday morning." He wagged a finger at Paul like an old schoolmarm. "What a naughty fellow you've been."

Paul still said nothing.

Van Fester continued. "As for your second unspoken question, that is to say, your immediate future, I can only tell you it is being debated. But we'll know soon enough."

"Where are you taking me?"

"Well, you know, Mr. Jenssen—may I address you as Paul? Splendid—Paul, June is such a lovely month in Europe that we thought Switzerland would be just perfect. Well, actually Liechtenstein, a proverbial pimple on the face of Switzerland. We have arranged very attractive accommodations for you. I hope you'll be pleased."

Paul furiously watched the man smirk. "What have you done with Beth?"

Van Fester's smile turned to blankness. "Whom? I don't follow you."

"Beth Danniken and her father, Pieter Danniken. The two innocent people your goons kidnapped."

Comprehension flashed across the old man's face. "Ah, but of course, the Dannikens. Lovely people, but quite misguided and naive politically, don't you agree?" Not waiting for Paul's response, he continued, "I am led to understand that the Danniken family, *pere et fille*, are vacationing with some friends of mine for an undetermined duration. They are, however, quite comfortable and quite healthy, I promise you."

Paul strained against the confining rope. "I want you to know that if so much as—"

Van Fester interrupted. "My dear boy, such faithful and protective sentiments are certainly noble, but I believe that, on reflection upon your present situation, you will also agree that they are empty and perhaps even a trifle silly."

Paul said nothing, but turned to face the window. His head throbbed violently. He closed his eyes.

As if reading his thoughts, van Fester said, "The frightful headache which you undoubtedly are experiencing at the moment should disappear soon. It is a residual effect of the chemical sodium pentathol. I am sure that during your previous career with the Central Intelligence Agency you became acquainted with its curiously useful applications. You were quite, ah, chatty." He smiled tauntingly and rose. "Will you excuse me for a moment, please? I want to check on our progress. Please don't get up." Laughing at his own joke, van Fester edged his way to the fore of the cabin and disappeared to join the pilot in the cockpit.

Paul grimaced. If it was true, and his aching head seemed to bear it out, he had indeed been subjected to sodium pentathol. The miracle "truth drug," although by no means infallible or without risk to the injected party, was a staple of intelligence services throughout the world. He wondered if he'd told them everything he'd discoverd about them.

The first rays of dawn turned the sky a cold martian greenish red. Below, jutting through the cloud line, Paul glimpsed the shadowy, snow-covered peaks of the Austrian Alps, their silent jagged majesty crowning Europe's roof. The powerful G-2 began to bank, and soon it was descending rapidly toward nearby Liechtenstein.

In the cockpit, van Fester watched the pilot alert the controller in Vaduz to open the runway. The plane dropped lower, and several miles ahead, a string of pale blue lights appeared on the now treeless strip. He mused out loud, "You know, it's funny, all these years, all that gold, and I never once made the trip. Quite an impressive piece of work."

The Afrikaner pilot nodded in agreement.

In a few moments, they were on the ground. Van Fester emerged from the cockpit and clapped his hands together. "Well! Are we ready?" The pilot and copilot appeared behind him.

Paul didn't bother answering. He sat immobile while the pilot and his assistant placed handcuffs on his wrists and removed the rope.

Van Fester continued to gloat, leaning forward in his teasing manner. "You know, Paul, there's an advantage to being tied up, in that you don't have to worry about those uncomfortable seat belts. Don't you agree?"

Deciding to play the man's game, Paul smiled and said, "Getting tied up can actually be lots of fun, don't you think, Jan? I'll bet you and Mrs. van Fester have a blast together."

Van Fester's smile evaporated. He turned away and stepped out of the cabin through the now open hatch. The copilot eased Paul to his feet, and they followed the old man outside, where a fuel truck was already refilling the plane's tanks.

The chill of the early alpine morning made Paul wish for something warmer than the thin cotton oxford he was wearing, his sweater and windbreaker having disappeared. The pearl-gray sky foretold a dank, chilly day.

A Rolls Royce Grey Ghost, painted pine green, was waiting next to the G-2. A liveried driver held the rear door open, and van Fester gestured to Paul to get in. The old man then took the seat next to Paul. The driver closed the door, walked around the car, and seated himself behind the wheel.

The Rolls glided bumplessly along the narrow

road, the soaring alpine firs bordering on both sides. Paul observed the weird trolleylike rollers, each supporting a number of the gigantic trees, ready to slip soundlessly back into place when the rough strip was no longer needed.

In moments, the grand parapets of the castle appeared. The estate's lawns, clipped every three days, were uniformly and lushly green. From the highest tower, the red, blue, and gold flag of Liechtenstein flapped gently in the clammy breeze. The moat surrounding the castle's outer wall, no longer used for protection but for decoration, was home to thousands of brilliant orange Chinese carp.

The car rolled onto the now permanently open drawbridge and came to rest in the massive octagonal courtyard, where the enormous iron doors leading into the main structure were located.

Paul was herded inside through the massive reception hall and up the imperial stone staircase. From the ceilings, baronial banners hung in faded but regal glory, some dating to the heydays of the Holy Roman Empire of which Liechtenstein was once a part. It was magnificent.

Van Fester accompanied him into a second-floor bedroom whose heavy furnishings of solid oak would make unlikely weapons. "Paul, I do hope you will be comfortable here during your stay. In many ways, it's a little like a five-star hotel. We even have room service around the clock. Just knock on your door, and somebody will be there, rest assured." He strode to the solitary window, looked out on the courtyard, and turned. "Paul, come here. As you can see, you have a precious, precious view, marred only by these irritating iron bars. Magnus!" He addressed the driver, who stood at the door. "Magnus, how long have these bars been here?"

"Always, sir."

"Well, then, I guess we'll just have to leave them. I'm so sorry, Paul. I do hope they won't be too unaesthetic for you, but it simply wouldn't do to go about ripping the place up every time we have a houseguest." He smiled patronizingly and tapped Paul on the shoulder. "So sorry."

A door slammed on the opposite side of the courtyard. Paul looked out and almost cried out in surprise. Pieter Danniken, hands tied behind his back, was walking slowly across the castle's octagonal center. Beside him was Beth, supporting her father with one arm. She was unshackled. Paul wanted to bang on the window to attract their attention, but his bound hands would not penetrate the iron grill covering it. The Dannikens were closely followed by a pistol-toting guard. The three disappeared through a side door.

Noticing Paul's gaze, van Fester remarked, "I see that you recognize your two fellow guests. The Dannikens arrived yesterday. This is their first visit to Europe together, and we are trying awfully hard to make it a success."

He paused as if he'd thought of something. "Do you know, Paul, I've just remembered that today, May thirty-first, is Republic Day in South Africa. I think there's a certain poetic justice in that, don't you? But I guess you wouldn't understand. . . . Anyway, I know you must be hungry, so I shall leave you alone to enjoy your breakfast. Again, dear boy, such a pleasure to have you here." Van Fester walked out, followed by the driver, who shut the door behind them. A bolt slid into place from the outside.

Seconds later, the bolt clicked again and the door opened to reveal a white-clad nurse bearing a breakfast tray. She nodded curtly, set the spread on the sturdy desk, and withdrew. The door locked behind her.

After debating whether or not to eat the food, Paul realized that his captors could drug him if they wanted to. He sat down at the desk to eat the eggs, croissant, and coffee.

Shortly after he had finished, the nurse returned, carrying a small black leather case. Paul watched with alarm as she withdrew a syringe and a glass vial filled with a clear fluid.

"You will please roll up your sleeve," the nurse, a fiftyish Afrikaner with a stern, impassive countenance, ordered in a gruff monotone.

Paul stared at her and smiled. "Really, ma'am, I'm feeling great. And I already had my tetanus shot."

She was not pleased. "We can do this the hard way—" she nodded toward the door, indicating the guard, "or the easy way. You decide."

"What do you intend to inject me with?"

"It is Nembutal, a barbiturate. It is a sedative.

You will sleep. There is nothing to worry about. It is harmless. You are not being poisoned, I assure you."

"Please, won't you let me pretend to sleep? I promise I won't cause you trouble." He smiled pleadingly at her.

She returned his gaze, stonefaced. "You overestimate your charm. Listen, Mr. Jenssen, I will tell you something. Eight years ago, a young man of twenty-five and his wife were walking with their three-year-old son on DeVilliers Street in Johannesburg. The parents had just taken him to visit the Railway Museum.

"A few steps from the museum, there was a bank. Its president was a powerful man in the Johannesburg financial district. His car was parked in front of the bank. At four o'clock, he left his office and stepped into his car.

"Under the hood of the car, Mr. Jenssen, a bomb was wired to the ignition. When the banker turned the key, his car exploded in flames, instantly killing him, as well as eighteen innocent bystanders. The bomb had been placed in the car by the African National Congress. The ANC.

"Three of those innocent people were the young man, his pretty wife, and their beautiful baby boy. That young man was my son, my only son, Karl, and in that moment, I lost the only grandchild I shall ever know. The people, the animals, who took them from me are the same people you help. So, no, Mr. Jenssen, I am quite immune to any plea for sympathy or pity you may attempt. Roll up your sleeve, please."

Paul bared his arm, and the nurse injected him with the sedative. He moved to the bed and within a few minutes became rapidly drowsy. His eyes refused to stay open. Stretching out on the bed, he was soon swallowed in dreamless drugged sleep.

13

Days passed in a hazy, cyclical progression of force-fed meals, injections, and unconsciousness. Time blurred. During Paul's few moments of relative awareness, he realized he had to break out, but the powerful sedative was impossible to fight. They were carefully timed so as to allow him no interval of lucidity between injections.

Then, finally, it happened. His captors grew careless. The nurse, either through forgetfulness or incompetence, did one of two things, Paul was never sure which. She either administered less sedative than usual, or she showed up late. In any event, the result was the same. By the time she reappeared, Paul was, for the first time, in a relatively conscious state of mind. As she entered the room he pretended to sleep, drawing the slow, measured breaths of heavy slumber.

She was carrying his dinner, anticipating feeding her groggy patient and then returning him to unconsciousness. Nonchalantly, through half-closed eyes, he watched as she set the meal on the desk and then extracted the ubiquitous syringe from the bag attached to her white belt. She always prepared the injection before feeding him, so that it would be ready while he was still incapacitated. She sank the needle into a vial of the sedative and set the syringe on the night table next to Paul's bed.

As she turned her back on him to get the meal, Paul silently sat up and dealt the woman an expert chop to the back of her neck. She collapsed to the floor noiselessly.

Shakily, he stood up. The effect of what must have been days of sedation had left him weak and dizzy. He tried to lift her, but found his strength insufficient. He was drained.

Paul rested for a few minutes, breathing deeply. Slowly, the murky fogginess lifted. He was enfeebled, but not paralyzed. He staggered over to the desk and as quickly as possible devoured the meal. He would need the food to recover.

Returning to the unconscious woman, Paul struggled again with her dead weight. Gradually, with several much-needed breaks, he managed to hoist her onto the bed.

Just then she began to come around. Paul reached for the syringe. He whispered, "And now, ma'am, a little taste of your own medicine. Sweet dreams." He injected the needle's contents into her upper arm. She ceased to stir, lapsing speedily back into insensibility. The question now was how to get past the guard.

Paul pulled the covers up over the insensate

nurse. The bed would be the first object to appear in the guard's field of vision when he opened the door, so it was important that there be a body in it.

He then searched the room for a serviceable weapon. There was none, everything being either too heavy to effectively wield or too insubstantial to do the job. The attack would have to be unarmed.

Paul walked to the hinged portion of the door and positioned himself. He anticipated that it would not be long before the guard realized the nurse had been inside for quite a while.

Ten minutes elapsed, seeming more like an hour. At last, the sound of the bolt's scraping indicated that the guard's curiosity had been piqued. The knob gently turned, and the door slowly opened. Paul hovered behind the door, his right hand raised.

As soon as the guard saw that the bed was occupied, the door opened more quickly; the prisoner obviously was still out cold.

The guard stepped into the room, perplexed. He could have sworn the nurse had come in to deliver dinner to the prisoner. And there was the tray sitting on the desk, so she ... *wham!* Paul executed another effective neck chop. With a choked cry of surprise, the guard tumbled to the cold stone floor.

Paul dragged the guard, a tall Afrikaner in his thirties, inside and shut the door. He removed the man's heavy sweater and rolled up one of the sleeves on the heavy flannel shirt. Once again, he administered a shot of the sedative, filling one of the dozen unused syringes from the nurse's black bag. His two keepers would be out at least until morning.

Paul removed the pistol hanging at the guard's holster and set it on the dresser behind the door. He stripped off the hospital gown he was wearing and, discovering that his own clothes were not in the room, undressed the unconscious guard. The man was almost the same size as Paul; the guard's clothes fit almost perfectly.

Remembering first to grab the remaining syringes and the three vials of Nembutal from the nurse's bag, Paul eased open the door. The dark hall, musty with centuries of dampness, was empty. A single dim wall lamp illuminated the passage. He slipped out of the room and silently shut the door, bolting it locked.

The castle was hushed, the thickness of the chilly stone walls efficiently muffling any noise in the myriad rooms. Paul moved to the left, toward the staircase leading down to the main floor. He pressed his back close against the sides of the corridor, firmly grasping the pistol in his right hand.

All of the doors lining the hallway were closed. Paul listened carefully at each, but there was no sound from within. The upstairs was empty. He crept to the stone steps.

The banister lining the magnificent double staircase was a masterwork of carved stone, a relic of the ornate Gothic style of the Holy Roman Empire. Peering over the railing at the top, Paul was conscious of a faint hum, the murmur of voices carrying across the first floor.

Grateful for the gloom of the poor lighting, Paul moved speedily down the stairs to the foyer and paused to listen. The humming sound was slightly louder, but there was nothing else. No one had heard him.

On both sides of the foot of the staircase, the foyer opened onto stately drawing rooms. The baronial motif was prevalent in both, with enameled crests and coats-of-arms of long-extinct families adorning the walls. Full suits of armor with chain mail leggings stood upright in several corners. Banners and flags were everywhere.

Paul followed the sound of the distant voices through the chamber to the right. It was like a walk through the Middle Ages.

The voices gradually grew louder and more distinct. There seemed to be at least four or five different men deep in conversation. They sounded fairly close now.

At the end of the room, a door, slightly ajar, allowed Paul to overhear the heated discussion in the library, which was situated next door to the medieval chamber. Paul peered through the crack.

He saw five men, all in their sixties or older, seated at a round malachite table. Its dark green surface was littered with files, papers, and cups half filled with cold coffee. The men were engaged in heated debate. The faces of two of the men were not visible, as they were facing away from him.

". . . have to stay there until after they detonate. Otherwise who'd be there to run the government?" The speaker looked irritated; his high-pitched voice sounded petulant.

Someone else spoke up. "Yes, Freddy, we've been over it a thousand times. Why are we continuing this discussion? Because it's too late to reconsider: The last of the membership were out of the country as of ten o'clock this morning." He paused and then added, "Imagine—the country's twelve thousand most important men and their families suddenly take a vacation abroad. How bizarre."

Another man, pursing his lips, remarked ironically, "Well, seeing as we've put a rein on the media, no one's going to put it all together in time to realize something big's happening."

"It's just that I'd feel terrible if something goes wrong with one of the bombs and something happens to the president or a member of the cabinet." A fourth man peered nervously around the table.

The irritated speaker whom Paul had first heard patted his concerned colleague on the shoulder and said patronizingly, "Freddy, you know we all feel the same way you do. But the experts have assured us that because the explosions are so far underground, the radiation won't affect more than a mile or two of land surrounding each mine. Pretoria won't feel a thing."

Freddy looked slightly reassured.

The remaining man at the table glanced at the other four and queried, "Well, then, are we all quite clear on everything?" Paul stiffened, recognizing the nasal aristocratic voice of Jan van Fester.

Freddy piped up again. "And there's absolutely *no* danger to any Brothers?"

Van Fester purred soothingly, as if comforting a child. "Certainly, Freddy. It's quite simple, and the president and the cabinet will be in absolutely no danger, I assure you. We've made sure of it. In four hours, at exactly midnight, the detonation code will be transmitted from Chur. The belfry of the cathedral there is fitted with all the necessary radio equipment. The president and the cabinet will be on a plane by the time the bombs go off, but as you heard, even if they're delayed, there's no radiation danger whatsoever."

Freddy nodded his gray head several times, following this explanation closely.

Paul stood by the door, in shock. They were monsters. They were going to endanger the lives of thousands of South Africans in the areas surrounding the mines. At all costs he must stop what promised to be a holocaust. But how?

He uncapped five of the syringes he had taken from the nurse and carefully filled them from the vials of clear tranquilizer. Placing these in his pocket, he grasped the pistol tightly and gradually opened the door wider. No one noticed. Finally, standing in the threshold, he pointed the pistol at the table and shouted in Afrikaans, "Freeze! Move a muscle and you're dead."

The eyes of the men snapped up at him in shock and horror. One of the group without thinking started to get out of his chair. Paul adjusted the gun so it pointed at the man and yelled, "You! Sit down, now, before I blow your head off." The man seated himself hurriedly.

"Now, you're all going to follow my instructions very carefully and very slowly, and nobody will get hurt. Is that understood?"

There were nods around the table from all except van Fester, who turned in his chair to stare haughtily at Paul. "You will be unable to stop us, young man. Why not give yourself up now? I offer you my word that you will be treated well and, when it is safe, released."

Paul snorted derisively. "Quite an attractive offer, Jan. Unfortunately, I always was a fool when it came to good deals. I'm going to have to pass. Now I want all of you, slowly, slowly, to stand up, keeping your hands on the table."

They rose carefully. Ten sweaty hands smudged the polished surface of the malachite table.

"Now, one at a time, strip down to your shorts. Jan, my dear fellow, why don't you lead off?"

Glaring balefully at Paul, van Fester slowly removed his jacket and tie, shirt, and trousers. His spindly white legs sprouted from his pink boxers. "Nice shorts, Jan. Now put your hands back on the table."

Van Fester complied, warning, "You'll never get away with this absurdity."

"I'll take my chances. Now shut up. Next!"

The old men divested themselves of their

clothing one by one and placed their hands on the table, palms down. Paul thought they looked rather pathetic, shivering in their skivvies.

"Now, while the other four remain motionless, I want the aristocratic Mr. van Fester to come here by me."

Van Fester shuffled to where Paul was standing, bravely pretending to be unconcerned. His comrades watched with interest.

"Mr. Treasurer—I mean Jan—I am going to inject you with a tranquilizer, the same one Florence Nightingale has used to keep me out for . . . what is today?"

Someone said, "June fifteenth."

". . . for two weeks. You will feel no pain, and you will awake in the morning."

Van Fester turned defiantly to Paul. "I will not permit this."

Paul stared into the old man's eyes. Without looking away, he placed the barrel of the pistol at van Fester's temple. "Then you leave me no choice."

His bluff failing, the haughty Afrikaner irritably held out his scrawny left arm.

Keeping careful watch over the group while clenching the gun in his right hand, Paul inserted the needle into the man's white flesh. He then walked him over to one of the many armchairs scattered around the richly furnished library.

Everyone watched as van Fester's head suddenly tilted back so that it lay against the headrest. He began breathing deeply and regularly.

"Next." Paul gestured with the revolver at Freddy. He repeated the process until, like a quintet of Rip van Winkles, the five Afrikaners sat sleeping soundly in their armchairs. They would be out at least until dawn.

Paul searched their clothing and collected their five wallets. They contained a total of several thousand Swiss marks, the currency used in Liechtenstein. In van Fester's jacket pocket he also discovered his and the Dannikens' passports.

The house was now completely silent. Outside, the lights in the courtyard dispelled the darkness which had fallen after the late-spring sunset.

Paul opened the connecting door at the far end of the library and found himself in an ornate dining room. An impressive chandelier hung above a highly polished table capable of seating twenty. The rug, a subdued gray-green, matched the walls, upon which were painted alpine scenes: turn-of-the-century mountaineers, cows grazing on a hillside, a snowy dale. The colors were cold—pale blue, white, gray, and violet. It gave the room an air of old aristocratic wealth.

The dining room was sandwiched between the library and the kitchen. Paul continued into the latter, careful not to make noise as he stepped across the cold flagstones. The kitchen occupied a corner of the first floor and, passing through it, led left into a hall similar to the one upstairs. It too was lined with closed doors.

Halfway down the corridor, a guard sat on a

bench reading a newspaper. He was leaning back against a door.

Paul ducked back into the kitchen. The guard did not look up. Taking a dish from one of the cupboards, Paul flung it onto the hard floor. It shattered. He pressed himself against the wall next to the threshold.

The guard dropped his newspaper, startled. Hearing no further sound, he rose and walked to the kitchen, his curiosity aroused. He stood in the doorway, staring down at the shards.

Paul extended his arm, pressing the revolver to the man's temple. "If you act smart, you'll live to see tomorrow. Do you understand?"

The guard nodded delicately. His ruddy face had turned pasty white.

"First, let me relieve you of that gun." Paul carefully stretched his free hand to the guard's hip and extracted the revolver hanging from his belt.

"Now remove your shirt. Slowly."

The guard complied, his eyes flicking sideways at the gun barrel.

Taking another syringe from his pocket, Paul filled it with two hundred milligrams of the barbiturate and injected it into the guard's arm, first reassuring him of the contents by showing him the vial. The man was asleep on the floor in several minutes.

Warily moving down the hall, Paul arrived at the door. Pistol extended, he turned the knob and pressed the door open.

Inside, Pieter and Beth Danniken were playing rummy with a dog-eared deck of cards. They looked up casually when the door opened, expecting the guard.

The Dannikens stared uncomprehendingly at Paul. Then Beth was in his arms, while Pieter clapped him joyfully on the back.

"But how did you find us?" Beth finally broke away from the embrace long enough to ask.

"I didn't." Paul smiled at her. "They found all of us. I've been here for two weeks, drugged. I saw you both when I first got here, but couldn't do anything to let you know."

"How did you escape?" Pieter asked.

"They screwed up on my anesthesia. I revived." He held up a bottle of the Nembutal. "There are about a half dozen fascist Afrikaners lying sprinkled around this castle, all dozing soundly."

The Dannikens listened agog while Paul explained how he had disarmed their mutual captors. Then, remembering van Fester's chilling words, he asked, "What time is it?"

Pieter looked at his watch and said, "Five after nine."

"Then we've got less than three hours." He quickly recounted the horrifying plan he had overheard.

"Now, if they're going to send the launch code at midnight from the Chur cathedral, we may still be able to stop them. I think it's a little less than halfway between Liechtenstein and St. Moritz. We could probably make it there in an hour."

The three slipped into the hall, sidestepped

the unconscious guard by the kitchen door, and silently entered the courtyard through a connecting door from the kitchen. They were on their guard in case Paul had missed someone, but they heard and saw no one.

There were several cars and trucks parked in one corner of the spacious quadrangle, most painted dark green. In one of them, a Mercedes sedan, a set of keys hung in the ignition. They climbed in and gingerly closed the doors, carefully making no noise. Paul turned the key, put the gears into reverse, and in seconds was gunning the car over the drawbridge to the street outside. They were free.

Pieter, sitting at Paul's right, opened the glove compartment. It contained several maps, one of which was of eastern Switzerland. Peering at it, Pieter muttered under his breath, trying to find Chur. Paul stretched a finger to a point due south of Liechtenstein.

Pieter said, "Ah, I see it. Hmm . . . we could probably make it there in about an hour."

"I seem to recall someone already saying that," Beth commented from the backseat.

Pieter looked at Paul and said, "It's a pity when children show their aged parents no respect. What hard times are these in which we live." He shook his head mournfully. Beth leaned forward and tousled his silver hair.

The car sped smoothly southward, the road frequently running parallel to the meandering Rhine River. Its surface shimmered in the moonlight like black metal. The car passed Bad Ragaz, a pretty spa and mountain resort, the healing properties of whose spring waters have been reputed since the days of the Roman Empire.

The Mercedes rolled into Chur, the capital of the canton of Grisons and the oldest continuously inhabited site in Switzerland. The commercial part of the city was virtually deserted, its hard-working citizens having already returned to their homes. Chur's medieval buildings stood dramatically floodlit against the black sky. The mighty Rhine lay less than two miles away.

Paul pulled to the side of the street and switched off the motor. "We need to talk about our game plan."

Beth and Pieter waited attentively.

"I suggest that you both check in at a hotel here. I will go to the cathedral. It will be better that way."

Pieter and Beth simultaneously said, "Nonsense."

Pieter continued, "That, dear boy, is absurd. You may need help, and if I'm in the hotel I can't very well provide it. I shall accompany you."

"And I," said Beth.

"Beth, that is *not* a good idea. It is very important that you not go so that if Paul and I get into a pinch and don't show up there will be someone to phone the Swiss police." Pieter spoke in a firm tone.

"Well, then, why don't you stay and I'll go with Paul?" She was not pleased.

Paul interrupted. "Beth, without being sexist,

if anyone's going to accompany me, I'd prefer it to be your father. If strength is needed, he is quite definitely stronger than you. It just makes more sense. Please accept the logic."

She sat with her arms folded across her chest, saying nothing for a while, and then resignedly threw up her hands. "All right, fine, seeing as you two have it all worked out."

Paul restarted the car and drove through the city. He saw a uniformed policeman walking his beat and pulled up alongside him.

"Guten Abend." Paul wished the man a good evening.

"Guten Abend," the officer answered.

"I'm looking for a hotel. Could you please direct me to one nearby?"

"Certainly, sir. The Duc de Rohan is about the best in town. The grub's something special, too, if you can afford it." The policeman's accent was the twangy German of Switzerland's eastern Rhineland. Paul strained to understand him.

They followed what they hoped were the correct directions and arrived at the large and comparatively modern Hotel Duc de Rohan. Paul reached into his pocket and handed to Pieter most of the cash he'd taken. "Pieter, don't check in under your real name. If they want passports or I.D., just tell them you've had an accident and they've been lost and that you're reporting it tomorrow to your ambassador. Pretend you're from Hamburg—you speak German, right? If the clerk gives you any grief, demand to see the manager and insist loudly that he register you. He'll do it to keep you quiet. I'll wait here in the car. And Beth, if we're not back by two A.M., get the police and tell them everything. We'll be at the cathedral."

She nodded, blew him a kiss, and accompanied her father into the hotel. In five minutes, Pieter returned. "That was a breeze. The manager just asked us to fill in our names and addresses." He shut the door and they drove through the sleeping town toward the cathedral, in Chur's center.

The huge structure captured the essence of medieval architecture. Its windows and doors were all cut in the distinctive, pointed-dome style that typifies Gothicism. Gargoyles leered menacingly from the bases of the spires, their batlike faces contorted and infernal. In the shadows created by the floodlighting the satanic goblins looked particularly evil.

The cathedral sat on its own asphalt island, surrounded by two semicircular streets running in opposite directions. The island was fenced with iron posts. At the back, a simple lever gate allowed access; it was primarily for the use of the bishop and his staff. It was unlocked.

Paul parked the car in back and the two men let themselves in through the gate, slipping in as unobtrusively as possible. The area was deserted.

The clerics' entrance at the rear of the building proved to be open as well. It led to the bishop's office and the robing room at the foot of the stairs to the belfry.

The interior was dark, illuminated only by the glow from the streetlights shining in through the ew windows. Pieter and Paul softly climbed the stairs, cautiously listening to make sure they were the first to arrive. They heard nothing.

The staircase, a stone spiral without a banister, climbed more than one hundred feet. At the top, a wooden-floored room housed the ancient and enormous iron bell which weekly summoned the devout to prayer. The bell's sturdy hemp rope dangled in the center of the attic.

The men halted, holding their breath. Still there was no noise. If whoever was to send the launch code wasn't sedated at the castle in Liechtenstein, then he hadn't arrived at the cathedral yet. It was now only a quarter past ten—almost two hours to go.

They explored the attic warily. Its musty spaciousness was interrupted by the many supporting beams sprinkled around the interior. Cobwebs hung in several of the upper corners, while the air smelled stale. Aside from a few wooden tables jammed into a corner, the attic was empty.

Set into the wall farthest from the stairway was an iron door. In the shadowy light the lock glinted, its newness not in character with the rest of the attic. Pieter tested the handle; the door was bolted shut.

Paul looked around in vain for something with which to pick the lock. They would have to wait.

"We'd better move one of those tables so we'll have something to hide behind when our mystery guest shows up." Paul pointed at the splintery furniture, and the men eased a table onto its side. They sat on the floor behind it and settled in for the wait.

Neither man said anything. They concentrated on the silence, listening for the creak of a door or the soft thud of a footstep far below. Paul could hear Pieter fiddling with his watch. Paul had observed the older man's habit of buckling and unbuckling the band when he was nervous or excited.

The minutes crept by. Eleven o'clock. Eleven-thirty. Paul consulted his watch every three or four minutes. Still no sound. Pieter shifted uncomfortably, his legs becoming cramped.

At ten minutes to twelve, the two men froze, hearing a small noise far below. It sounded like a click, possibly the slap of shoe leather against stone, or of a door shutting. They strained to listen.

Hearing nothing more, Paul placed a finger to his lips and tapped Pieter on the shoulder. The older man nodded while Paul rose and edged to the top of the spiral staircase. In his right hand he grasped the revolver he'd taken from the guard at the castle. He peered into the gloom. The shadows offered no clue.

At the base of his neck, Paul felt the metallic iciness of a pistol barrel. In his ear Pieter Danniken whispered, "Slowly, very slowly, I want you to place your gun on the floor."

"Pieter, what in hell are you doing?" Paul asked, looking straight ahead.

"What does it look like? I am disarming you. You have already meddled in our affairs too

uch. I have no intention of allowing you to
poil our grand design. Now do it."

"You! You're one of them? But ... your ..."
e placed his gun on the floor.

"My political views? All an elaborate charade,
necessary cover against prying eyes like yours.
The pretense of being a liberal academic has
roved extremely useful." His lips curled dis-
ainfully. "You and everyone else believed I
vould sooner turn my country into a wasteland
uled by Zulu Marxists than be accused of rac-
sm. Well, let me tell you something. South
Africa *is* going to fall, and the world will see
ow poorly the blacks govern. Africa will give
irth to another squalid dictatorship. But we are
ot going to allow them to confiscate the profits
or which we have worked so hard all these
ears."

Paul was overwhelmed with shock. "But the
ombs—don't you care that you're going to
aporize all those people?"

"What are you talking about?"

"I heard them say in the castle that nuclear
ombs were going to be detonated underground
n South Africa. Why do you have to do that?"

"You don't have the whole story, Paul. Those
veapons are going to go off, that is true. But
hey haven't been placed in population centers.
They're located in every important gold mine in
he country. The bombs have been placed at the
ptimum depth for detonation. The mines will
e destroyed, while the toxic levels of radiation
vill ensure that the ores in the mines will be

useless to man for decades. A minimal loss
life will occur. We have done all we can
ensure that the mines and the outlying areas a
deserted at the time of detonation, which I a
going to initiate in ..." he consulted his watch
"exactly eight minutes. Our little military exe
cise can only be triggered by my radio sign
from faraway Switzerland."

"So you're taking away the country's greate
source of income just to show the world the
can't govern?"

"My dear boy, we're not that spiteful. N
we're doing it purely for profit. The value of ou
vast gold reserves in Switzerland will soar, pe
haps as much as eight- or tenfold, upon th
destruction of the South African mines. A worl
gold shortage will occur. We are merely enhanc
ing the value of our own financial portfolio. An
that is why you are now going to take from you
jacket the sedative which you lifted from you
nurse and inject yourself with a generous dos
of it."

"What do you intend to do with me?" Pau
was stalling for time.

"That's an interesting question. I must tell yo
frankly that, after your escapade at van Fester'
house, we attempted to prod the CIA into assas
sinating you. Rather deviously, too, I thought
You see, there was a secret and historic entent
between your Franklin Roosevelt and our Dr
Malan which would be most embarrassing t
your country were it to surface now. I happer
to be in possession of the documents signed a

the time—1939. I keep them hidden in my Bible. In any event, we sent a telegram to Langley pretending you'd uncovered them and were blackmailing your government. I gather it worked.

"However, prior to our flight to Liechtenstein, I learned that my daughter has fallen in love with you. That changed things. My daughter's happiness is important to me.

"Therefore," he continued, "when you awake, you will have two alternatives. Option number one: You may keep silent about what you have learned, abandoning your book project and its research. You will be given a settlement of one hundred thousand dollars in cash. We will make sure the CIA understands that you were not trying to blackmail the U.S. government. If you choose to pursue your relationship with my daughter, you may do so, but you will never reveal to her your knowledge of her father's true role."

Paul said nothing. The cold metal pressed at the nape of his neck.

"Option number two: Should you fail to comply with any portion of option one, we will kill you. Do not think that by telling everything to my daughter you will protect yourself. On the contrary, should Beth subsequently show an inclination to go public with the knowledge, she too would be eliminated." Seeing Paul flinch, he added, "Yes, rest assured that our purpose is greater than any individual or family. Nothing supersedes the security of the community. Not even the daughter of the Treasurer."

Paul jerked as if he'd been slapped. Danniken pressed the gun tightly against his neck. "Don't move. Yes, the Treasurer. You were confiding in him from the beginning."

"But the initials—"

"The initials contained in Hendrik Verwoerd's correspondence are correct. They belonged to my predecessor, my father, who died eight years ago. He was born in Johannesburg in 1905, the son of German immigrants, and his name was Edmund Freilinghoff. In 1935, he went to Germany and worked for the Nazis until almost the end of the war, when he managed narrowly to escape. He returned to South Africa, where he changed his name to Danniken to avoid his Nazi past. Through a combination of luck and talent, he came to the attention of Dr. Malan, the first Afrikaner president. Malan made him secret custodian of the *Broederbond*'s treasury, which was named Elizabeth. We added steadily to it each year, always in gold. The treasure now sits in the vaults of the United Bank of Switzerland in Zurich."

"When did you become Treasurer?" Paul asked.

"Sixteen years ago, it was decided that the time was ripe for me to replace my father, who was then almost seventy. I had been prepared all my life for the position; the person whom the world knows as Professor Pieter Danniken was an elaborately contrived cover to allow maximum secrecy under which to operate." Danniken clearly enjoyed his own importance.

"And the handcuffs I saw you wearing? And your kidnapping, and your guard?"

"The handcuffs and the kidnapping were all part of the charade, and in no small measure for your and my daughter's benefit. The guards were to protect me, the Treasurer, not to imprison me."

"What about van Fester? And Falkenhaus?"

"Jan van Fester is one of the four members of the Executive Committee of the *Broederbond*. As such, he keeps a ledger of the Elizabeth fund, which you so brashly stole from his study.

"As for Ernst Falkenhaus, he, along with Feldberg and Fortner, are all members of the *Broederbond*, but no more. That is to say, none of them has held office in our fraternity. But when called upon they were ready and willing to play their parts. We still don't know what happened at Falkenhaus's house. It was all quite peculiar.

"Anyway, I'm sure that you thought you'd found your man, but the real Treasurer was near at hand the whole time. Although there is a safeguard to ensure that the codes are not lost in the event of my death, I, and only I, know the access sequence to Elizabeth.

"And now I have a radio broadcast to make from the next room, so it is time for your injection. I want you to remove your jacket and roll up your right sleeve, keeping your right arm motionless. Do not make any sudden movements or attempt anything foolish. As much as I am fond of you personally and have grudgingly come to admire your resourcefulness, I will not hesitate to shoot if need be."

Paul unzipped the jacket and rolled up his sleeve. He let the jacket which he'd taken from the guard drop to the floor.

"Now, Paul, I want you to lean down, slowly, and remove a syringe and the sedative from the jacket pocket."

Paul did as he was told, the gun pressing firmly against his skin as he bent forward. He probed the voluminous pockets of the jacket for the vial. His hand touched another bottle. It was cologne, nearly full. It had an atomizer. He extracted a syringe and slowly straightened. In the dim light the cologne was indistinguishable from the sedative.

"Now fill it and inject yourself. Hurry up."

Paul peeled the wrapper from the syringe, while simultaneously turning the bottle so that the nozzle of the atomizer was aimed at himself. Then, lifting the bottle as if to plunge in the needle to fill it, Paul pressed hard on the cap.

A powerful fog of fragrant alcohol shot over Paul's shoulder into Danniken's face. He screamed in pain, his eyes burning. Paul dropped to the floor in a full judo roll, grabbing his jacket from the floor as he moved away.

Blindly, Danniken focused on the sound and fired. The bullet embedded itself in the wooden floor half a foot from Paul's feet.

Silently, Paul circled toward Danniken's back. The Treasurer was trying to listen while coping with the excruciating pain caused by the cologne. His gun gyrated wildly.

Paul maneuvered to within two feet of Danniken. From the jacket he pulled the gun and jabbed the barrel against Danniken's back, saying, "Drop it."

For a split second, the older man hesitated. Then, impetuously, he tried to whirl. Paul pulled the trigger. Danniken collapsed awkwardly to the floor. The Treasurer was dead.

Paul stood still for a long while. From another church somewhere in the city, the twelve bells of midnight pealed solemnly.

Paul knelt. The corpse's eyes were half closed, as if squinting at a far-off object.

Realizing Danniken must be carrying a key, Paul searched the body's pockets.

In the back of Danniken's pants, Paul found a small brass key. Grasping it, he walked to the locked door on the other side of the garret. He inserted it into the keyhole below the doorknob. The lock turned; he swung open the door and gaped.

He was looking into a tiny room, hardly more than a closet. Against one wall sat the most powerful radio transmitter Paul had ever seen. Next to it were a receiver, a keyboard, an amplifier, a separate scrambler, and an assortment of atlases, radio manuals, and other reference books. A wooden table and stool served as a makeshift desk and chair.

Feeling along the threshold, Paul's hand located a switch. He closed the door behind him and flipped it on, bathing the radio room in pale yellow light. On the desk lay a single sheet of paper.

At the top of the paper was typed, *Instructions.* Beneath this was a step-by-step guide for the transmission of a radio signal to a signal relay station in the Caprivi Strip in upper South Africa. The last step read *Punch in code—refer to manual.*

Paul flipped open a binder labeled DETONA-TION CODES. It too contained only one sheet of paper, on which was written a half dozen menu options and a corresponding code number. *Detonate as planned* was *111. Change detonation time of specific targets* was *222 + specific target + new time.* The last option, *Universal disarm and self-destruct,* was *777.*

Paul turned on the power to the radio. It crackled to life. Following the instructions on the first page, he adjusted the dials on the transmitter and then pressed 777 on the keyboard. He then hit the send button.

Several seconds elapsed. Then a computerized mechanical voice issued coldly through the receiver. "Please confirm instructions by repeating them."

Paul punched in 777 again.

This time the voice eerily answered, "Thank you. These instructions will be implemented in fifteen minutes. They are irreversible. This station will now be unable to receive incoming signals." The voice was replaced by static as the frequency went dead.

Paul rose and left the room. He walked to the corpse and proceeded to lug it down the stairs, its heaviness rendering the task difficult and awkward.

The square outside was still deserted. Lifting one limp arm around his neck, Paul carried the body to the car as if it were a friend who had drunk too much. He placed it in the front, strapped it in with the seat belt, and placed himself behind the wheel.

It suddenly occurred to Paul that it was highly likely that Danniken had carried somewhere on his person the access code to Elizabeth. He reached across the seat and methodically searched the corpse's pockets, finding nothing but some small change. He removed Danniken's shoes and examined them thoroughly by the dashboard light, but they yielded nothing.

And then the silver band of Danniken's watch glinted dully in the pale light. The memory of the dead Treasurer's nervous tic rushed to Paul's mind.

Paul removed the watch from the cold wrist and examined it. Outwardly, it seemed perfectly normal. It was an Audemars-Piguet, a handsome Swiss windup.

He placed the watch on the floor of the car, lifted a foot into the air, and brought his heel down hard. It smashed the crystal.

Paul picked up the ruined chronometer and picked away the slivers of glass. He pried back the little paper circle on which the hours were printed.

On the reverse side, in pale green ink, a non-sensical series of letters and numbers were scrawled in a semicircle around the edge. The key to Elizabeth.

Paul drove to a pay phone and called the hotel. He asked to speak with Beth.

She came on the line breathlessly. "Paul?"

"Hi. Can you meet me in the lobby, not outside, in ten minutes?"

"What's wrong?"

"Beth, just meet me. I'll . . . I'll explain there."

Paul drove quickly back to the Duc de Rohan and parked in the shadows beneath a large tree. He slid the corpse on its side so that it was not visible.

Inside Beth was pacing across the lobby. She rushed to him when he entered. "Where's Pa?"

"We need to talk." He led her to a group of chairs near the front entrance.

"He's dead, isn't he?" she asked suddenly.

Holding her hand, he said, "Yes, he is."

In a dull voice which seemed to contain no emotion, Paul told her exactly what had happened at the cathedral. She listened silently. Tears began to stream down her cheeks. Finally she placed her head on his shoulder and wept. The night concierge looked away discreetly and busied himself with some papers.

"Oh, Paul, he was so . . . Sometimes, little things would happen, he'd get angry over nothing or he'd say something that seemed so out of character, and I'd be afraid." She sobbed chokingly. "I never knew him. He never let me in. He never let me in."

He held her. Her tears came in spurts. At last she wiped her eyes and said, "I'm okay."

"Yes, you are. And strong too."

She gazed tearfully at him. "Yes. I'm strong too. We have to go, don't we?"

"Yes. We're going to have to go back to Liechtenstein. If we leave your father there, with the *Broederbond*, they won't dare call the police when they wake up. They'll hush it up and try their best to find us before we plunder the account. We'll have to cross into Austria or Germany. Do you think you're up to it?"

She nodded.

The border guard accepted the two passports and peered at them, bored. It was just after four in the morning, and the graveyard shift at this outpost was always quiet. He gave the documents a cursory glance and handed them back to Paul. He made a *move along* gesture with his hand and the car sped away toward the frontier town of Bregenz. Paul held Beth's hand and squeezed it hard. They were in Austria.

Epilogue

The caller was adamant. "I don't care if the little weasel is meeting with the president. He's going to want to talk with me. I urge you, for your own sake, to find him and tell him that he has a call from Switzerland and that he'd better get his devious ass on the telephone or he'll live to regret it."

The secretary punched the hold button with a mixture of irritation and titillation. On one hand, the foreign caller was both unpleasantly pushy and refused to identify himself; on the other hand, nobody, but *nobody*, spoke about the director of the CIA in such a manner, much less about his "devious ass." She scurried off to find her boss.

Several minutes later, she located him in the office of the assistant director. Grumpily, he told her to stop looking like a scared mouse and transfer the call. When it rang, he pressed the speaker box and groused, "Yes?"

"Mr. Sullivan?" The fuzz of the overseas call was exaggerated on the microphone.

"Yes, Sullivan here, with assistant director James Bell. Who the hell is this?"

"Mr. Sullivan, I must inform you that this conversation is being recorded. My name is Hans Singer. I am an attorney, and I am calling on behalf of my client, Mr. Paul Jenssen." The two spies stared at each other, alarmed.

Singer continued. "This telephone call is to advise you of several facts concerning my client about which you ought to be aware." The Swiss lawyer's English was clipped and precise. "First, your employee, Mr. Ellison, whom you instructed to assassinate my client, was himself killed two weeks ago. You probably are aware of this development, but Mr. Jenssen thought you might be interested to know."

Bell tried to interrupt. "I don't know who the—"

"Second," the speaker went on, "my client wishes to make very clear to you that at no time did he ever send to you any communication which threatened to embarrass, or compromise the security of, the U.S. government. Mr. Jenssen recently learned that a third party, an enemy of his, sent you, Mr. Sullivan, a telegram spuriously authored by Mr. Jenssen. Apparently it promised to reveal the existence of a secret, rather embarrassing accord between the United States and another country which Mr. Jenssen has not identified to me. Although Mr. Jenssen has since learned about the accord, he wishes me to emphasize as strongly as possible that as far as he is concerned, the matter is dead.

"He also wished me to add at this point, and I quote: 'That guy at Langley may be an asshole, but I wouldn't blackmail him. I'm not a traitor.' Specifically, the asshole Mr. Jenssen was referring to was you, Mr. Sullivan. Mr. Jenssen was both saddened and appalled that you would trust in the veracity of a single untraceable telegram enough to order his execution, without even confronting him first. For that excellent reason, he feels that your powers of judgment are no longer what they once were, or may have been. Therefore, for the good of national security, you will resign the office of director immediately. Should you decide to continue in your post, or should some foolish further attempt on my client's life be attempted, the entire story will be leaked to the press in half a dozen cities simultaneously, through protective measures already in place. The entire story includes not only the existence of the accord, but also the U.S. government's attempt to hush it up, your authorization of the kill order for Mr. Jenssen, and an explicit and rather damaging tape-recorded interrogation of Mr. Ellison made shortly before his death. You have two days in which to resign. The choice is yours: with dignity intact, or later, in disgrace."

The lawyer paused for breath and asked, "Are there any questions?"

After a long pause, Sullivan managed to squeak, "Who the hell do you think you are, making threats to me. Do you know what you're—"

The lawyer from Switzerland cut in. "Two days, Mr. Sullivan. This conversation is concluded. Good day." He clicked off. The director of the CIA glared at his deputy. Unable to think of any constructive course of action, he slammed a fist onto his thigh and shouted, "Son of a bitch."

In his modern office in Zurich, decorated in muted gray tones and with abstract paintings, Hans Singer gently replaced the telephone and smiled across the desk at his client. "Do you think it will work?"

Paul Jenssen smiled back, his green eyes glinting. "I'm inclined, Counselor, to think that it will."

At a quarter past eight, John Lewis shut the door of his Volvo and headed across the parking lot toward the administrative building at CIA headquarters. The July morning air was already warm, even for Virginia.

Just inside the building's main doors, a guard sat at a metal desk, checking I.D.s. To his right on a pair of folding chairs against the wall were seated two men. They had been waiting since seven-thirty. Both wore innocuous gray suits. Well-groomed, clean-cut, with short hair and polished shoes, they looked like stereotypical G-men. In fact, they worked for the CIA's Internal Security Office.

When Lewis walked through the doors, he already had his wallet open, his I.D. ready for the guard's routine inspection. Instead, the two men in gray rose, walked to either side of Lewis and gently but firmly escorted him back outside to a plain gray Buick; he didn't ask about the charge. The espionage days of John Lewis were abruptly at an end.

At roughly the same moment, in a time zone five hours to the east, Alistair Crowley's lunch was interrupted by a sharp rap on his office door. He was eating in, being even more behind on his paper shuffling than usual.

"Yes?" he shouted grouchily. He had told his secretary he did not wish to be disturbed all afternoon.

The door opened, and in walked three men. One was dressed in civilian clothes; the other two were London bobbies. They were not smiling.

Crowley looked up from his papers, his mouth still filled with cheese sandwich. His eyebrows rose questioningly.

The man in business attire addressed him. "Alistair Crowley, I hereby place you under arrest for violation of the Official Secrets Act of Her Majesty's government and for passing classified information to a foreign power."

Alistair Crowley's throat refused to swallow the chunk of cheese sandwich in his mouth.

In the First Family's living quarters on the second floor of the White House, the president of the United States sat in his bathrobe across the breakfast table from his wife, reading the morning paper. Periodically he would mutter or chuckle. Between articles, he would stop long enough to shovel in a few mouthfuls of the healthy and utterly tasteless oat bran cereal the First Lady force-fed him. He would give her a meaningless artificial little smile and then resume his reading.

He snorted derisively. "Listen to this:

" 'CIA Director William Sullivan resigned yesterday, citing a desire to spend more time with his family. The White House issued a statement saying that the president accepted the resignation "with great regret." The president went on to praise Sullivan's service as director, adding that the Agency experienced a period of increased efficiency and responsibility during Sullivan's administration.

" 'Sullivan resigned less than a day after John Lewis, a midlevel CIA employee, was arrested and charged with passing information to a foreign government. The scandal widened with the related arrest of a British intelligence official, Alistair Crowley, who purportedly received classified information from Lewis and passed them on to the Soviet Union. It is not yet known if Lewis was aware of the ultimate destination of the leaked information.' "

The president made a curious sound by blowing air sharply through his nose. "Great regret, indeed. That man set a new record for incompetence. It's a godsend he's resigned."

The First Lady smiled encouragingly.

"I think I'm going to keep Bell on."

"That's nice, dear. Now finish your cereal before it gets soggy."

"You mean soggier." The president did as he was told.

At nine A.M. sharp, the bolt behind the front door of the United Bank of Switzerland's main office was thrown back. The bank was open for business.

A quarter hour later, an old man, stooped with the burden of many years, walked slowly up the steps to the bank's entrance. He held a cane in his right hand.

Holding his left arm was an old woman, also humbled by the passage of time. She walked with a slight limp.

The aged couple, dressed expensively but conservatively, entered the bank, peered myopically through their Coke-bottle glasses at the directory just inside, and headed for the elevator. The woman pressed a button with apparent difficulty and the elevator silently lifted the pair to the fourth floor, where the offices of the bank's chairman and top staff were located.

A receptionist, an attractive and beautifully dressed blonde, smiled at the elderly couple and prepared to redirect them to the tellers, located back on the main floor; these were not the sort of people who would have business with the chief officers of the United Bank. "May I help you?" Her broad Zurich accent slightly mellowed the choppy German.

The woman quaveringly said, "Yes, you

may, young lady. We would like to see Herr Neuhaus."

Surprised, the receptionist inquired, "Do you have an appointment?"

The old man lifted his white head and squinted. Behind his glasses his eyes shone greenly. "No, we do not. But we must speak to Herr Neuhaus on an urgent and confidential matter."

The blonde smiled gently. "Perhaps someone else could help you, no?"

They both shook their heads. The man continued. "We must meet with Herr Neuhaus. It will take only a minute of his time, but he must see us. It concerns a great deal of money."

The receptionist, nonplussed at this firmness, disappeared through a door, only to reappear a few seconds later. "I'm very sorry, but Herr Neuhaus is extremely busy right now. Maybe if you can tell me what it's about—"

The old man interrupted her. "I cannot. I'm afraid that this is entirely unsatisfactory. We shall wait here until Herr Neuhaus sees us." He crossed his arms across his chest; the old woman held one of his elbows to support him.

The receptionist was bewildered. She disappeared once again, this time returning accompanied by a young, smug-looking man in pinstripes. "*Mein Herr, meine Damme,* I must ask you to leave this floor. It is impossible that Herr Neuhaus interrupt his schedule today."

The old woman piped up. "We respectfully refuse."

"You *refuse?*" The man repeated the word as if it were from another language.

"Yes, we refuse." Her tone was adamant.

"Then, regretfully, I will have to have you escorted from the building." His eyebrows bunched into a frown.

"Then, regretfully, I will place myself upon the ground immediately in front of the entrance to this building, where my husband will bend over me, as if I have been stricken with a fainting spell or a heart attack. I suspect, *mein Herr*—" she winked at him, "that you can imagine how quickly a crowd of our civic-minded fellow Zurichers will gather around me. My husband will beg for help, saying that the brutal, bullying guards of the United Bank manhandled me and pushed me down."

She gestured at herself and the old man. "You see that we are well dressed, obviously not riffraff or bums. We look like everybody's grandparents. People will believe us. You will have a rather nasty publicity incident on your previously respectable hands." She smiled sweetly at the banker.

The smugness had evaporated from the troubleshooter's face. He stared at the couple, aghast. Then, saying nothing, he staggered through the door, leaving the stunned receptionist alone to stare appalled at the monsters.

Five minutes elapsed. The door reopened, and the man strode angrily to the elderly pair. "You will have exactly one minute with the chairman, on the condition that you promise to leave this building immediately afterward." He gritted the words through clenched teeth.

Nodding their agreement, the pair followed him through the door, where a security guard frisked them for weapons. Terrorists were not unknown in Switzerland.

Padding after the infuriated banker, they were led to a surprisingly simple office furnished in modern functional style. Behind an immaculate desk, the well-fed and rotund Gerhard Neuhaus rose to greet his guests, intrigued. It was rare that anything exciting happened at his job. He gestured for them to be seated in two chairs on the other side of the desk. "I understand you have an urgent matter you wish to discuss?" He smiled politely.

The old man turned in his chair and gazed pointedly at the flunky still standing at the door.

With a wave of his hand Neuhaus ordered the door closed; the three were now alone. His curiosity was thoroughly aroused.

The old man spoke first. "You are Gerhard Neuhaus, chairman of the United Bank of Switzerland?"

Neuhaus smiled at the formality of the question and nodded.

"Then you will please read this." The man extended a piece of paper to the chairman, who unfolded it and began to read. After two sentences, he gasped and looked up sharply. "Who are you?"

The old man answered curtly, "That is irrelevant. Please finish reading the letter."

Submissively the chairman lowered his head and concluded the document. He then raised his eyes again. "Do you have—"

Silently the woman passed him a sealed envelope. The chairman placed it unopened on the desk and walked to a small but exquisite oil by the Swiss artist Paul Klee. Although it appeared to hang like any other painting, it was in fact attached to the wall by hinges; Neuhaus swung the painting to the left, revealing a safe embedded in the plaster.

Turning the dial, he hurriedly unlocked the vault and removed an envelope. It was sealed with black wax.

Not bothering to shut his safe, the chairman returned to his desk with the envelope. Using a steel letter opener, he slit its spine and extracted a fragile, slightly yellowed slip of paper. On it was nothing but a series of numbers and letters that ran K–3661–LK–2–$8XMC935$.

Placing the paper delicately on the desk, Neuhaus reached for the envelope the woman had handed him. He slit it open and withdrew the paper lying inside. It too contained only numbers and letters.

Placing the two sheets side by side, the chairman meticulously compared them. They were identical.

He stared at his guests, amazed. "I always wondered when you would come, what you would look like."

"There will be no difficulty should we wish to

make a withdrawal?" The old man leaned forward intently.

Neuhaus shook his head slowly. "No, none whatsoever. We can sell it for you, if you like."

"Sell it?"

"Yes, on the gold market. The bullion. Not all at once, of course; your little horde could cause a significant drop in gold prices." He coughed nervously. "Will you, ah, be making a withdrawal?"

"That remains to be seen. But there will be no problem, as you said, Herr Neuhaus?"

"This is correct, sir. My apologies for any discourtesy you were shown in getting through to me. My staff could not have known."

"No need to mention it. Come, my dear." The aged couple struggled to their feet and were ushered out by the chairman, who rode down with them on the elevator and saw them out personally.

Hailing a passing taxi, the old pair seated themselves in the back and were driven to the nearby train station. There they parted, heading slowly for the restrooms.

A quarter of an hour later, Paul Jenssen seated himself at a table in Zurich's Café de la Gare. A waiter handed him a menu, and he flipped through it, not really reading.

A woman seated herself at Paul's table. Her glossy golden hair was drawn up into a bun. Several men in the restaurant turned to look at her.

"Hi, old-timer. How's your lumbago?"

Paul smiled at her. "Beth, I'm glad to see your

face-lift went so well. It's taken years off your appearance. Would you like some breakfast?"

Beth Danniken shook her head. "Let's go meet him now. He should be awake. We'll get it over with."

The two walked out and hailed a cab. It took them to the chic Dolder Grand, a castlelike hotel commanding a superb view of Lake Zurich. They entered the lobby and Beth watched Paul speak to the switchboard operator on the house phone. He waited, and then began talking. The conversation lasted only a few seconds.

Paul rejoined Beth. "He says to come on up. Suite three-twelve." They rode the lift to the third floor and found the room.

An enormous black man jerked the door open. He did not smile, but stood aside as much as his bulk would allow. Paul and Beth squeezed past him into the room.

Inside, on a velour couch in the sitting area, perched a slender, almost emaciated old man. His chocolate-colored skin was a vast network of fine wrinkles, while what was left of his hair was completely white. He smiled and bade them be seated.

The old man gazed at his guests for a few seconds before speaking. When he did, they were startled at the cracked voice, the result of many years in a damp prison cell. "I ask myself, can this really be true? I do not permit myself to believe it yet."

Paul said, "I assure you, it is true. The gold is sitting there, waiting. A hell of a lot of gold."

The old man was quiet for a while, and when he spoke again his voice had a discernible quaver. "It is funny, you know, after centuries of harassment, torture, slavery, and general mistreatment by the white man, that when the black man has finally thrown off his oppressors in South Africa, he is helped most by a white man. And woman. I have no words to properly express the thanks of my countrymen. You, who could have kept this for yourselves, are doing more good than you can know. Will you not accept a gift as a sign of our gratitude?"

Beth said, "A gift would be most appreciated." Paul looked at her, surprised.

The black man said to her, "Name it. We owe you so much; I read today in the papers that the members of the *Broederbond* are accusing each other of embezzlement—no one knows who has their treasure. I become giddy just thinking of this."

"How does one tenth of one percent sound?" She met his gaze without flinching.

The African grinned and told Paul, "Your woman is a businesswoman." Then, turning to her, he added, "I do not think one tenth of one percent will be sorely missed. So be it—you may regard it as your finder's fee. Please deduct it from the reserves when you transfer them to our account." He passed them a sheet of paper on which was written the name of a different Swiss bank, an account number, and the name Republic of South Africa.

The old man extended a withered hand to both

of them and then saw them to the door. "And when you come next to South Africa, you will be official guests of the state."

In the elevator down to the lobby, Paul began to chuckle. "What a nervy lady you are."

"I wouldn't bitch about it—my nerviness just netted us about a hundred and twenty million U.S. dollars."

"How nice."

"How very nice, indeed. Now, Mr. Jenssen, how about something to eat? Do you think you can afford to buy me some lunch?"

"Wouldn't a piece of cake taste better? You know, one of those nice tall ones with about nine layers, all frosted in white? Maybe a couple of plastic dolls perched on top?"

Beth closed her eyes, considering.

She chose the cake.

In her tiny office at the consulate, Pat Ryan opened the official-looking document addressed to her attention. A small piece of paper fell to her desk. She ignored it and read the letter. It was typed on corporate letterhead from a Swiss law firm based in Zurich.

July 10

Dear Ms. Ryan:

My client, Mr. Paul Jenssen, has asked me to initiate inquiries into the cumulative financial differential between "early" and "full" retirement from employment with the U.S. government. This I have done.

Mr. Jenssen has asked me to submit to you a draft in that amount so that you may retire from your current employment with the U.S. government four years earlier than you would normally be eligible for a "full" retirement pension, should you wish to do so.

Mr. Jenssen's gift is not dependent upon your "early" retirement. Should you wish to do so, you may continue working for the U.S. government until you are eligible for a "full" retirement pension without jeopardizing this gift, which will be made regardless, assuming you wish to accept it.

Mr. Jenssen hopes that you will share in his recent good fortune and accept this token of his gratitude for your recent invaluable assistance and hospitality during his stay in Johannesburg.

If you accept the gift, please endorse the enclosed cheque and deposit it into your savings or checking account.

Should you have any questions, please do not hesitate to call me.

Sincerely,

Hans Singer, Esq.

Pat Ryan picked up the slip of paper that had fallen out from the envelope and gawped at the amount written after *Pay the sum of* . . . She rose, walked to her door, shut it, and let out what could best be described as an Indian war whoop. Then she began to cry.

About the Author

Douglas Easton was educated at Wesleyan University. The twenty-eight year old author has traveled widely throughout Africa, Asia, Europe and the Americas, and now lives in New York City. THE MIDAS ACCORD is his first novel.